Truth

Truth

Makilien Trilogy - Book 1

Molly Evangeline

Living Sword Publishing

www.livingswordpublishing.com

Truth
Makilien Trilogy – Book 1
Copyright © 2011 by Molly Evangeline

Published by Living Sword Publishing

www.makilien.com
www.mollyevangeline.com

Cover Design and Map
© Molly Evangeline

Cover Images
© Molly Evangeline
© tirc83 - istockphoto.com

ISBN 13: 978-0983774006
ISBN 10: 0983774005

Contents

CONTENTS

To the One who is truth who took a story I loved, but didn't believe I could do anything with, and showed me how to use it for His glory.

And to my cousins who gathered around years ago to hear the original telling of this adventure.

"And you will know
the TRUTH, and the TRUTH
will make you free."
- John 8:32

:Chapter One:

Prisoners

Makilien glared, her intense eyes switching from a half-finished charcoal sketch to the subject of the drawing. The steady, unchanging trickle of the shallow stream should have been a soothing sound, yet it grated on every single one of her nerves. No longer able to bear it, she dropped her piece of charcoal and picked up a stone. With all her might, she flung it into the stream. The splash and ripples it caused only interrupted the natural flow momentarily before it returned to normal.

Scowling, Makilien stuffed her sketchbook and charcoal into the pouch at her side and leaned her head back against the tree. In the silence that followed, she sensed a concerned gaze. Finally, her eyes turned to the dark haired young man, two years her elder, and her closest friend.

"I don't know how much longer I can take this, Aedan. I have sketched this stream from almost every possible angle over the years. I'm tired of doing it just to pass the time."

Aedan kicked at the dirt. In his heart, he agreed, but what could he say to give her encouragement or change any of it? They went through this nearly every day, and even that was monotonous, but as far as he knew, change was impossible.

Nothing ever changed in the village of Reylaun. The butcher, the bakery, the inn—everything stayed exactly as it had been for over a century. And the people were just as unchanging. They were born, lived their quiet lives, and eventually died. Every day the same. Day after day.

After a long moment of frustrated silence, Makilien stood, mumbling, "I should go home. Mother might have chores for me."

Aedan rose with her. "Me too."

Makilien envied him in a way. At least he had some purpose to his life in shouldering the responsibility of caring and providing for his mother and younger sister. They relied on him as the man of the house since his father's untimely death years ago, the result of a hunting accident, or so they had been told.

The two friends walked a short ways together before they came to a split in the road, one way leading to Makilien's house, and the other to Aedan's.

"I'll see you later, Makilien."

"Bye, Aedan."

Going their separate ways, Makilien soon reached the house of her family's small village farm. Inside the modest dwelling, she found her mother Hanna already at work on supper while little six-year-old Leiya swept the floor. Hanna looked up from her meal preparations when the floorboards creaked.

"Makilien, the animals' water trough is low. Will you please take Leiya to the well?"

"Yes, Mother."

Makilien held back a sigh, knowing her depressed mood would only make her mother upset.

With buckets in tow, Makilien led her younger sister through the dreary, gray village they called home. *Not a single thing ever changes,* she lamented on their way to the well, a task she'd performed nearly every day for most of her seventeen years.

As they passed by, she glanced at the two guards who stood on either side of the village's one gate. Tall men, dressed entirely in menacing black, they wore large, angular helmets that covered most of their stony faces. Makilien's skin prickled at the sight of them.

No one went in or out of Reylaun without permission. If anyone wanted to visit a nearby village or go out hunting, they had to have an escort. Zirtan, the ruler of the country of Aldûlir, declared it to be for the good and safety of everyone—to protect them from the vast evilness of Dolennar outside their borders. Zirtan, a ruler no one had ever seen—a ruler who seemed to have been around for years far past those of an average Human.

Makilien and Leiya soon arrived at the nearest public well. A guard stood there too. Even their water consumption was monitored. The guard watched them with piercing dark eyes as they lowered their buckets into the well.

Living in Reylaun was like living in a prison, but to speak in such a way would be considered treason. One could be put in the stocks, beaten, or worse for any word or deed that questioned the all-powerful Zirtan. But most people insisted life was good and that Zirtan only did what was best for them. They were content that Reylaun had never been attacked by the evil outside, and everyone could live their lives quietly. *They are fooling themselves,* Makilien thought bitterly. *We are no better than prisoners.*

As she lifted her last bucket, she glanced once more at the guard, glad he could not read her mind else she would have been dragged away to the center of the village and punished for all to see. But this thought did not scare Makilien as much as her parents said it ought to. All the desperate questions and laments in her heart cried to be shared and answered, but she held her tongue, if only for her family's sake.

With Makilien's two buckets full and one small enough for Leiya to carry, the two of them turned for home. After they had passed the gate, Leiya whispered, "They scare me."

Makilien took a quick glance over her shoulder at the guards. "Don't worry, I wouldn't let them hurt you."

When they reached home, Makilien carried her buckets of water around the house to a small stable. In a paddock stood three sheep, some chickens, and an old milk cow and her calf. Makilien dumped the water into the trough and watched them drink.

"We're not much better off than you," she murmured.

At the deep sound of her father's voice drifting from the house, Makilien turned away from the animals. Inside, the family gathered for their evening meal. As the food was passed, Hanna asked her husband, "Did work go well today, Néthyn?"

"Yes," he answered with only a satisfied nod and no details concerning his labor at the mill.

Quietness settled over the table. Makilien glanced at each of her parents as she poked at her supper with her fork. Neither appeared to have anything more to say. She hated when it was like this, and it seemed to be so more and more lately, at least to her. When she could no longer bear the silence, she asked, "Did anything unusual happen?"

Her father gave her a questioning look. "Unusual?"

"Anything different? Something interesting you could tell us about?"

"No."

Makilien's shoulders sagged with a sigh. They never had anything of any interest to discuss at the table because nothing happened in Reylaun unless it was something bad and, right now, even that would have been welcome.

Finally, Makilien pushed her plate toward the center of the table.

"I'm not hungry," she muttered.

Everyone paused. Néthyn and Hanna looked at each other across the table, sharing a look of discouragement.

"What is wrong this time?" Néthyn asked with a sigh, weary of his daughter's increasing discontent.

"This, right here, is wrong," Makilien answered, her voice rising a little. "We don't have anything to talk about. What are we living for? Just to live? What is the point? Don't you think there should be a purpose?"

"Makilien, stop," Néthyn told her firmly.

But Makilien's frustration had built too far. "Don't you ever wonder what more there is to Dolennar and why Zirtan is trying to hide it from us?"

Hanna gasped, and Néthyn looked hard at his daughter, caught between anger over her outburst and fear for her.

"Lord Zirtan is protecting us. There is nothing but evil in the world, and you should be grateful we are shielded from it."

"What if the evil is right here, not out there? Don't you feel the fear and dread creeping into you whenever you are near his guards? What if *they* are the evil ones—"

"Makilien, that is enough," Néthyn commanded. "Do you want our family to be seen as traitors? Do not speak in such a way again. Outside of our borders *is* evil."

A tense and uncomfortable silence followed, and the family continued their meal. Knowing she would not be granted permission to leave the table, Makilien crossed her arms and glared at her lap until the meal ended.

After the sun had dropped below the horizon that night, Makilien sat on the steps of the front porch and stared up at the stars. *I wonder if they are the same in faraway places as they are here or if they are different. Will I ever find out? Will I even know what is just beyond the border of our village or will I die here uselessly just as everyone else?*

"Makilien, will you take me to hear Mornash's stories tonight?"

The sound of Leiya's sweet voice brought an interruption to Makilien's depressing thoughts, and she looked up at her sister with a sigh.

"Don't you get tired of them?"

"No." Little Leiya crawled into Makilien's lap, her large brown eyes illuminated by moonlight. "Can you take me, please?"

Makilien still hesitated, but she could not say no to Leiya's pleading expression. She dearly loved her little sister, and at least it could be one of her life's goals to make her happy.

"All right, let's go."

Leiya clapped excitedly as Makilien set her on the ground and rose to her feet. Makilien had to smile as Leiya took her hand, and the two of them walked toward the village square.

The dancing light of a bright fire lit up the center of town, and they joined the many people already gathered there. Mornash, a short, plump, undesirable man who reminded Makilien of some sort of rodent, stood with the fire behind him as he faced the crowd. He had been the village storyteller for as long as Makilien could remember, and she harbored deep dislike for him, though most people loved to hear his stories.

Makilien took a vacant seat on a bench and set Leiya back on her lap to listen as Mornash told his tales. Most were scary stories—stories about sneaky goblins, giant, fire-breathing dragons, Elves that were evil beings who tricked unsuspecting people into danger, and many other horrible creatures. They were all stories of the evil world told to fascinate adults and both scare and delight the children. But Makilien had never enjoyed the stories, not truly believing them. She believed the evil creatures were real, but she also believed there had to be more than that—more that Mornash never shared with them.

The storytelling lasted for over an hour, but then the people began to disperse to get their children to bed. Amidst the sound of children begging for one more story, Makilien left Leiya for a moment and found the courage to walk over to Mornash. She'd never talked to him personally before because of her dislike for him, but tonight she was just worked up enough to ask him a few questions.

"Mornash, how do you know about all those creatures if we are never allowed to leave the village?"

7

Mornash blinked his beady eyes in surprise and then answered smoothly, "I am a loyal servant of Lord Zirtan and go wherever I am requested. I am not so fortunate as you to have been sheltered in this village all my life."

"What is out there?" Makilien asked, her heart pounding with a desperate hope that she just might learn something from this man, undesirable or not.

"Have you not listened to my stories?" Mornash questioned, placing his hands on his hips with impatience.

"Yes, but there must be more." Makilien's desperation leaked out in her tone. "If there are so many evil creatures, how have we stayed safe?"

Mornash tensed and narrowed his eyes. "Lord Zirtan is a powerful ruler, quite capable of protecting his people from evil. You should not be speaking as you do about things you do not understand. Be thankful for Lord Zirtan's protection."

Makilien wasn't satisfied, but she now realized Mornash wasn't the one to talk to. He surely wouldn't hesitate to get her in trouble if she kept after him. Disappointed, she turned away, but before she returned to her sister she ran into Aedan.

"I thought you hated Mornash's stories," Aedan said with a smile.

"I do," Makilien muttered, "but Leiya doesn't."

"Yeah, Rommia still likes to listen to them too," Aedan said, looking over his shoulder to locate his own sister. Turning back to Makilien, he asked, "What were you talking to Mornash about?"

Makilien's face soured. "I wanted him to tell me what more there is in Dolennar, outside of our village."

"I'd like to know that too, but I don't think I'd go to him for answers." He was surprised Makilien had tried it.

"I know, but he's the only one who knows besides the guards, and I'd sooner ask him than one of them."

"Be careful. You don't want to get into trouble."

"It might be worth it to know," Makilien murmured.

Aedan nodded slowly, but said nothing. Too many people still lingered around them. They would have to wait to speak freely another time.

:Chapter Two:

The Stranger

With each unchanging day that passed, Makilien grew more and more despondent. Her family and friends all sensed it, but no one, not even Aedan or Leiya, could do anything to lighten her mood.

Several days later, Makilien reluctantly agreed to a walk around the outskirts of the village with Derrin, a young man about Aedan's age. It was well known throughout the community that Derrin had been taken with Makilien for years. She, however, had no interest despite everyone's attempts to see them together.

"What's wrong, Makilien?" Derrin asked after failing miserably in an attempt to have a conversation with her. "You're so quiet."

"I'm always quiet," Makilien muttered.

"Not this quiet."

Makilien crossed her arms and kicked at a pebble. "You know how I hate life here. I want it to have some sort of purpose, but it doesn't."

"Perhaps it could," Derrin said, his words tentative. "Maybe . . . if you had your own family . . ."

"Stop, Derrin," Makilien snapped, a little more harshly than she meant to. "I know you have your heart set on marrying me, but I'm not interested. Neither do I have any interest in raising a family who will just exist as we are."

With their walk over as far as she was concerned, Makilien strode away leaving the young man to follow behind in disappointment. By now they had nearly reached the gate. When it came within her view, a most unusual sight halted Makilien. A stranger stood at the gate, speaking to the guards. Standing behind him was a proud dapple gray horse, quite a rarity since the only horses she had ever seen were the pure black ones belonging to the guards.

Makilien inched her way closer, straining to hear the men's words.

". . . you are not to speak with the villagers," one of the guards instructed, his voice sharp with warning.

The man merely gave a casual shrug.

"You will get your supplies and leave in the morning, understand?"

"That's all I asked."

"Remember, keep away from the villagers," the guard reminded him threateningly.

"Yes, sir," the stranger replied with a hint of sarcasm.

The two guards stepped out of his way, and he turned to his horse. After mounting, he rode slowly into the village. Makilien was riveted. It was rare for a stranger to come in who was not a servant or subject of Zirtan, and clearly he was not.

The stranger rode right past Makilien who could only stare. He turned his head to look at her as he passed and nodded courteously. His short, dark hair and beard were flecked with gray, showing his years, but his eyes made him seem even older. They were the eyes of someone who had seen many things—things Makilien longed to see. An incredible urge to follow him gnawed at her, but the guards were watching closely. Resisting, she turned for home.

It truly was her intention to head straight for her house, but the urge to see the stranger became overpowering, and she changed course once the gate was well out of sight. Instead, she headed for the livery stable where he would have to bed down his horse. Avoiding everyone along the way, Makilien finally made it to the stable and took a cautious step inside. The stranger stood in a stall brushing and talking to his horse. Silently, Makilien approached him.

"Just what could a young woman like you be thinking by sneaking alone into a stable with a complete stranger who could kill her for all she knows?"

Makilien froze. The man's back was to her, and she didn't know how he could have possibly heard her coming. With a wry expression, he turned around.

"How did you know I was here?" Makilien came to only one conclusion. "Magic?"

The man scoffed. "Hardly. There is no such thing. I heard you coming."

Makilien frowned deeply.

"To a trained ear, you are not nearly as silent as you think you are," the stranger said with a flicker of amusement in his eyes.

Makilien's cheeks flamed with embarrassment, but she asked, "Who are you?"

"My name is Torick, but I suggest you leave here before someone sees you. Apparently, I am not permitted to speak with the villagers here and that means you."

13

"I'm sure I would not be permitted to speak to you either, but I'm not afraid to do it anyway."

Torick smirked. "You're quite a spirited one, aren't you?"

"I just want to know the truth."

"Truth?" The man's eyes narrowed keenly.

"Yes. The truth about what is out there, beyond this village, and whether or not there is any purpose to life."

Torick paused and contemplated her words. "Were you born here?"

"Yes, and so were my parents, my grandparents, my great-grandparents, and probably my whole family since the beginning of time when Dolennar began," Makilien answered in a dark and miserable tone.

"Well, I'm sure that's not quite true." Torick turned back to his horse.

"Please, tell me what is out there." Fearless, Makilien walked into the stall with him, determined not to leave without answers. "Is it all evil like I've been told?"

Torick looked at her again, finding himself intrigued by this young woman with rich brown hair and striking green eyes that hungered for knowledge. Something about her piqued his interest, something he just could not ignore.

"What is your name?"

"Makilien."

"No, Makilien, it is not all evil."

Then it is a lie! Makilien's heart jumped at the knowledge.

"What else is there?" she asked eagerly, wanting to know everything all at once.

"It is true that evil can be found everywhere, but there is much good also. There are good beings fighting the evil."

Makilien knew how dangerous her next question would be, but she had to know. "Is Zirtan evil?"

Torick's eyes were hard with seriousness. "These questions and the answers could lead to very serious consequences." *For both of them.*

"I *need* to know," Makilien replied, holding his gaze steadily.

"Yes, Zirtan is evil . . . he is the root of all evil . . . evil itself. He is the deceiver of all Dolennar."

Makilien hardly dared to breathe. "Is he Human?"

"No."

"What is he?"

"I told you, evil."

Makilien wasn't sure she understood this, but one thing she did understand well. "We are his prisoners."

"Yes, you are," Torick confirmed gravely. "He does not want you to know the truth and will keep you from learning and accepting it no matter what it takes. He uses his lies to convince people that he is doing what is best for them, but unfortunately, at the end of life, these people will realize they never believed the truth and will be separated from it forever."

A dreadful chill raced through Makilien's body. "What can I do? I want to know the truth."

"The truth is available to anyone who will believe it."

"Tell me more," Makilien requested. Gaining answers to the questions she'd struggled with for years only made her want to know more.

Torick glanced uneasily over his shoulder. "Now is not a safe time or place."

"I need to know more," Makilien pleaded with him.

Torick sighed. "Tell you what, you meet me here at dawn tomorrow. By that time I will have found a place for us to talk."

Makilien grinned. "I'll be here."

She left Torick and snuck away from the stable with more to think about and consider than she ever had in her life. Makilien wished desperately to share the information, but she kept it to herself for the time being. She would tell her parents after she learned more from Torick. The more information she had, the easier it would be to convince her family it was true.

Word of Torick's arrival spread through every corner of the village in no time at all. Néthyn had heard all about him by the time he arrived home from work, and the family finally had something to discuss over supper.

"Everyone hopes he leaves quietly in the morning like he is supposed to," Néthyn said, passing a bowl to his wife.

"So do I," Hanna replied. "The last thing we need is trouble."

"Why do you think the stranger would cause trouble?" Makilien asked, trying to keep an innocent demeanor.

"Strangers almost always mean trouble," Néthyn told her.

Speaking cautiously as she spooned peas onto her plate, Makilien suggested, "Maybe he can tell us things about other lands."

"Yeah, he can tell us stories like Mornash," Leiya piped up.

"No." Their father gave them each a stern look. "No one is to talk to him. Anyone who does will be punished."

The thought of punishment made Leiya's young face become sober and fearful.

"What could be so terrible about talking to him?"

16

Everyone's eyes settled on Makilien, and she shifted in her seat.

"Strangers like him tell lies," Néthyn spoke with surety.

"How could you know they were lies if you've never left the village to see for yourself?" Makilien found herself asking.

Néthyn's stern look returned to her. "Makilien, I have already said we will not discuss such things. There will be no more talk of the stranger."

"Yes, Father," Makilien murmured, wondering how she would ever be able to convince her parents of what she believed to be true.

Tossing and turning, Makilien could hardly find sleep for fear of not waking at dawn. All through the night her mind raced with the questions she wanted to ask Torick and the answers she'd already gained. For a long time she dwelled on what he'd said about believing the truth. The thought of being separated from it forever scared her. She had to find out what it was.

At last, the barest hint of light peeked through the windows, and Makilien threw back her covers. She dressed quickly and snuck out of the house, careful not to wake anyone.

No one was around this time of the morning, yet Makilien used all caution on her way to the stable. She was willing to risk punishment to see Torick, but she certainly wanted to avoid it.

Creeping into the stable, Makilien looked around. Torick's horse stood where he had left him, but she could find no sign of Torick.

She whispered his name.

Only the soft snort from his horse came as an answer. *Maybe he's on his way*, she thought, realizing in her eagerness she had arrived a little early.

Makilien walked over to the horse who watched her curiously, but with calm eyes. Gently, she ran her hand down his smooth face. She had only seen a couple of horses in her lifetime. No one in Reylaun had any use for them. All they had were ponies and donkeys for pulling carts. Makilien longed to ride a horse and dreamed about what it would be like to ride Torick's magnificent, gray stallion.

A long while passed, marked only by the steady breathing of the horse and straw rustling in the corner from mice, but Torick did not appear. Makilien frowned and looked out the window as the sun climbed up over the trees. *Where is he? Maybe he didn't actually think I'd come*, she grumbled. *Or he never intended to come in the first place.*

The stable door creaked open, and a shaft of pale sunlight poured in. Makilien's heart jumped, and she ducked down out of instinct. A stableman walked in to feed and care for the stabled ponies. Makilien grimaced. Staying low, she crept out of the stall and to the back door. Holding her breath, she slipped out and pressed herself up against the building. After a moment, she blew out a sigh when no one came after her.

Looking both ways, she dashed away from the stable. Once the building was out of sight, she relaxed and slowed. The villagers were used to seeing her walk in the early morning and would not suspect her. In the middle of the main street, she paused, wondering why Torick had not come to see her. *Well, if he won't come to see me, I'll find him.*

Makilien hurried to the inn, which was really just a gathering place for the townspeople since it was so rare to have visitors. Inside the large, gloomy building, Makilien spotted Keni, the innkeeper at work. She searched the room and, when she saw no one else around, she walked up to the bar.

"Hello, Keni," she said cheerfully.

"Hello, Makilien, what're you doin' in here?" the bald and somewhat short and rounded man asked.

Makilien shrugged. "I was just taking a walk." She purposely let a moment of silence pass. "Hey, Keni, did the stranger leave yet like he said he was going to?"

Keni sent her a serious look. "You ought not to be askin' questions 'bout him."

Makilien shook her head as if it was of no importance. "I was just curious if he was gone since everyone was hoping he would leave without trouble."

"Oh, he's gone all right," Keni answered with a quick nod.

Makilien frowned. "But I thought I saw his horse still at the stable."

Keni leaned closer to the bar and spoke in a low voice. "Late last night, guards came in and took him away."

Makilien's stomach twisted. "Why?"

Keni shook his head. "Guess they thought he was stirrin' up trouble."

"What did they do with him?" Makilien asked breathlessly.

"Who knows? Maybe they took him to Lord Zirtan."

Remembering what Torick had said about Zirtan made Makilien shudder. If Zirtan was nothing but evil, what chance did Torick have of surviving?

"Somethin' wrong, Makilien?" Keni asked when he noticed her look of distress.

"No," Makilien lied, quickly hiding her emotions. "I'm fine. I think I should be getting home for breakfast."

She turned and left the inn with an awful feeling of hopelessness. Now that Torick had been taken away, how would she ever learn the truth?

:Chapter Three:

Escape

The news of Torick's capture pulsed at the very center of Makilien's mind; however, her family had no reason to believe her sullen mood to be anything more than what she'd been suffering for days. But to Makilien, it was worse than ever. Now that she knew about Zirtan and the true state of those in the village, she wanted desperately to do something, but what could she do? If only she had been able to speak more with Torick!

Later on that day, Makilien followed her mother and sister to the town square to do their market day shopping. It was one of the only days that offered any change or a chance for entertainment, but this day Makilien's mind was not on their task. Hanna continually had to reclaim her attention, and even then Makilien was preoccupied.

Only a short time after their arrival in the bustling center of town, a sudden commotion startled everyone. Makilien looked up. Several guards stormed into the square. Between them, they dragged a young man. Makilien gasped and horror gripped her.

Hanna and Leiya turned at the sound.

"Aedan!" Leiya cried with the same distress that ran like ice through Makilien's body.

Everyone who had gathered in the market grew still. Gasps and murmurs punctuated the stillness before everything became deathly quiet. The guards dragged Aedan into the center of the square and halted.

Sweeping his cruel eyes over the crowd, one of the guards declared, "This man was seen speaking with the stranger, an enemy of His Majesty, Lord Zirtan, after warnings were issued not to do so. He will therefore face the consequences."

With a rough shove, Aedan stumbled toward a tall post, and Makilien knew what was coming even before she spotted the whip in another guard's hand. Her throat and chest tightened. Could she just stand there and watch her best friend be punished for something she too had done? Without knowing what she could possibly do, Makilien rushed toward Aedan.

"Stop! Please don't!"

The iron grip of one of the guards clamped down on her arm and jerked her back.

"Stay back, girl!" he growled.

Makilien struggled against him. "No! Please!"

Her eyes caught Aedan's. He shook his head with grave urgency.

"Makilien, don't."

But Makilien had to do something. She had to. She pulled hard against the guard, but she was no match for his strength. Before things could escalate to the point she might share Aedan's fate, someone took her by the shoulders.

"Makilien, come with me," Néthyn said firmly.

The guard released Makilien to her father, but her eyes stayed fused with Aedan's as Néthyn half-dragged her back to where her mother and sister waited. But she could not bear to stay, and the moment he released her, she ran for home, tears blurring her vision. When at last she reached the confines of her bedroom, the tears spilled over, pouring down her face. Overcome with frustration and pain, she beat her fists against the wall until finally she slid down against it, spent. Burying her face in her arms, she wept bitterly.

"This isn't right!" she choked out, hardly able to bear the despair that crushed her heart. "It shouldn't be this way!"

She cried in agony for a long time and barely noticed when her family returned home. Quietly, her parents stepped into her bedroom, and her mother knelt beside her.

"Makilien," she coaxed, laying a hand on her shoulder. "Will you come downstairs and have lunch with us?"

Makilien gave no response.

Hanna glanced uncertainly at her husband, and Néthyn said, "Makilien, you must understand. Aedan chose to ignore the warnings we are all given for our own good and had to face the consequences."

"No, the warnings weren't for our own good!" Makilien burst out. She rose, eyes flashing. "We are prisoners, and Zirtan is just trying to hide the truth from us."

"Makilien, what has gotten into you?" Hanna asked, shocked and frightened at what her daughter's behavior could bring upon her in light of what she had just witnessed in the square. "How can you dare to say that?"

"Because, it's true! I talked to the stranger too," Makilien declared, and her mother paled. "He told me Zirtan is evil and we are his prisoners. He's deceiving us into thinking he's doing what is best for us, but he is just hiding the truth. It isn't just evil outside our borders. There is good out there fighting the evil."

"The stranger told you lies," Néthyn tried to make her understand. "That is why we were warned not to speak with him."

"No," Makilien insisted stubbornly. "That is exactly what Zirtan wants us to believe. Torick was telling the truth."

Néthyn just shook his head, frustrated at his inability to make her understand and as fearful as his wife of the consequences. "Makilien, unless you stop this right now, you will not leave your room until you do."

But Makilien would not be swayed. "I won't stop searching for the truth."

"You are going to get yourself punished just like Aedan or worse," Néthyn warned her. The last thing he wanted was for that to happen to his daughter.

"If I find a purpose to my life it will be worth it."

Néthyn didn't know what else he could say. Hoping time would bring Makilien around, he and Hanna gave up and left the room, closing the door behind them.

Tears still falling, Makilien sat by her window and stared out at the forest, past the palisade. For hours she did not move. Evening crept into the village as the sunlight faded. At suppertime, Makilien's door opened again, and she glanced back. Her mother stepped into the room with a tray of food.

"I'm not hungry," Makilien murmured almost inaudibly.

"Makilien, you haven't eaten since breakfast. You must eat." Hanna set the tray of food down on Makilien's bed and looked pleadingly at her daughter. "Please eat it."

Makilien didn't reply and turned her face back toward the window. With a sad sigh, Hanna turned and left the room again. Still, Makilien did not move. From her chair, she watched the stars appear and the moon rise above the trees, but her mind was far from idle.

At last, Makilien stood and opened her window wider. She crawled through it and climbed down the tree growing next to the house, something she'd done frequently over the years. With all caution, she crept through the village, careful to stay well away from the patrolling guards. Shortly, she came to the small cottage where Aedan, Rommia, and their mother lived. Makilien snuck around the back of the house to Aedan's bedroom window. The curtains were closed but light peeked through.

She stepped up to the window and whispered, "Aedan."

When no answer came, she tried again a little louder. Finally, the fall of footsteps approached. The curtains parted, and Aedan looked out. He wore no shirt, but most of his torso and shoulders were wrapped with bandages. Makilien's stomach churned.

"Makilien, what are you doing?" Aedan asked, frowning down at her.

Makilien shrugged a little. "I wanted to see if you were all right."

Thinking she was acting very strange, Aedan looked at her oddly. "I'll be fine. You could have used the front door. Mother would have let you in."

"I know, but . . ." Makilien hesitated and looked to be certain no one was around. "Aedan, when did you speak to Torick?"

At once, Aedan turned very serious. "How do you know his name?"

"I spoke with him too," Makilien murmured.

25

Concern clouded her friend's eyes as he too scanned the area. He motioned for her to come in and helped her climb in through the window. Quietly, he shut it behind her and drew the curtains.

"When did you speak to him?" Aedan asked in a low voice.

"Yesterday in the stable, just after he got here."

"Are you sure no one saw you?"

"I don't think so. I'm sure they would have come after me by now."

"What did Torick tell you?" Aedan wanted to know.

"That Zirtan is evil and we are prisoners."

"He told me that too."

"What else did he tell you?" Makilien desperately hoped Aedan had learned more information than what she had been able to obtain.

"He said there are people and creatures fighting to end Zirtan's rule."

"Did he give you any details?"

"Not much, but he did say Zirtan is preparing to attack them. The army going against him is not as strong as Zirtan's, but they are trying to rally more help."

A sudden tingle of excitement raced through Makilien's body as she thought of being part of the fight. "Is that all he told you?"

Aedan nodded. "We were going to speak again, but then . . ."

Makilien sighed. "I was supposed to meet him at the stable this morning and talk more too. Where did you talk to him?"

"At the inn. I didn't think anyone else was around, but I guess I was wrong. Someone must have seen us talking, but I don't think it was Keni."

"No, he wouldn't tell on you." Makilien took a deep breath. "What do you think, Aedan? Do you believe what Torick said?"

"Yes, I do believe him," Aedan answered with certainty.

"What are we going to do?"

"What can we do?"

"We can leave," Makilien murmured.

The thought had for years floated around in her mind, but never this seriously.

Exhaling, Aedan shook his head in regret. "I can't just leave, Makilien. I'm all Mother and Rommia have. I can't walk out on them."

Makilien understood his position, but that didn't change the decision she'd already made. "I am going, Aedan . . . tonight."

The young man's eyes widened. "Tonight?"

"Yes. You know how I feel, and it's worse now than it has ever been. I *must* find the truth. I can't stay here and just accept I am a prisoner. I have to try to do something about it."

"Do your parents know?"

"No . . . and I don't think I can tell them. I know they would stop me from going. I told them what Torick said, but they won't believe it."

"Where will you go?" Aedan asked, wondering if she had any plans beyond her escape.

"I'm not really sure. I figure my best chance is to head south since Aldûlir is called the North. That's all I know," Makilien answered. How could she know any more than that?

"I wish you luck, Makilien, and you know how much I wish I could go with you."

Makilien smiled. "I know. Thank you, Aedan." She turned back to the window. "I'd better get back home and get ready. I want to get as far as I can before morning."

But Aedan stopped her. "Wait. Before you go, I have something I want you to take."

He walked over to a chest on the floor and dug through its contents. Makilien was shocked when he pulled a dagger out of the chest and placed it in her hands. Weapons were forbidden in Reylaun. To know someone who possessed one was rare.

Makilien gazed in awe as she wrapped her fingers around the polished, deep red mahogany handle. Pulling it out of the sheath, her eyes took in the shining, razor sharp blade, slightly curved and about as long as her forearm. It had a snake-like design etched along the top edge.

"It was my father's," Aedan explained, "but I want you to take it."

"Oh, Aedan, I couldn't if it was your father's."

Makilien tried to hand it back to him, but he refused it.

"You need to have some protection, Makilien. You're going to need it much more than I am."

Aedan walked over to the window and opened it again. He peered out carefully before helping Makilien climb out.

"Be careful," Aedan whispered, almost afraid to speak out loud. "Torick said there was good, but there is also evil. You don't know what is out there."

"I know," Makilien murmured. After a pause, she told him, "Aedan, I am going to come back, and I'm going to come back with the truth."

Her friend nodded gratefully at her promise.

"Goodbye, Aedan."

"Goodbye, Makilien," he said, his eyes expressing the deep longing to join her.

Wishing she could have him at her side as she began this dangerous and uncertain adventure, but knowing she could not, Makilien turned and ran home. She climbed back up the tree and through her bedroom window. Listening, she heard nothing and suspected her family had gone to bed.

Careful not to make any noise that would wake them, Makilien pulled a pack from under her bed and packed clothes and a few of her belongings into it, including her sketching supplies. She reached for her belt and buckled the dagger Aedan had given her around her waist along with a small pouch of coins she'd been saving.

With most of her preparations done, Makilien sat down at a small table in the corner of her room and wrote a note to her family, explaining her reasons for leaving and promising she'd be back for them. She placed it on her bed with her uneaten supper and snuck downstairs into the darkened kitchen. She'd left just enough room in her pack for enough food to last a couple days, hoping she'd be able to find more by the time it ran out.

Once Makilien had filled a waterskin and packed a couple useful items, it came time to leave. Taking one last look around the house, Makilien quietly walked to the back door. Just as she reached it, a voice broke the silence.

"Makilien?"

She spun around. Leiya stood in the kitchen doorway.

"Leiya, what are you doing up?" Makilien whispered.

"I'm thirsty," Leiya told her innocently.

Makilien filled a cup with water and handed it to her. After Leiya had taken a long drink, she looked at her sister curiously.

"What are you doing?"

Makilien sighed and explained, "I'm going on a journey."

"A journey?" Leiya perked up. "Like in stories?"

Makilien nodded.

"Do Mama and Papa know?"

"No, they don't," Makilien answered hesitantly.

"Won't they be mad?"

Makilien grimaced. "I hope not. Now, Leiya, you have to go back to bed quietly, okay?"

"Makilien, will your journey be dangerous?"

"It might be."

Deep concern clouded Leiya's face. "Will you come back?"

"Yes, I'm going to come back," Makilien assured her.

"When?"

"I don't know."

Leiya's face drooped sadly. "I'm going to miss you."

Her expression melted Makilien's heart. She got down on her knees and hugged Leiya. "I'm going to miss you too." When she let go, she said, "All right now, go on back to bed."

Leiya turned and went quietly to her bedroom. Having seen her little sister made it difficult for Makilien to leave. But finally, she let herself out the back door and hurried past the paddock and through the side streets until she reached the palisade. She would never be able to leave by the gate, which was closed at night, but she knew one of the stakes that made up the wall was loose. When she was much younger, she and her friends used to dare each other to sneak outside the village and then, of course, come right back in. She hoped she could still squeeze through the gap.

Scanning the entire area for guards before she moved, Makilien dashed from the shadows of the buildings to the palisade. Kneeling down, she put her fingers around one of the wooden stakes and pulled hard. Finally, the stake moved a little. Eyeing the gap, she shrugged off her pack and pushed it through first.

Makilien glanced over her shoulder once and squirmed through the gap. On the other side, she pulled the stake back into place, grabbed her pack, and stood. If she took just one more step, it would be the first time she had ever truly left Reylaun in her entire life.

Taking that one step, relief and a sense of freedom swept through her. She wasn't a prisoner any longer and was determined never to be one again. That thought sent her hastily into the woods for cover, and she began her journey south.

:Chapter Four:

The Village

With the passing of the night hours, Makilien put several miles between her and Reylaun. Once daylight came and her parents realized she was gone, the search for her would begin. Zirtan's men would no doubt come after her, and maybe even take her to Zirtan if they caught her.

When the pink glow of dawn spilled across the sky, Makilien pushed on even though she was overcome with weariness and hunger. Unexpectedly, the forest opened up, and she stumbled upon a dirt road. Only then did she stop to look both ways. One way led back north, and the other continued south. *If I follow the road it will probably lead me to a village where I can get some information*, Makilien reasoned. But, to be safe, she stayed off the road and followed it from the safety of the trees.

Finally, when the noonday sun had caused Makilien to become uncomfortably warm, she stopped in a group of tall ferns not far from the road. She opened her pack and ate hungrily, but had to be sparing. Who knew how many miles the road would go on without reaching civilization?

Just as Makilien had packed up again, a sound echoed from up the road. She froze. The sound grew louder, and she realized it to be the clamor of horses approaching fast from the north. *They're after me!* Heart racing, Makilien scrambled to her feet and bolted farther into the forest. She ducked down behind a big tree and peered around it, just able to still see the road. In only a few short moments, five riders appeared—guards from Reylaun. Makilien nearly stopped breathing when they halted just yards away and peered into the trees. *They can't know I'm here.* She rested her hand on the hilt of the dagger Aedan had given her and tried to control the terror building inside of her.

The group's leader turned to the other four, gesturing. "We'll continue south. You two go back and check between here and Reylaun again. If you find her, restrain her until I've returned and, if she puts up a fight, kill her."

Makilien gulped as her heart hammered in her chest. *Please don't let them find me!* She had never before prayed and hadn't any knowledge of who she might be praying to but felt she had to ask someone for help. If she was caught now, she would surely be killed one way or another.

Two of the guards spun their horses around and galloped back the way they had come. With one last penetrating look into the forest, the leader and the two remaining guards rode south. Still, Makilien waited for a long time after the hoof beats had died away before she dared to stand, trembling a little, and moved on, her senses on high alert. Now she would have to be especially careful on her journey and stay as far away from the road as she could without losing it.

For the rest of the day, Makilien only stopped when she had to. She stayed well within the forest, listening and watching for even the faintest sign of the guards. When evening came, she was forced to stop since the road was no longer visible. In a small hollow, she sat in a bed of leaves and reached into her pack for food. Goose bumps rose on her arms at the chill in the air, and she wished she could build a fire, but she did not dare to. After her hunger was satisfied, she wrapped herself in a blanket and huddled against a tree in the stillness of the dark.

The night before, she had not even thought about what could be in the forest, but now Aedan's words echoed in her mind. *"You don't know what is out there."* This night, every sound startled her and prevented her from sleep. She wished she would have at least thought to climb a tree when it was still light enough, but even in a tree she didn't know if she'd be safe.

For a long time, Makilien sat wide awake, clenching the hilt of her dagger in a desperate attempt to be brave as she listened to the rustling around her. *It's probably just deer or raccoons and other small animals,* she tried to tell herself. *Harmless animals.*

Suddenly, leaves and twigs crunched and something bounded toward her. With a jolt of terror, she jumped up and pulled out the dagger. But all that appeared in the dim moonlight was a small fox. It stopped and looked at her curiously before bounding off again into the darkness. Makilien blew out her breath and looked at the pale glow of the dagger's blade. Her legs shaking, she sank down again feeling exhausted and a bit uncertain as to whether or not this had been the right decision.

The lively birdsong echoing through the trees roused Makilien from the slumber she had found sometime late during the night. She was quite relieved to look around the sunny forest and know nothing terrible had befallen her during the night.

She packed away her blanket and pulled food from her pack for breakfast. Taking stock of what she had left, Makilien found enough for another two days, possibly three if she was very sparing. She looked to the north where she had come from and contemplated the uncertainty she'd felt during the night. But the memories of the meaningless years she'd lived, and all those she would yet live if she went back, drove away the uncertainty. She would not go back. Not without something that would give life a purpose—for her and for her family and friends.

Well clear of the road, Makilien continued on her course, though she realized the road had veered more to the southwest now. She wondered just how large the forest might be and when it would eventually end. One mile after another stretched before her and again evening came with no sign of Human population. Neither did Makilien see the guards she'd encountered the previous day. By this time the weather had changed. Dark clouds gathered in the sky and thunder rumbled slow and menacingly from the northwest. She dreaded the thought of spending the night in a storm.

Yet, just as Makilien decided she should search for some sort of shelter for the night, she realized the trees ahead were becoming sparse and the ground rose steadily uphill. Curious to know what lay beyond the hill, Makilien hurried on. She could always return to the forest.

Climbing the rise, she reached the open hilltop a few minutes later and stopped. Just below, Makilien gazed upon a village. The gathering of wood and stone buildings were nestled close together, closer than most in Reylaun. A plank wall ran along the perimeter. Makilien's eyes dropped to the gate to which the road led. No guards appeared to be on watch, and she came to the conclusion that the village must not be directly controlled by Zirtan.

For several minutes, she just looked at it, contemplating. She desired to go and find a place to stay out of the rain, but what if the guards from Reylaun had come here and would spot her? Makilien looked back at the forest. She did not want to spend another night out there, especially if it stormed. This feeling was compounded as a sharp crack of thunder sounded and the clouds opened to spill heavy raindrops.

Makilien pulled up the hood of her cloak. *I'll try to blend in with everyone else,* she thought, making up her mind. Confidently, she strode down the hill, though at the gate her caution returned, and she peeked in first to assure herself there truly were no guards. Satisfied, she stepped inside the village and paused to take in the surroundings. Many more people inhabited this village than Reylaun. The streets were full of people noisily hurrying about. Makilien didn't know what to do next. *I need to find an inn, but where?* Her only option was to start walking and hope she came upon one. It seemed logical an inn would be built somewhere on the main street through the village so she did not deviate from that path.

After a good fifteen minutes of navigating through the pushy crowd and muddy road, Makilien's eyes landed on one of the many signs hanging at the entrances of the buildings. Fastened to the sign was a great pair of antlers, gray and cracked from years of exposure to the weather. Below the antlers read *The Black Stag Inn.* Makilien sighed in relief, and a little spark of hope kindled inside her. Anxious to be out of the elements, she pushed open the door.

The strong, pungent odor of ale and smoke struck her, causing her eyes and nose to sting. She coughed a little, and her gaze swept the large, open room. A rowdy, noisy mass of men populated the tables. Makilien's hope was instantly snuffed out by apprehension, and she wondered if she would rather sleep in the forest. Yet, not having shelter didn't appeal to her either. Before moving from the door, she studied each individual to see if she could spot any of the guards, but she found none with their familiar black clothing.

Taking a deep breath and resisting the urge to cough again, Makilien approached the counter where a slim little man with white hair stood filling mugs. She drew herself up in an attempt to appear confident.

"Excuse me." Her voice came out sounding rather small compared to the noisiness all around her, but she continued, "I'd like a room please."

The man peered at her, his brows lowering at the oddity of a young woman like her traveling alone.

"What are ya doin' here?" he questioned gruffly.

"That's none of your business," Makilien answered, taking offense.

The man narrowed his eyes. "How long are ya plannin' to stay?"

"I don't know yet. A day, maybe two." *Not long if I'm only met with suspicion.*

"Well, I don't want ya causin' trouble while yer here, got it?"

"I don't plan on it."

"Good."

The old man turned to grab a key. Makilien followed him out of the common room, eyeing the men at the tables along the way, and into a hall dotted with doors. The innkeeper unlocked one door near the opposite end and handed her the key. Wearing a scowl that never seemed to leave his face, he left her without a word, and Makilien walked into the room he had just unlocked. It was dark inside so she lit a couple candles. Standing in the middle of the room, she looked around. It was small but cozy with a narrow bed, a table, and two chairs.

Glad to be indoors again, Makilien pulled off her wet cloak and laid it over a chair. Wearily, she sat in the other and stared out the rain-pelted window as daylight diminished, watching the few people braving the elements pass by.

She dug into her pack for her supper a short time later. Now that she could replenish her food supply, she ate until her stomach was contentedly full. Afterward, she grew sleepy and crawled into bed. It wasn't as comfortable as her bed at home, but it was a bed and not the ground. Wondering what the next few days would bring, Makilien drifted off to sleep listening to the rain, the echoing thunder, and the hum of voices still coming from the common room.

:Chapter Five:

Friend or Foe?

When Makilien woke the next morning, memories of the last two days were slow in coming, and it was not until her eyes took in the small bedroom of the inn that she remembered clearly where she was. Itching from the unpleasant straw mattress, she sat up and slipped on her mud-caked shoes. As she buckled her belt around her waist, her stomach growled. She had become tired of cold food by now and hoped she could get a warm meal here at the inn.

Leaving her room, Makilien walked down the hall and into the common room. It wasn't nearly as full as the night before, but several men still occupied the tables. Now, without her cloak and the darkness of evening, it was easy for them to see she was a woman. Apprehension grew inside her when she caught some of the men staring at her. Attempting to ignore them, she walked up to the counter and the grouchy old innkeeper.

"Can I get some food?" she asked.

"All I got made up right now is some soup," he told her shortly.

"As long as it's warm I'll take it."

The innkeeper ladled the thick soup into a wooden bowl and handed it to her along with a spoon. Makilien thanked him, to which he only grunted, and she turned around to look for somewhere to sit. An empty table sat in one corner farthest from anyone else. She hurried over to it and took a seat.

Makilien was cautious in taking her first bite of the soup, leery over how it might taste. To her surprise, she found it quite delicious after what she'd been eating on her journey here. In a short time her bowl was emptied.

Now what? Makilien wondered. She needed to decide her next move. Reylaun was much too close for her to feel comfortable staying in the village for long. She would have to move on, but to where? *I should try to find a map. Then at least I'll know what is out there.*

Makilien stood, intending to do just that. She headed toward the door, but her way was blocked by two burly men. Stopping abruptly, Makilien looked up at their harsh faces. She swallowed hard. Their eyes settled on the pouch of money she still had hanging from her belt. Alarm gripped her. *How could you be foolish enough to leave it there for all to see?*

Trying not to panic, she took a step backward, but they came after her. Dashing forward, Makilien barely slipped past them and bolted for her room, but the men trailed not far behind. Makilien flew around the corner into the hall and sprinted toward her room.

Without warning, a door opened, and a strong hand caught her by the arm. In spite of her momentum, she was easily pulled into the room, and the door closed before she could react. Her scream was cut off by a hand covering her mouth. The greatest fear and panic she had ever experienced filled her with desperation. She struggled mightily to break free of the iron-like arm pinning her arms to her sides, but her captor was just too strong. It was impossible to escape.

"It's all right," a man's deep voice whispered in her ear, "I'm just trying to help you."

The words penetrated her terror, and Makilien stopped struggling but stood stiff with fright, breathing hard as tears threatened to spill from her eyes. For a moment, nothing happened, but then pounding footsteps stopped outside the door.

"Which room is hers?"

"I don't know."

Silence followed for a long moment.

"I'll wait for her in the common room and you can watch the back door," the first man instructed.

Once their footsteps had died away, Makilien's captor released her. Fearing for her life, she pulled out her dagger and spun around to face the man. When her eyes settled on him, she realized only a dagger for defense would do little good if this man intended to harm her. He was tall, like her father, with dark hair that came to his shoulders and a dark beard. His clothing was worn and suited for travel, but Makilien's gaze lingered for a long moment on the sword hanging from his belt. Swallowing hard, she looked up to his face and found that, despite his rough appearance, kindness warmed his gray-green eyes.

"I'm not going to hurt you," the man said in a gentle voice, keeping his distance so he wouldn't frighten her further, "but you do have to be careful. Andin is notorious for thieves and murderers."

Makilien didn't know what to say. Could she trust him? She eyed him warily, the boldness she'd possessed when first meeting Torick nowhere to be found. Finally, she stammered, "Wh-who are you?"

"I was about to ask you the same question. You are not from around here, are you?"

"No, I'm not and . . . I don't know who I can trust," Makilien spoke truthfully.

At the uncertainty in her voice, the man gave her a reassuring smile. "My name is Halandor. I am from Eldor."

Makilien hesitated. With no knowledge of what Eldor was, the information was of no help. Finally, she thought to ask, "Are you for or against Zirtan?"

"Against," Halandor answered with a confidence that gave Makilien little doubt he spoke the truth.

Feeling a bit more sure he truly didn't intend her harm, she said, "My name is Makilien."

"Makilien," Halandor repeated, an unexpected sadness tingeing his voice.

She nodded, wondering at his tone, but it was gone when he asked, "Where do you come from, Makilien?"

"Reylaun."

Now surprise entered Halandor's eyes. "You came here from Reylaun?"

"Yes, I left two days ago."

"Not many people leave Reylaun or villages like it, and those who try rarely succeed."

"I know. There are guards looking for me. I've been trying to avoid them." Makilien glanced nervously out the window. "Do they come here?"

"They could."

Makilien's fear grew again.

Knowing she was ill-prepared to be on her own, Halandor asked, "Where are you headed?"

"I don't know," Makilien admitted, suddenly feeling a little hopeless. "I don't know where I am, and I know nothing about Dolennar outside of Reylaun."

With compassion in his voice, Halandor explained, "Well, to begin with, we are in the village of Andin. It is one of the only villages this far to the north that is not directly controlled by Zirtan. I am traveling south to my home country of Eldor. It is a country most opposed to Zirtan's rule. If you'd like, you are welcome to come along with me."

He didn't want her to wander around on her own. She surely would never make it without help.

Makilien thought long and hard before answering. She needed help if she was going to survive and would eventually have to trust someone. She couldn't know for sure if Halandor was telling her the truth, but something told her he was.

"All right, I would like to go with you," she decided.

"Good. I'll do all I can to get you there safely," he told her.

Makilien's hope returned.

"Thank you."

Halandor smiled and then looked at her money pouch. "If you will trust me with it, I think it would be safer for me to carry your money."

Makilien took the pouch from her belt and weighed it in her hand. It was all she had, but she gave it to him. He bent down to pick up his pack from the floor. Putting her money into it, he lifted the pack over his shoulder.

"Do you have anything in your room?"

Makilien nodded, and Halandor opened the door. After she retrieved her own pack, Makilien followed him back to the common room.

Knowing the other men would be waiting for Makilien, Halandor said, "Just stay close to me."

Makilien did as instructed. When they entered the common room, she immediately spotted one of the two men who had been after her. He sat at a table where he could easily watch the door. Halandor saw him too and gave him a warning look. To Makilien's great relief, the man didn't make any move to come after her again. He only glowered at her, disappointed she was no longer alone, and she was increasingly glad she had agreed to go with Halandor.

Walking up to the bar, the innkeeper scowled at them.

"Is this girl a friend of yours, Halandor?" he asked unpleasantly.

"Yes, Rindal, she is."

"Then next time she wants to stay here, you be here with her. I don't like givin' out rooms to just anyone, 'specially troublemakers."

Rindal looked hard at Makilien, and she couldn't believe he blamed *her* for the trouble with the other men.

"I will," Halandor assured him.

"You'd better," Rindal grumbled.

Ignoring the innkeeper's foul mood, Halandor asked, "How much do we owe you?"

Rindal mumbled the amount, and Halandor paid for both rooms from his own money. As the innkeeper pocketed the coins, Halandor thanked him for his hospitality. Rindal's scowl only deepened at this, and Halandor led Makilien out of the inn.

Outside, she asked, "Is he always like that?"

Halandor smiled at the question. "Yes. He's easily put off by people, especially strangers."

"But he's an innkeeper," Makilien said, puzzled.

Halandor only shrugged, but then looked around cautiously, becoming serious.

"We must be careful to watch for the guards who are after you."

Makilien nodded, wondering what might happen if they did run into them.

"We will need to buy supplies before we can leave here," Halandor went on. "It's a long journey to Eldor, and this is the last village on the road we'll be traveling."

"How far is it?"

"About a week on foot."

Makilien could hardly imagine it. Even just two days from Reylaun and she already felt a world away.

Halandor led her familiarly down a few side streets, checking every so often to make sure she stayed close. He motioned for her to follow him into what seemed to be just a random building, but when Makilien walked in, she found it was in fact a shop. Inside were all manner of items and supplies anyone could need to begin a journey. A lovely woman with chestnut brown hair and pretty hazel eyes met them just inside the door.

"Halandor," she said in a sweet voice. "It's been quite some time."

"Hello, Laena," Halandor replied with a smile. "It has indeed."

"Are you here for supplies?"

"Yes, we are."

Always interested in news and such, Laena asked, "Where are you headed?"

"Back to Eldor."

"I hear there could be fighting there soon," Laena said, echoing the rumors that had been circulating for weeks.

"Unfortunately, that's true. That's why I need to get back as soon as possible."

"You know I have no love for Zirtan or any of his underlings so I hope you beat him, and beat him good," Laena declared. It was then she noticed Makilien and smiled at her. "Who's your friend?"

"Her name is Makilien," Halandor answered.

For a reason unknown to Makilien, Laena's expression was one of surprise. "Really? Well, what can I get the two of you?"

"Food, mainly, but Makilien could use a few more supplies."

Halandor looked at Makilien. "I would suggest new clothing for the journey."

She looked down at her homespun farm dress. It wouldn't last a long journey as it had already sustained quite a bit of wear on the journey from Reylaun alone.

"You're right, I do need something different."

"Find her whatever she needs, Laena," Halandor instructed.

"Right this way," Laena told Makilien kindly.

The other woman led Makilien into a crowded back room. Clothing lay everywhere.

"These ought to fit you well enough," the woman said as she chose several articles of clothing and handed them to Makilien. "Go on and change behind that curtain, and if they fit nicely, I'll pack more for you."

Makilien stepped behind a long curtain in the corner and changed out of her dress. The clothing Laena provided was much different than what she was used to. There was a pair of dark, leather pants and the dress, made of strong, dusty blue linen, was constructed with a skirt that was split up the front and back and along the sides, clearly for ease of movement and riding horses. Over the top went a sleeveless overdress with a lace up front and sides. The long skirt was split just like the dress. This was made of dark brown leather. All constructed of sturdy material that would last months of heavy travel.

She stepped out from behind the curtain feeling like a different person in the new clothing.

"Everything fits well," she told Laena.

"Good," Laena said with a pleased smile, and turned to pack a couple more pairs of the same kinds of clothing into a new, larger pack. Lastly, she picked up a pair of leather boots. "Try these on for size."

Makilien slipped her feet into the boots that came up to her knees. She took a few steps and nodded. "They fit too."

"Very good, now we just need a few more things."

Laena gathered a cloak, a new wool blanket, and anything else she thought Makilien might need. Finally, they returned to Halandor, and Laena provided their food supplies.

"How much do I owe you?" Halandor asked when she finished.

"That will be twenty for the food and one-hundred for the clothes and other things."

Halandor started counting out his money.

"I want to pay for my things or at least some of it," Makilien said. "I'm not sure I have enough."

Halandor gave Makilien her money and she counted it.

"I only have seventy-eight," she said regretfully.

"I can pay the rest," Halandor offered.

But Laena shook her head. "I'll take the seventy-eight."

"Thank you very much," Makilien said gratefully.

Now, with all the supplies they would need to take them to Eldor, Makilien and Halandor said goodbye and turned for the door.

"Wait," Laena stopped them. "I just thought of something I'd like to give you before you go."

Makilien and Halandor turned back as she disappeared into the back room again. They heard some rummaging around and then Laena's muffled voice.

"Ah, here we are."

She returned carrying a long object wrapped in cloth and handed it to Makilien. Curiously, Makilien unwrapped the heavy item. The cloth fell back to reveal the hilt of a sword. Surprised, Makilien pulled the cloth completely off, realizing the sword wasn't as large as Halandor's. It was just the right size for her. She studied the two handed hilt, admiring the simple design wrapped with black leather and topped off with a round pommel. The silver cross-guard was straight and rounded at the ends.

"I've had that laying around forever now," Laena said. "Someone traded it to me a few years back. It's too small for the men who come to buy weapons so I've never known what to do with it, but something tells me you could put it to use."

"But I don't have any more money."

"I'm giving it to you," Laena said gently. "No need to pay me."

"Are you sure?"

"Certainly."

Makilien could hardly believe the woman's kindness.

"Thank you."

Laena smiled. Halandor thanked her again as well before he and Makilien left the shop.

:Chapter Six:

On the Road

Just outside the shop, they paused so Makilien could fasten the sword to her belt. Before they moved on, Halandor handed her a folded piece of parchment. Glancing at him questioningly, she unfolded it and found it was a map of Dolennar, something she'd only ever dreamed of seeing.

"This is Andin, here." Halandor pointed to a village in the northwestern portion of Dolennar. "We are going to follow the road southeast, through the forest of Eldinorieth, and here, on the other side of this river, is Elimar, our destination."

"Is Elimar a city?" Makilien asked.

"Yes, an Elven city."

"Elven!" Makilien looked at Halandor, her eyes widening in alarm.

Halandor nodded slowly, but his eyes showed understanding.

"You've heard stories of Elves being evil, haven't you?"

"Yes."

"None of those stories are true. Elves are not evil. In fact, they are the only race who does not have any of their people actually in league with Zirtan."

"Why is that?"

Halandor smiled a little. "They are much wiser than most Humans."

Makilien found it all very interesting and turned her eyes back to the map, fascinated. At last, she refolded it and held it out to Halandor, but he told her to keep it, which pleased her enormously.

With everything in order, they followed the streets to the village's southern gate. From there they traveled the dirt road leading into open country as far as Makilien could see. She'd never seen anything like it before. Only tall grass blowing in the wind with occasional clumps of trees spread far apart.

All day Makilien and Halandor walked, and she was able to ask all the questions she wanted. Halandor told her much about Eldor, a country shared by Elves and Humans. It was ruled by a Human king named Darand who Halandor spoke of with high esteem. Minarald was the capital city. Elimar, the Elven city, which was their destination, was ruled separately by an Elven-lord named Elnauhir.

Once most of Makilien's immediate questions were satisfied, Halandor was curious to know more about her so she told of her life back in Reylaun. When she came to the arrival of Torick, she was surprised to learn Halandor knew him well and they had traveled north together. She could see his deep concern when she told him of Torick's capture.

Torn, Halandor looked over his shoulder, back the way they had come. Had Makilien not been with him, he would have gone back to try to find and rescue his friend, but he couldn't abandon Makilien now. Nowhere was safe until they reached Eldor. Conflict disquieted his mind. Makilien would probably be safe with Laena until he could come for her if he went after Torick. But could he reach

Torick before his friend fell into Zirtan's hands? Four days had passed already.

"Is that the forest?"

Makilien's question pulled Halandor back from his dilemma. He looked ahead at the dark line on the horizon.

"Yes, Eldinorieth, one of the largest forests in Dolennar."

"What kinds of creatures live there?"

"Many different kinds."

"Dangerous creatures?" Makilien asked warily.

"Some are dangerous." Seeing she wanted to know more, Halandor continued, "There are trolls, mountain wolves, and now with threat of war from Zirtan, goblins too."

"Do you think we'll see any?"

"Most stay deep in the forest. Last time Torick and I were through there we didn't see anything."

Makilien hoped not to see anything either. As she thought about the nasty beasts, Halandor again considered his choices. Dusk was almost upon them. It was too late to get far if they turned back, so he decided they would make their camp in the forest that night, and then he could decide which direction to choose in the morning.

The trees cast long shadows across the road when they arrived at the edge of the thick, dark woods. A short ways in, Halandor stopped.

"We'll camp here tonight." He looked to the right. "The river is just that way. We can catch some fish for supper."

Makilien followed him a short distance into the forest, and they reached a clear, sparkling river, wider and deeper than the one flowing through Reylaun. Leaves floated south along its slow current, and Makilien wondered where they would end up.

Halandor put his pack down and pulled out a wound up line with a hook tied to the end. He looked at Makilien.

"Have you ever been fishing?"

Makilien laughed a little. "More times than I want to remember."

Halandor pulled out another line and handed it to her. They walked over to an old rotten log and rolled it over. Underneath, worms and bugs scurried around in a panic. Makilien and Halandor each put a worm on the end of their hooks and went to the riverbank where a huge willow tree stood whose roots grew into the river.

Halandor lowered his line in on one side and Makilien lowered hers on the other. Not many minutes later, Halandor pulled out a large, fat trout. Shortly after, Makilien too caught one. It turned out to be much more fun than in Reylaun. In another little while, Halandor had caught two more and Makilien one more, plenty for their supper.

On the way back to their campsite with their catch, Makilien watched Halandor pick a few plants she guessed were for seasoning the fish. Back at the road, she helped him set up their camp for the night. They gathered wood and cleared a spot for a fire. As soon as it burned well, Halandor cleaned the fish and put them and the plants in a pan from his pack to fry over the flames. All through the process, Makilien watched closely.

"Halandor, could you teach me?" she asked after a while.

"Teach you what?"

"How to survive out here? How to find food, what plants are edible, and how to hunt?"

Halandor smiled. "I'd be glad to."

Quite happy, Makilien looked down and her eyes snagged on the sword Laena had given her. "There's something else too."

"What's that?"

"Well, Laena gave me this sword, but . . . I don't know the first thing about using it. With the creatures we could meet, I want to be able to defend myself."

"We can start on it as soon as we're finished eating," Halandor told her, to which she smiled in thanks.

A short time later, Halandor dished up the fish and handed a plate to Makilien. The trout was some of the best fish Makilien had ever eaten. Much tastier than any fish she'd had in Reylaun. The herbs Halandor seasoned it with gave it a mouthwatering flavor.

Just before they had emptied their plates, something caught Halandor's attention, and he looked back up the road.

"Someone's coming."

Makilien couldn't hear anything at first, but listening closely she finally picked out the sound of a horse coming in their direction.

"Could it be the guards?" she asked in alarm.

"I don't think they'd come this far, and there is only one horse," Halandor reassured her.

He stood, resting one hand on his sword as he waited for the rider to appear. Even just standing there he appeared intimidating, for which Makilien was now glad. She too got to her feet and picked up her sword. Though she couldn't use it she wanted to appear as though she could defend herself. They waited for a few moments more until their eyes picked out movement in the dark. At last, the rider reached the light of the fire. Makilien's mouth dropped open.

"Torick!"

He smiled down at her from atop his stallion. "Well, well, you made it." Dismounting, he came closer. "Halandor," he greeted, nodding at the other man.

"Torick, it's good to see you're all right," Halandor said, wonderfully relieved at the sight of his friend. "Makilien said you'd been captured in Reylaun."

"I was," Torick acknowledged with a nod, "but I escaped."

"How?" After seeing the way the guards had come after her and overhearing their conversation, Makilien could hardly imagine how one would escape once captured by them.

"I haven't lived to be as old as I am without having a few tricks up my sleeve," Torick told her with a smirk. He paused, but he could see how much she wanted him to elaborate. "The guards in Reylaun transferred me into the hands of Shaikes, and I was able to escape them."

"What are Shaikes?"

"Beings in the service of Zirtan. They're brutes who are hired to kill mercilessly, and they do their job well, but fortunately, most are not very intelligent."

"Did you learn anything from them?" Halandor asked.

"Little we don't already know. They talked of Zirtan still at his fortress up here, but beyond that, nothing."

"At least he is still preparing. It gives us more time to do the same."

Torick agreed.

"Is he really going to attack?" Makilien joined the conversation once more.

"Yes, that much is certain," Halandor answered. "We just don't know when."

"Are you prepared for him?"

"As prepared as we can be . . . we could use more men."

"Maybe if the men of Beldon would open their eyes and see that if Eldor falls, they'll fall, we'd have more of a chance," Torick grumbled.

Halandor only nodded in silent agreement.

"What's Beldon?" Makilien asked.

"The country south over the mountains from Eldor," Halandor answered.

"They don't want to help?"

"No."

Torick unsaddled and tied his horse to a tree before sitting down with Makilien and Halandor. Halandor offered him the leftover fish, and Torick accepted graciously. After he'd taken a few bites, he looked at Makilien.

"So tell me about your journey thus far," he requested. "When I went back to Reylaun to get my horse, I talked briefly to your friend, and he told me you had left."

"Aedan?"

"Yes. You caused quite a stir in that little village of yours. It's the only reason I was able to get back in and get my horse out. The guards were shorthanded and very distracted."

As Torick ate, Makilien told him all about her escape and her adventures in Andin.

"You're very fortunate Halandor was at the Black Stag," Torick said. "Those men likely as not would have killed you."

Makilien shivered at the prospect. "I know. That is why I want to learn to defend myself."

"Would you like to start now, before it gets too late?" Halandor asked her.

Makilien nodded and they rose. She slid her sword out of its leather scabbard and, though it hadn't been sharpened in some time, the steel blade was flawless. Halandor pulled out his own sword and, facing Makilien, he taught her the basics of swordplay. It was difficult, much more so than Makilien had expected. She hadn't thought much of the weight of the sword when she was just holding it, but when she was actually wielding it, it felt much heavier.

For well over an hour, they went slowly over different stances, attacks, and defenses until Makilien thought she would never be able to remember everything. At that time, they decided to call it quits for the night. Sitting down heavily by the fire, perspiration made Makilien's hair stick to her face and neck.

Torick looked at her with a knowing smile. "How do you feel?"

Taking a deep breath, Makilien blew a wisp of hair away from her face. "Exhausted and like my arms are going to fall off. I don't know how I'm ever going to learn, but if this is what it takes, I'm willing."

"Don't worry, in a few days you'll get used to the weight of a sword and start to get familiar with what I teach you," Halandor promised her as he too sat down.

I hope so, Makilien thought to herself.

A short time later, the three of them unrolled their blankets for sleeping. By now, Makilien could barely stay awake long enough to spread hers by the fire. She'd never walked so much in one day before in all her life, and between the incident at the inn and the training she'd done with Halandor, she was in desperate need of rest.

"Do you want me to watch first or do you want to?" Halandor asked Torick.

"You've had to walk all day. I'll watch," Torick told him.

Makilien couldn't help but be glad neither of them said anything to her about standing watch. Lying down, she curled up in her blanket next to the warm fire and fell almost instantly to sleep.

:Chapter Seven:

The Forest

Dawn was just breaking as Makilien woke from a refreshing night's sleep. She opened her eyes to find Halandor and Torick already up and busy. Halandor sat preparing their breakfast by the fire while Torick packed their supplies onto his horse. Pushing back her blanket, Makilien sat up.

"Good morning."

Makilien smiled at Halandor. "Good morning."

She rolled up her blanket and tied it again to her pack.

"Bring your pack here, Makilien, and I'll put it with the others," Torick told her.

Makilien brought it to him, and he secured it to his horse's saddle. By now, Halandor had breakfast ready for them. While they ate, Makilien contemplated all that had happened in the short amount of time she'd been away from home. She'd already learned so much, yet her desire for knowledge was far from satisfied. So many questions and wonderings still filled her mind. One question in particular jumped ahead of the others, and she looked at Halandor who sat across from her.

"Halandor, why did you and Laena react to my name?"

Looking up from his food, Halandor answered softly, "Makilien was my daughter's name."

"Oh," Makilien murmured. She had never considered that possibility. She hesitated. "What happened to her?"

"She was killed . . . by goblins." Halandor fell silent for a moment, memories, still quite fresh, stirring in his mind. "Makilien and I lived in the Elven city of Elindor. My wife died when Makilien was just a small girl. A little over a year ago the city was attacked by goblins. We held them off for as long as we could, but there just weren't enough of us. The city was overrun. Those who could fled. Before we could make it out of the city, Makilien was shot. It was too late by the time I found help."

Makilien couldn't imagine how horrible it must have felt for him to lose the two people closest to him. "I'm sorry, Halandor," she said with a deep remorse. "I'm sorry if the name Makilien is painful for you to hear and use again."

Halandor shook his head, and the faraway look in his eyes disappeared. "No, it's all right. I do not mind. It is a lovely name."

"Yes, a lovely name with a lovely meaning," Torick added.

Makilien looked at him curiously. She did not know names had any meaning. "What does it mean?"

"Touched by God."

Makilien sat silent at these words. They gave her an inexplicable feeling inside as if in anticipation of some event. She pondered it for the rest of their short meal, and before long they had packed up the last remnants of their camp and were on their way.

Makilien's curiosity soon returned as they traveled the well-worn path through the dense and wild, but beautiful Eldinorieth. With Torick now part of the group, Makilien had questions particularly for him.

"Torick, what were you doing in Reylaun anyway?"

"Spying for the most part. Halandor and I came north to gather whatever information we could about Zirtan's whereabouts and his plans."

Mention of Zirtan sparked another question. "In Reylaun, you told me Zirtan was evil itself, what did you mean by that?"

"Just what I said, Zirtan *is* evil," Torick told her in his usual matter-of-fact, no-nonsense way. "He is the source of evil throughout Dolennar."

It shocked Makilien to learn he had so much power. "Is he a god?"

"No, not at all. There is only one true God—Elohim, the Creator of Dolennar. He created everything and everyone."

"Even Zirtan?"

"Even Zirtan, and then Zirtan, in a quest for power, turned against Him."

"Is Zirtan more powerful?" Makilien asked.

"Than Elohim? No," Torick answered, shaking his head.

Makilien cocked her head in confusion. "Then why doesn't Elohim stop him?"

"He will someday, but this is all part of His plan. We may not understand it now, but one day He will stop Zirtan and evil will be no more."

"But if He could stop Zirtan, why wait and let evil things keep happening?" Makilien asked, a bit of indignation sharpening her tone.

"Because He is God, and He knows and sees what we cannot," Torick told her, sounding sterner. "He knows every tiny thing that has happened from the beginning of Dolennar until now and what will happen in the future. All we can see is what is around us, but He sees the whole picture in its entirety.

Adversity can help people grow and make them stronger. Like I said, He has a plan in all that happens."

Feeling she'd been reprimanded for her indignation, Makilien was contritely silent as she considered what Torick so adamantly believed. Finally, she looked up to ask more about Elohim, hoping to gain better understanding.

"What about the evil creatures like Shaikes? Did Elohim create them?"

This time Torick let Halandor answer.

"Yes, but he did not create them to be evil. They chose that. You see, a long time ago, Shaikes were not hostile. They kept to themselves in the area we now call the Black Lands. Centuries ago, Zirtan came to them pretending to be the god they had made up to worship. Most believed him, and those who did not were enslaved or killed. The majority of Shaikes today are born into Zirtan's service and don't have knowledge of how they lived in the past."

"So how does Elohim feel about us and other creatures who are not in league with Zirtan?"

"Elohim loves everyone more greatly than we can even comprehend. He gives guidance and protection to those who have trusted in Him."

Makilien took a moment to think on this. When she'd first considered Elohim, she'd thought of Him only as some all-powerful being who just controlled the world around her, but Halandor made Him sound more like a loving father who would love her and protect her if she let Him. But still, it confused and overwhelmed her.

"Why would He bother? We must hardly seem of any importance."

"That is as far from the truth as it can be," Halandor told her gently. "We are very precious to Him. He is a great artist, and just as an artist loves and enjoys his creations, so does Elohim."

Referring to Elohim as an artist had a powerful effect on Makilien. She considered herself an artist as well. She could sketch the most realistic and breathtaking drawings that awed whoever she shared them with. Makilien took great pride in them and loved every one she'd sketched. Now she could understand, in a way, how Elohim felt about His creation.

"Then He loves me," Makilien realized out loud.

"Yes, He does," Halandor confirmed. "And He wants you to love and trust Him too."

Turning her head to look at Halandor's face, she asked, "Do you love and trust Him?"

"With all my heart," Halandor answered with deep conviction.

Makilien looked to Torick who nodded in agreement with Halandor.

"Have you seen or heard Elohim?" Makilien asked them.

"Not in the traditional sense," Torick answered.

"Then how can you be sure of Elohim and His love if you have never seen or heard Him?" Makilien wanted to know.

"We have faith in Him and believe even if we do not see," Torick told her more quietly than usual. "Evidence of Elohim is all around us in His creation. And we have scrolls and books that have been written by men and Elves He chose and inspired to write His words. Through them He does speak to us, and we have faith in His words."

Can I have that kind of faith? Makilien wondered. She had grown up with so many uncertainties and lies that now all she wanted was to be able to see before she believed. She wondered what made Halandor and Torick so sure and believe so deeply and hoped sometime perhaps she could understand.

As evening approached hours later, the threesome had just begun to discuss where to set up a camp when a faraway echo reached Makilien's ears. She stopped.

"Did you hear that?"

Halandor and Torick nodded as they too halted. All three waited to see if they could hear it again. This time, Makilien was able to identify the noise—a shrill, panicked whinny of a horse coming from somewhere deep in the forest to their left.

"It's a horse," Torick stated.

Halandor looked at him. "Someone could be in trouble."

"Let's go," Torick said without further discussion.

They turned into the forest, and Makilien was delighted they did not tell her to stay behind and wait for them to return. As they made their way into the trees, the whinnies grew louder. When Torick's own horse started getting nervous, he tied him to a tree and they continued. Before long, voices mingled with the whinnies, and they crept along more stealthily.

Finally, they reached the bushes around the edge of a clearing where a crackling fire spit sparks high into the trees. Makilien's eyes grew large as she stared from her position, crouched next to Halandor behind the brush. Gathered all around the fire were the most hideous creatures she'd ever seen. Some were quite short, shorter than she was, while the others were even taller than Halandor and Torick.

Immediately, she suspected the shorter creatures were the goblins she'd heard so many tales about. The ugly creatures stood a few inches shorter than she did. They had inhumanly long arms that were unnaturally skinny. Their pale skin was stretched taut across their limbs, and their bodies were covered in thin grayish brown hair. They had large animal-like eyes and long pointed ears. To Makilien they resembled giant, wingless bats with raspy, high-pitched voices.

The other, larger creatures were the very opposite of the goblins. Their limbs and torsos were thick and heavily muscled. The skin showing through the black armor they wore was dark brown in color, and strange angular tattoos marked the arms of some. Situated atop thick, muscled necks, their broad faces were much more human-like than the goblins, but still monstrous, with fierce yellow eyes and the points of two stained teeth jutting up over their top lips. Most had their heads shaved, though some left strips of black hair growing. Makilien guessed these were the Shaikes Torick had told her about.

Once she conquered the initial shock of seeing such creatures with her own eyes, she located the source of the terrified whinnies they'd heard. Tied securely between two trees was a horse. Underneath layers of dirt and mud and numerous oozing wounds from mistreatment, he bore an ebony coat. His mane and tail were long and thick, and feathering grew from his fetlocks. The poor animal whinnied again, flattening his ears against his head in anger, and tried to rear up; however, the two ropes around his neck yanked him back to the ground.

One of the Shaikes growled in the horse's direction. "I say we kill it! If it won't carry our things, it's useless for anything more than a meal."

"Yesss!" a goblin hissed. "Kill it!"

The whole group roared and hissed in agreement. Makilien looked at the struggling horse and spun around.

"We have to stop them," she whispered desperately to her companions.

Halandor looked at Torick and they came to a swift decision.

Looking down at Makilien, Halandor asked, "Do you think you can use a bow?"

Makilien nodded quickly.

"When I give mine to you, shoot any goblins and Shaikes that you can," Halandor instructed. By now the creatures were preparing to kill the horse.

Both Halandor and Torick pulled out their bows and nocked their arrows. Holding her breath, Makilien watched one of the Shaikes approach the horse with a long, jagged sword. The horse whinnied in terror, and then Makilien heard the sudden twang of Halandor's bowstring. The Shaike roared in pain as he was struck fatally in the back by the arrow and collapsed with a thud. For a moment, the other Shaikes and goblins only stared at their fallen comrade.

And then, all at once, they scrambled for their weapons. Before they could even reach them, Halandor and Torick dropped a couple more and continued to shoot into the panicked fray. Finally, the creatures gathered their wits and rushed toward the bushes where Makilien, Halandor, and Torick hid. Halandor put his bow and a handful of arrows from his quiver into Makilien's hands and rose with Torick.

The two men pulled out their swords and left the bushes to meet the goblins and Shaikes.

As Halandor and Torick clashed into combat, Makilien hurried to follow Halandor's instructions. She nocked an arrow and stood up to shoot. Grasping the string, she pulled it back toward her face. Halandor's bow had a much stronger draw weight than what she was used to, but she managed to pull it back enough and aim at the foul creatures who tried to surround her friends. After only a second to aim, Makilien released the arrow, and one of the goblins dropped with a shriek. Realizing they were up against more than just two opponents, they became disorderly again, and it gave Halandor and Torick an advantage.

With one successful shot, Makilien continued firing rapidly, never missing a target, and taking down any goblins and Shaikes who came her way. In only a few minutes, every one of the creatures lay dead around the campsite. Slowly, Makilien stepped out of the bushes to join Halandor and Torick. She took a deep breath, letting her adrenaline filled body calm.

A soft blowing noise came from across camp, and Makilien looked at the horse. He was much calmer now and stared at them with large, curious eyes. Makilien returned Halandor's bow and approached the horse. She didn't know whether he might be wild or if he'd trust her, so her movements were slow and unthreatening.

"Hello there, boy," she spoke soothingly.

When she came within a few feet of him, Makilien extended her arm. The horse lifted his velvety nose and touched her hand. Right away, she felt a special attachment to him. She ran her hand up his face and gently stroked his neck with her other hand.

Halandor and Torick joined her. The horse watched them, but didn't seem to feel threatened. Inspecting the ropes around the horse's neck, Halandor shook his head.

"These ropes are awfully tight. We'll have to cut them off."

Makilien looked down the horse's neck. In his struggles, the rope had rubbed right into his flesh and was stained with his blood. The cruelty of the goblins and Shaikes caused anger to bubble up inside Makilien.

"Halandor, you stay here with Makilien, and I'll go back for my horse. I have some rope we can use for a halter that is much less rough than what is here," he said.

Halandor nodded, and Torick hurried away. Slowly, Halandor pulled out his dagger, and, as Makilien kept talking softly to the horse, he cut through the two layers of rope around the horse's neck.

In a short time, Torick returned with a halter he'd made out of his rope. He slipped it over the horse's head and handed the end of the lead to Makilien.

"He seems to trust you the most."

"We should take him back to the river and get him cleaned up," Halandor suggested. "There we can tend to his wounds."

Leading the horse along, Makilien followed Halandor and Torick back to the road. By the time they reached it, the sunlight was fading, and they began their search for a good campsite. A short ways from where they left the forest, Makilien spotted a beautiful little area surrounded by ancient willow trees along the river. The ground was carpeted with soft green moss, and groups of cattails grew along the river and rustled in the breeze.

"What a beautiful place," Makilien breathed.

Halandor agreed. "We can set up camp here tonight."

Makilien smiled, happy to be able to stay in that spot.

"Why don't you try to lead the horse into the river and get him clean?" Halandor said. "I'll get a fire going and make something for his wounds."

Makilien pulled off her boots, rolled up her pants and sleeves, and tucked the skirt of her dress up into her belt to stay as dry as possible. Glad it was a warm spring evening, Makilien stepped into the cool river, and the horse followed quietly. Halandor tossed her a rag to wash the grime and blood from the horse. The horse's strong muscles rippled and twitched beneath his smooth coat as she worked, and Makilien tried hard not to cause him pain.

"I'll see if I can scare up a few rabbits," Torick told Halandor after he'd unsaddled his horse. "I won't go too far."

The campsite fell into silence as Makilien and Halandor were both occupied with their tasks. Getting the horse clean was a slow process, but Makilien didn't mind in the least. She loved standing beside the amazing animal. Now she realized how very big he was. His withers came to well past her own shoulders, and she had to stand on tiptoes to see over his back. *What would it be like to ride him?* she wondered.

Torick returned with his catch of two rabbits just as the last bit of light disappeared, and Makilien finished with the horse. She led him out of the water and admired him now that his sleek black coat was showing, but still the ugly sight of his wounds remained. As Torick cleaned the rabbits for their supper, Halandor walked over to Makilien and the horse with a wooden bowl in which he had mixed together some sort of herbal paste.

71

"This will help the wounds heal more quickly and guard against infection," Halandor explained.

Makilien stuck her fingers into the thick concoction and carefully rubbed it over the horse's wounds. When she and Halandor finished covering them all, they sat down around the fire with Torick who was cooking the rabbits. From her seat, Makilien stared at the horse as he munched contentedly on a lush patch of grass. Finally, she looked at Halandor.

"Where do you think he came from?"

Halandor shook his head. "I don't know. There are no villages nearby he might have wandered from."

Makilien waited a moment and then asked, "What are we going to do with him?"

Halandor looked up at the horse who was now staring at them. "Well, since we have no way of knowing where he came from, we'll have to take him along with us." He turned back to Makilien. "Torick already has a horse and I have one in Elimar so I guess that would make him yours."

Makilien's eyes lit up with surprise and excitement. "Really? I can have him?"

Halandor smiled. "Yes."

Makilien looked up at the gorgeous horse she could call her own. It was a dream come true.

"What should I call him? I don't really know any suitable names for such a beautiful animal."

Halandor and Torick both silently thought about it, and then Torick suggested, "How about Antiro?"

"Antiro?" Makilien repeated.

"That was the name of a great Eldorian general," Halandor explained.

Makilien smiled and repeated the name again. It was a strong and proud name. "I like it. I think that is what I'll call him."

Feeling quite content, the three travelers had their meal of cooked rabbit and herbs. It was just as good as the trout Halandor had prepared the night before, and Makilien was so glad she was fortunate enough to be traveling with the two of them.

"I had no idea you were so proficient with a bow, Makilien," Torick remarked in between bites. "Where did you learn to use one?"

"My father taught me," Makilien answered. "He always promised to take me hunting sometime . . . we never had a chance to, but I used to practice almost every day. It was one of the few activities that gave me any satisfaction."

"Now as soon as you learn to handle a sword you'll be well able to defend yourself."

Makilien looked forward to knowing she could and was eager to begin an evening of practice with Halandor. When both of them had finished eating, they stood and Makilien drew her sword. Now she really noticed how sore different muscles in her arms were, but she tried to ignore it. However, several minutes into the training, Makilien winced and looked down at one of her hands. From the last two nights of practice they had become blistered. Quietly, Halandor walked over to his pack and dug around inside it. When he came back, he handed her two strips of soft leather.

"Wrap these around your hands until they become calloused."

Makilien gratefully followed his instructions and was able to continue her training.

:Chapter Eight:

Mountain Wolves

In the days that followed, Makilien, Halandor, and Torick traveled at a fast pace through the forest. Every night Makilien kept up her training with Halandor, and he had also begun teaching her about the forest and survival just as he'd promised. Makilien proved to be a fast learner and quickly retained all he taught her.

Four days after they left Andin, Halandor announced only another three days lay between them and the comforts of Elimar. Makilien enjoyed the beauty of the forest, but she was ready to sleep in a bed again and have a meal at a table.

That night as Halandor prepared supper and Makilien and Torick gathered extra firewood, the echo of a low, eerie howl that sent icy chills down Makilien's spine broke the silence of the darkening forest. She knew it must be a wolf, but it sounded different than any wolf she'd ever heard howling outside the walls of Reylaun.

"Great," Makilien heard Torick mutter under his breath.

She followed him back to the fire, dread churning in the pit of her stomach.

"What was that?" Makilien asked them, trying to keep the fear out of her voice.

Halandor glanced at Torick with a grave look and answered, "A mountain wolf."

"What exactly are mountain wolves?"

"They are larger and much more aggressive than any normal wolf," Torick explained.

"I didn't expect them to have come this far south yet," Halandor said.

Shaking his head, Torick mumbled, "Between goblins, Shaikes, trolls, and wolves, it's a wonder anyone survives the journey through here."

"Halandor," Makilien regained his attention. "Will they bother us?"

Halandor looked at her and hesitated. He didn't want to worry her, but he could only tell her the truth. "I haven't known them yet to keep their distance."

"What are we going to do?" Makilien asked, doing her best not to seem frightened. After all, Halandor and Torick had clearly faced the wolves before and lived.

"We must build up a good fire and make sure we have enough wood to last through the night," Torick answered. "Fire won't completely deter them, but it might help. They won't show themselves until dark so we have to gather as much wood as we can while we still have some light."

The three of them immediately went to gather wood and stacked it next to the fire. A cold dread consumed Makilien as she filled her arms with as much wood as she could carry. She tried to keep her mind focused on the task, but she had to wonder what the night hours would bring. If they were attacked by a pack of mountain wolves, how much defense did they really have?

Light faded far too quickly, and they gave up their hunt for wood to stay close to the fire. With nothing to do but wait, Halandor returned to fixing their supper. Torick untied his horse and Antiro from the nearby trees to bring them closer to the fire as well. He then picked up his bow and quiver, which lay next to his pack, and handed them to Makilien.

"If we're attacked, use my bow and shoot as many of the wolves as you can. They are quick and agile so it won't be easy, but if we can bring down enough of them, the rest may give up. I will stay close to the horses and protect them."

Makilien was glad to know Antiro would have protection.

During their meal, they stared uncertainly into the dark forest. Every little while a howl pierced the silence, each one sounding closer, until finally they were just outside the light of the fire. The horses shifted and snorted anxiously. Makilien clutched Torick's bow in one hand and kept her sword lying next to her.

Minute by minute, the hours passed, but no wolves showed themselves. As the night grew late, Makilien found herself growing sleepy, yet, just as her eyelids started to droop, movement caught her attention. She barely had time to realize it was a wolf before several more sprang out of the forest from all directions.

Makilien was momentarily stunned by the size of the animals. They were huge—about as large as a good sized pony—and their thick fur was coal black. Makilien scrambled to her feet with Halandor and Torick. She and Halandor raised their bows and nocked arrows while Torick took a stand near the horses.

Makilien drew back the bowstring and aimed at one of the wolves as it bounded by her. Panicked, she released the arrow before she was ready. To her frustration, it sailed right over the wolf. She grabbed another arrow and took a deep breath to steady herself before letting go. This time the wolf yelped and fell.

Makilien didn't pause to celebrate her small victory. She immediately grabbed another arrow, but before she could fire again, something hit her from the side with such force it knocked her right to the ground. Gasping for the air that had been forced from her lungs, she found herself staring up at a snarling wolf. Saliva dripped from its vicious, bared teeth, and its cold yellow eyes glinted in the firelight. Makilien threw her arms up for protection as the wolf's head dropped toward her face. She let out a cry of pain as the wolf's teeth sank into her right arm. Halandor shouted her name. The wolf let go and was about to lunge for her neck when it yelped loudly and stumbled away, eventually falling with an arrow in its side.

Makilien scrambled upright and heard an almost unperceivable swishing as more arrows flew out of the darkness behind them, one right after another at an almost inhuman speed. Each one found its target with astonishing accuracy, and the wolves dropped as fast as the arrows appeared. Finally, the last few turned and fled into the forest.

For a moment, no one moved, but then all together they turned and looked into the forest behind them. Out of the darkness, a figure appeared almost as if he'd materialized from the shadows. Approaching them gracefully, clad in clothing of various shades of dark green, brown, and gray, he moved without a sound, not a single leaf or twig crunching under his soft leather boots.

Forgetting the rudeness of it, all Makilien could do was stare. This new being joining them appeared to be Human, but she knew he was not. His long flaxen colored hair was very straight and smooth, and he had the clearest blue eyes Makilien had ever seen. He turned his head for a moment to scan the forest to his left, and Makilien almost gasped. The being had pointed ears. *He must be an Elf!* She was awed. This was certainly not how she'd ever imagined Elves when she'd heard Mornash's stories.

The world, which had seemed to be going in slow motion, suddenly sped up again as the silence that settled over camp was broken.

"Loron!" Halandor exclaimed, both with surprise and gladness.

The Elf reached the fire in only another couple of strides, and by this time, Halandor had turned his attention to an injured Makilien.

"Let me see your arm," he said as he knelt next to her.

Makilien had forgotten the pain and sensation of oozing blood when she'd seen the Elf, but as she lifted her arm, the pain returned. She grimaced. Carefully, Halandor rolled up her sleeve revealing the bleeding wounds caused by the wolf's teeth. He reached for his pack and pulled out a clean cloth. Makilien groaned as he pressed it down on her wounds.

"I'm sorry," he apologized, "I want to stop the bleeding."

Makilien nodded, understanding.

Looking over his shoulder, Halandor asked, "Torick, would you heat some water?"

Torick emptied one of their waterskins into a pot to heat by the fire. As soon as it was warm enough, he set it down next to Halandor who used it to clean the wounds. Once this was accomplished, he wrapped a clean bandage around Makilien's arm.

"There," he said. "The wounds should heal quickly. They are not serious."

Makilien was relieved. The last thing she wanted was an injury that would inhibit her from her training with Halandor.

Helping her up, Halandor said, "Now, I think it's about time for formal introductions. Makilien, this is our good friend, Loron." He gestured to the Elf, and Makilien turned to him with a smile. "Loron, this is Makilien. She is from Reylaun. We met in Andin."

"I am very pleased to meet you, Makilien," Loron said kindly.

"It is a pleasure to meet you as well, Loron."

He smiled at her, and the four companions took seats by the fire.

Poking at the embers with a stick, Torick glanced at Loron and asked, "What are you doing out here? I thought you were back in Elimar."

"I came out looking for you and Halandor. Lord Elnauhir and I thought you might need help," Loron answered.

"Well, you showed up just in the nick of time, as usual."

Loron chuckled and raised an eyebrow in amusement. "Elohim must have gifted me with the ability to sense whenever my friends are in danger."

Torick too chuckled, and then Loron told him and Halandor, "I also came out with news. It's been confirmed that Zirtan has put a man in charge of his force—a general by the name of Zendon. Zirtan has given him command of all his armies, and Zendon is the one who will lead the attack."

"That could be a move in our favor," Halandor remarked. "I know many were concerned about coming up against Zirtan face-to-face."

Loron agreed.

"Did you learn how soon he'll attack?" Halandor asked.

"No, what about you?"

Halandor shook his head. "No. We know he's still at his fortress in the North and seems still to be gathering his armies so that gives us at least a couple of weeks yet."

"Any extra amount of time will help us," Loron said.

Halandor and Torick were in agreement.

Makilien listened quietly. She seemed almost forgotten amidst the talk of such serious issues, but when a yawn escaped her, Halandor noticed.

"You should get some rest," he told her.

"Are you sure?" Makilien asked. "Do you think the wolves will be back?"

"No, they won't return without greater numbers, and they can't gather them tonight. Go to sleep."

The softness of Halandor's voice gave Makilien great comfort. He reminded her of her father when he used to put her to bed at night. Makilien was glad to have someone like him with her during this incredible, yet uncertain time.

"All right," she said with a small smile, for she was indeed very tired.

Wrapping her blanket around herself like a snug cocoon, Makilien lay down and closed her eyes. The crackling of the fire and the familiar sounds of Halandor and Torick's deep voices and the new, almost musical, flow of Loron's, put her to sleep within minutes.

The cheery calls of early rising birds echoed in the forest rousing Makilien from slumber. She stretched in her warm blanket and felt the weariness of the late night still in her muscles, but her mind was rested. Though her arm throbbed with a dull ache, it was not as painful as she might have expected. Around the fire, Halandor, Torick, and Loron spoke in quiet voices, and she smelled breakfast.

Rubbing her eyes, Makilien sat up. The entire forest stood shrouded in sparkling, silver mist making the trees appear as dark pillars rising in the fog. Around their camp lay the dark, lifeless bodies of the fallen wolves.

"Good morning."

Makilien turned to Halandor with a smile.

"Did you sleep well?" he asked her.

"Yes."

"How is your arm?"

"It aches a little," Makilien admitted.

Halandor reached for a cup, which sat by the fire, and handed it to her. "Drink this. It will help the pain."

Makilien sipped the slightly bitter herbal liquid and returned the cup to Halandor as she stood. The cool mist that had gathered on her skin made her shiver momentarily, but it felt good. The sun glowed through the trees now and created glittering shafts of light. It gave a mysterious beauty to the misty forest.

After stretching her tired muscles, Makilien walked over to the horses and rubbed Antiro on the nose.

"Good morning, Antiro."

The horse nickered and nibbled her sleeve playfully. Makilien smiled. Antiro looked much better than when they'd found him. Makilien kept him well groomed, and his wounds were healing well.

"Makilien, I do believe that horse can understand you," Torick said suddenly.

"Really?" Makilien asked in surprise.

Torick nodded. "He seems to listen when we're talking and reacts to the things you say to him."

Makilien looked into Antiro's face. "Can you understand me?"

Antiro nickered again and tossed his head.

"But how could an animal understand?"

"Occasionally, Elohim gifts certain common animals with the ability," Torick explained. "I would consider it a gift to you too."

Makilien glanced at him. Reluctance always sprang up in her heart whenever Elohim was mentioned. Halandor and Torick trusted and relied on Him so greatly. Their faith was admirable, but Makilien doubted she could have the same faith. She just didn't think she could let go of the need to rely on herself and her friends—things she could see and know to be real. And so she said nothing.

In a short time, the travelers ate their breakfast and went on their way while early morning was still upon them. The weather was ideal for travel. Bright rays from the sun streamed through the trees, burning off the fog and warming Makilien and her friends. Just off to the right of the road, the river bubbled and gurgled, slowly leading the way south as the foursome and their equine companions traveled along the well-worn path.

When midday arrived, Makilien felt the twinge of hunger in her stomach, and soon Halandor brought the group to a halt.

"We'll stop here for lunch and pick some jents," he said.

Curiously, Makilien followed his line of sight, and her gaze landed on the smooth gray bark and dark foliage of a tall tree growing beside the road. Her eyes traveled up to the branches. Growing among them were fruits unlike any she'd seen before. They were round, about the size of her palm, and had skins the color of pale blue like the sky. The breeze carried the sweet scent of the lighter blue blossoms, which still grew on the tree.

"I've never seen any fruit like this," Makilien said.

Halandor looked at her. "You haven't?"

Makilien shook her head. "No. I've only ever had fruit that was grown in Reylaun. What are they like?"

"They are very sweet and also have strong healing properties. They are used in many medicines."

Walking up to the tree, Halandor reached to pick one from a high up branch. He handed it to Makilien who found it had a velvety skin like peach. Curiously, she took a bite revealing the pale yellow flesh inside. Her eyes widened in delight. Never before had she tasted something so sweet. It tasted much like a plum, yet sweeter and without any of the tartness.

"Mmm, it's delicious."

Her companions smiled and picked some for themselves. Each of them ate their fill, and Makilien and Torick fed some to their horses. When they were finished, they packed a few extra jents into their packs for the remainder of their journey.

As they prepared to be on their way, Makilien turned questioningly to Halandor. "Could I ride Antiro? I've never been on a horse before, but I've wanted to ride all my life. Do you think he's healed enough and would let me?"

"I don't see why not," Halandor answered. "Why don't you ask him?"

Makilien turned to Antiro. "Do you mind if I ride you?"

Antiro shook his head making his long black mane ripple. Makilien smiled. "I guess you don't."

They tied the free end of the rope to Antiro's makeshift halter creating reins, and Halandor helped Makilien onto the horse's back. As she settled into place, she grinned, knowing immediately she would love it.

"Are you ready?" Halandor asked.

Makilien nodded. Halandor, Torick, and Loron walked on. Even though she'd never ridden a horse before, Makilien understood the basics. She squeezed her legs against Antiro's sides, and he started off at a smooth walk to follow the others. Makilien's smile could not be erased from her face at the joy of experiencing something she'd dreamed of for so long. Her friends smiled too at her bliss.

"When we reach Elimar, someone there can teach you more about riding," Loron told Makilien.

Eager to learn, Makilien asked, "How much farther do we have to go?"

"We'll arrive sometime around noon the day after tomorrow," Halandor answered.

"What plans do you have once we get there?"

"I plan to stay a few days to rest and then go on to Minarald."

Makilien wasn't sure whether he intended for her to go along or not. She disliked the thought of being left behind. Halandor had become like a second father to her, and she didn't want to have to say goodbye to anyone again so soon after leaving her family.

"May I come to Minarald with you?"

"If you want to," Halandor told her, though he warned, "Minarald will not be a safe place once Zirtan attacks."

But Makilien told herself she wasn't afraid. She wanted to do anything she could to fight Zirtan. "I would like to help, if I can."

:Chapter Nine:

Elven City

Makilien was still in awe of the sight that surrounded her. The day before, the trees of Eldinorieth had come to an end, giving way to beautiful rolling hills as far as she could see. Lush, knee-high grass covered the hills dotted with sprinklings of spring flowers. As much as Makilien enjoyed the forest, she was delighted by this change of scenery.

The sun had just passed its peak when she noticed part of the road branch off to the east. Instead of continuing to the south, her companions took this turn, coming to the edge of the river they'd followed all the way through Eldinorieth. Just across it lay a wondrous sight beyond anything Makilien had imagined. Amidst a wooded area stood the breathtaking Elven buildings she had waited so anxiously to see. The structures were constructed unlike any she'd witnessed in the past. The architecture was elegant and natural, blending well with the trees.

The travelers crossed the shallow part of the river with ease. When they arrived on the other side and entered the stunning city, it was as if Makilien were entering a dream. She could only stare in silent wonder.

Most of the structures were painted a creamy white with slate-blue shingles, and the winding streets were more just paths, carpeted with softly fallen leaves, which muffled their footsteps. The ground rose and fell along the way, matching the open, hilly terrain they'd just come from. Birds sang cheerful melodies from the towering maples and oaks surrounding them. Joining in was the gurgling of clear streams, which branched off the main river. Growing on the moist banks were bright yellow buttercups, but those weren't the only flowers. There were splashes of flowers everywhere, alive with butterflies.

Before long, they arrived at the biggest house Makilien had ever seen. At least as big as any four buildings in Reylaun combined.

"This is Lord Elnauhir's house," Halandor told Makilien. "All visitors to Elimar are welcome here."

After tying the horses to a hitching post, they walked up to the tall doors of the entrance. Without waiting, Halandor opened the door with familiar ease and walked in unannounced. They entered a spacious, marble-floored foyer whose ceiling rose up at least twenty feet, supported by beautifully carved pillars. Directly ahead stood a massive staircase leading to a second floor, and all around them were doorways to all the numerous rooms of the grand house. All was quiet, except for the sounds of birds through the open windows, which let in ample amounts of sunlight with no need for lamps during the daytime.

"It's good to be back," Torick said with quiet contentment.

Halandor agreed and shrugged off his pack. Everyone else did the same, setting them in a pile near the door. Makilien almost felt it a shame to spoil the look of such a beautiful and spotless area, but no one else seemed to mind. They obviously felt right at home.

"I wonder where everyone is," Halandor said as he looked around.

"They could be any number of places, and I'm not about to search the whole house. I'm going to do it the easy way," Torick replied. He raised his voice and called out, "Is anyone here?"

They waited for the space of a half a minute. Suddenly, Makilien heard a voice before she heard any footsteps.

"Loron, you found them! And they're alive!"

Looking to her left, Makilien saw a male Elf entering the foyer. He appeared to be a bit younger than Loron and had long, dark hair instead of blonde.

Torick rolled his eyes at the Elf's comment.

"Hello, Elmorhirian," Halandor said with a smile.

"I'm very glad to see you made it back all in one piece," Elmorhirian told them with a grin.

"You doubted?" Torick asked less humorously.

Elmorhirian smirked mischievously, but before he could comment, he noticed Makilien.

"Who is our lovely guest?"

Makilien smiled, and Halandor said, "This is Makilien. She came from Reylaun."

"It is a pleasure to meet you," Elmorhirian said graciously, "and an honor to have you here. I am Elmorhirian, son of Lord Elnauhir."

"I am very pleased to meet you, Elmorhirian." Makilien liked this Elf already. Though he seemed to annoy Torick, she found him amusing.

"Elmorhirian, where is your father and the rest of the family?" Halandor asked.

"I believe Father is in his study. Elandir and I just came in so I don't know where Mother or Vonawyn are. I'll go find them."

"We'll be in the living room," Halandor told him.

Elmorhirian hurried off, and Halandor led everyone else down a long hall and finally into another, larger room. This one was filled with many stuffed couches and chairs. At one end stood a huge fireplace with a beautifully carved mantel. On either side were massive bookcases filled with leather-bound books.

Weary from the long journey, everyone took seats, enjoying the comfort after so many days on the trail. Sitting beside Halandor, Makilien said, "You all seem so comfortable here. Do you come often?"

"This is our home when we are not traveling," Halandor answered.

"Oh. I didn't realize that."

"Yes, I've spent most of my life here. Loron also."

The four of them only had a few minutes to wait before Elmorhirian returned with an older and very wise looking male Elf. He too had dark hair, and the regality about him left Makilien in no doubt he was Lord Elnauhir.

"Welcome back," he told Halandor and Torick in a rich, kingly voice. "Do you bring any news?"

Halandor shook his head. "We weren't able to gather any specific information, but Zirtan still seems to be seeing to his preparations."

Elnauhir appeared pleased by this. "Good." His attention now turned to Makilien. She felt shy and rather lowly before the Elf-lord, but his gaze was kind, and Makilien relaxed.

"Elmorhirian told me we had a special guest. What is your name?"

"Makilien."

"I am Elnauhir, lord of this city, and I hope you will feel welcome here in Elimar."

"Thank you, Lord Elnauhir. I do feel welcome already."

"Good." Elnauhir smiled. "How did you come to be here, Makilien?"

Briefly, she told him of her escape from Reylaun and meeting Halandor in Andin.

When she had finished, the Elf-lord said, "I commend your bravery for leaving on your own even though you did not know what you would find."

Makilien shrugged. "I just wanted things to change so badly, and, after I talked to Torick, I knew I couldn't stay in Reylaun. I had hoped I wouldn't have to leave alone. My best friend, Aedan, wanted to come, but he's the only man in his family and has to care for them."

"Well, I'm very glad you made it here safely," Elnauhir told her with deep sincerity.

In the next moment, three other Elves stepped into the room to join them—the other members of Elnauhir's family. The one Makilien believed to be Elnauhir's wife was a lovely Elf woman with long, golden colored hair. The dignity of her appearance spoke of wisdom and maturity, yet she had a youthfulness about her. The second Elf Makilien guessed to be another of Elnauhir's sons. He had golden hair like his mother and seemed a little older and more mature than Elmorhirian, but still had the same impish look in his blue eyes. Lastly, was a beautiful Elf maiden who appeared to be about the same age as Makilien. She shared the same rich dark hair as the Elf-lord and his son.

Elnauhir turned to them with a smile. "Everyone, come and meet our guest. Her name is Makilien. She is from the village of Reylaun and has traveled here with Halandor and Torick."

He turned back to Makilien. "Makilien, this is my wife, Lorelyn, my son, Elandir, and my daughter, Vonawyn."

They each greeted and warmly welcomed Makilien to Elimar. Though she felt a little shy, their kind welcome made her feel right at home.

After the greetings, Elnauhir asked Halandor, "Have you had anything for lunch?"

"We had some jents from our packs along the way."

"I'll have a proper meal prepared for you, and you can eat once everyone's settled in." Elnauhir turned to his daughter. "Vonawyn, will you show Makilien to a room and see to her needs?"

"Yes, Father." Turning to Makilien, the Elf smiled sweetly. "Come with me."

Makilien followed her out of the living room and through the halls. Along the way, she stared in awe. It seemed right when she thought she couldn't see anything more beautiful, she did.

Vonawyn glanced over her shoulder, curiosity in her hazel eyes. "There aren't any houses like this in Reylaun, are there?"

"No," Makilien answered. "I'll probably get lost here."

Vonawyn laughed lightly.

"You wouldn't be the first, but don't worry, I will show you around."

"Thank you."

Soon, the two of them arrived in a most beautiful room, which was more than four times the size of Makilien's bedroom at home.

"This will be your room," Vonawyn informed her.

"All this for me?" Makilien asked in amazement.

Vonawyn smiled and gave her a nod. "Now, since you traveled so far, would you like a bath to wash up?"

"That would be very nice. Thank you."

"I'll have someone bring a tub and some water, and I'll get you some fresh clothes to change into once you're finished."

When Vonawyn left her alone, Makilien walked into the middle of the room and turned slowly in a circle to take it all in. She hadn't known such luxury existed. She stopped at the foot of the large bed. How good it was going to feel not to sleep on the ground that night!

Vonawyn returned with several other Elf women—some carrying a tub and others carrying water.

"Halandor told me about your arm," Vonawyn she said to Makilien. "When you're finished with your bath, I'll bandage your wounds with fresh bandages."

"All right." Having thought of Antiro just before Vonawyn walked in, Makilien went on to ask, "What about our horses? Torick and I left them tied up."

"They are being looked after," Vonawyn assured her. "My brothers will see that they are comfortable too."

After several trips, the Elves finished filling the tub with steaming water and some fragrant oils that filled the whole room with a flowery scent.

"I will be back in a little while to see if you're done," Vonawyn said. "Then I'll bandage your arm and show you to the dining room."

After she had left, Makilien got into the bath. Only now did she realize how dirty she and her clothes had become over the last several days of travel. The bath was just as heavenly as she had anticipated it to be, and at first, she simply sat and enjoyed it as the scent of the oils drifted around her with the steam. Finally, she picked up a bar of soap to wash.

Some time later, Makilien left the tub and put on a dress Vonawyn had left for her. She was amazed by how comfortable it was. The bodice and skirt were made of a light blue satin, and the flowing sleeves and sash were white. Makilien had never seen a dress made of such material.

Just as she finished tying the sash, a light knock sounded at her door, and she went to open it. Vonawyn stood on the other side with a pleasant smile. Makilien opened the door wider, and the Elf walked in with a handful of medical supplies. As she took a seat in a chair, Makilien pulled up her sleeve. By now, the wounds were healing nicely, and soon she wouldn't need a bandage at all. Vonawyn applied an ointment to the still visible bite marks and bandaged Makilien's arm lightly.

"Are you hungry?" Vonawyn asked as she was finishing.

"Yes, I am." Though the jents had been filling, traveling had increased her appetite.

"Good. The food is ready and everyone was just starting to gather in the dining room."

Makilien stood and followed. On the way to the dining room, Vonawyn pointed out different rooms, and Makilien tried to remember them, but she knew it would take more than one time to remember all of them.

Shortly, they came to the dining room with one long table sitting in its middle, which could easily accommodate many people. The room itself was large enough for a few more such tables. Places had been set for the travelers, and Elandir and Elmorhirian occupied two of them, sitting across from Halandor and Loron. Vonawyn frowned at her brothers as she and Makilien came to the table.

"What are you two doing? We've already had lunch."

"That was a *whole* two hours ago," Elmorhirian said dramatically.

Vonawyn shook her head and said to Makilien, "Trust my brothers to eat whenever food is present."

Everyone chuckled, and Makilien took a seat next to Halandor while Vonawyn sat down next to Elmorhirian.

"And just what are you doing here, little sister?" Elmorhirian asked Vonawyn, raising his chin and narrowing his eyes.

"Someone has to keep an eye on you and make sure you behave."

Makilien laughed at the comment as well as Elmorhirian's sour expression.

A few moments later, Torick joined them, all cleaned up and in fresh clothes as well. Elmorhirian looked at him and opened his mouth wide. "Look, Elandir, he's clean!"

Torick gave him a mock smile. "I know, shocking isn't it?" He sat down across from Makilien and looked at her seriously. "If there's one thing you should know about Elves, particularly these two, it's that they have a wicked sense of humor," he warned. "I'd watch them closely."

"Ah, come on, Torick, you don't have to make her wary of us," Elandir complained. "We're nice to guests, especially such lovely ones."

"And they are flatterers," Torick quickly added.

"Don't listen to the old man," Elmorhirian chimed in.

Torick scoffed. "Old man? I'm hardly more than half your age, you overgrown Elfling."

"That's true," Elandir admitted, but he flashed a grin. "Compared to us, Torick, you're practically just a child."

Torick rolled his eyes, and Makilien giggled. "Why don't you two just hush for once? Honestly, I'm beginning to think you're the ones to blame for giving Elves such a bad reputation in the stories told outside of Eldor."

"Now, Torick, you can't possibly pin that on us," Elmorhirian pouted. "We can't take all the credit."

By now, Makilien was laughing so hard she could hardly take a decent breath. She wondered if life in Elimar was this interesting every day.

Elandir turned his gaze to her. "Seriously, we're not as bad as Torick makes us out to be. We just like to have a little fun with him sometimes. You might not know it now, but trust me—Torick's sense of humor is just as wicked as ours."

This time, Torick smiled genuinely, and Makilien knew Elandir must be telling the truth.

"Yes, you should hear some of the stuff he's pulled on us!" Elmorhirian was quick to add.

Makilien's eyes turned to Torick who shrugged.

"What can I say? Someone's got to teach you two a lesson sometimes."

Everyone laughed again. Makilien had never had so much fun. She wished so much her family and Aedan were here with her. Aedan and Leiya would have especially loved it.

In just a few minutes, Elves brought food to the table. Makilien's stomach growled as soon as the aroma reached her nose. She couldn't wait to fill her plate and begin eating the food, which was sure to be delicious.

Elnauhir and Lorelyn also joined them at the table. As soon as the hungry travelers were served, they began telling of their journey. Makilien told them much about life in Reylaun and recounted the events leading up to her escape. Torick told of his escape from the Shaikes, and they all helped tell the story of rescuing Antiro and being attacked by the mountain wolves. It certainly had been an eventful time.

Once everything had been gone over thoroughly, Makilien chose a moment to pose a question she'd been pondering since Elandir and Elmorhirian had been joking with Torick.

"So, is it true then that Elves live forever?"

Elnauhir looked at her with a smile and shook his head. "No, that is one of the uncountable myths about Elves, but it is understandable. We Elves do live longer than Humans."

"How long?" Makilien wished to know.

"Around two-hundred years, twice as long as a Human," Elnauhir told her. "Another contribution to the myth is that Elves don't age quite the same way as Humans. We don't necessarily look very old when we die."

Makilien could hardly imagine what it would be like to live so long. She looked at Vonawyn. "How old are you?"

"This year I will be seventy-two."

Makilien tried not to look so stunned, but Vonawyn only smiled at her. "I know, if you have not grown up around Elves, it is a little strange and shocking."

"Yes, just think, we were around when *little* cousin Halandor was born," Elmorhirian threw in. "Vonawyn used to change his diapers!"

This remark sent everyone into waves of laughter, particularly the two Elf brothers. Once Makilien had regained her composure, she looked at Halandor questioningly.

"Cousin?"

Halandor nodded in confirmation. "Yes, it is true. I am their younger cousin."

"But how? You're not an Elf."

"My mother was. I am Half-Elf."

Makilien was shocked by this sudden discovery. "Really?"

Halandor nodded again.

"Do you have any Elven abilities?" Makilien asked.

"In some ways. My senses are a little more acute, but not nearly as much as an Elf's."

"Will you live longer?"

"Yes, but not as long as an Elf."

"Do you mind me asking how old you are now?"

"Fifty-eight," Halandor answered with a smile. "Actually, Torick and I are the same age."

Makilien looked between the two of them, amazed by the difference in appearance. She marveled over all the things she was discovering about life and beings outside of Reylaun.

Immediately after their meal, Makilien was given a grand tour of Elimar by Vonawyn and her brothers. They began inside the house and eventually made their way outside to tour the city. Makilien enjoyed every moment spent with the three Elf siblings. They had countless stories to tell, which made her laugh so hard at times her stomach hurt. How she loved it here already. It was such a stark contrast from the village she'd grown up in.

The tour lasted throughout the afternoon. Even though the Elven city wasn't really that large, there was so much to see. Many times Makilien felt the urge to get her sketchbook and draw what she saw. It was something she determined to do sometime during their stay.

When finally they returned to Lord Elnauhir's house, they received word that supper was about to be served. Elandir and Elmorhirian literally raced off to the dining room, pushing each other along the way as if the last one there wouldn't get as much to eat. Makilien and Vonawyn followed more slowly, chuckling at the antics of her brothers.

Once again in the dining room, Makilien sat down happily with her new friends and watched in delight as the food was brought to the table. This meal was much bigger than the one they'd enjoyed earlier. It was practically a feast. *I suppose with Elandir and Elmorhirian this much food is necessary,* Makilien thought, grinning to herself.

After everyone had filled their plates, Makilien heard Elnauhir mention prayer and everyone around the table bowed their heads. Makilien slowly did the same, still feeling awkward with the unfamiliar practice though her traveling companions had always prayed before meals.

"Elohim, our Creator and Lord," Elnauhir began with deep sincerity and reverence. "Thank You for this time we are able to share in each other's company and enjoy the food and comfort You have so generously provided for us. We thank You also for our guest, Makilien, and the opportunity for us to share our home and time with her. We ask that You guide and protect her and each one of us in this uncertain time in which we are besieged by our enemy. Help us to always be looking toward You for strength and guidance. Amen."

Amen was repeated around the table and everyone happily began the meal. However, Makilien was quiet at first. She'd never heard anyone pray for her before, unaware that Halandor and Torick had been doing it for days. It was nice to hear herself mentioned in a prayer, but, still uncertain of where she stood on the subject of Elohim, Makilien was also a bit uncomfortable. The discomfort did not last long though. She enjoyed being with everyone too much to let it affect her happiness.

:Chapter Ten:

Messenger

"Don't forget to keep your heels down," Vonawyn instructed.

Makilien made a few adjustments as Antiro cantered around the corral. She thoroughly enjoyed learning the basics of riding. It was now their third full day in Elimar and Makilien's third such riding lesson.

"Good, now bring him toward the center and change directions," Vonawyn said from the middle of the corral.

Makilien followed her instructions, Antiro smoothly obeying every command. She was already quite comfortable cantering in wide circles around the enclosure. She'd come a long way from the day before when she'd fallen off the first time she had tried.

A couple successful laps later, Makilien slowed Antiro to a trot and then a walk. She'd only lost her balance once during the exercise, and she was pleased. Now she halted Antiro at the fence where Halandor had joined Vonawyn. He smiled proudly at her.

"Your skills are improving. I haven't seen many take to a horse as quickly as you have."

Makilien's face radiated with excitement and pleasure. "I don't think I've ever enjoyed myself as much as I have the last couple of days."

Vonawyn walked up and laid her hand on Antiro's neck as she looked at Makilien. "Do you want to keep riding or stop for the day?"

Makilien would have loved to go on riding for the rest of the afternoon, but, until she'd started her lessons, she'd never realized how much energy it took to ride and by now she was tired and sore.

"I guess we'll call it quits for today," Makilien said reluctantly.

She dismounted and led Antiro toward the stable. Vonawyn and Halandor followed and lent a hand in removing Antiro's tack and brushing his sweaty coat.

On their way back to Elnauhir's house after the horse had been let out to graze, Makilien, Halandor, and Vonawyn were interrupted from their conversation by a sudden loud screech. At first, it sounded like an eagle, but Makilien realized it was deeper, almost a roar, yet still birdlike.

"What was that?" she asked, looking between her companions in alarm.

Vonawyn grinned. "It's Arphen."

"Who?"

"He's a messenger."

"But then *what* is he?"

Makilien couldn't imagine what had made the strange and rather frightening sound.

"He's another of the creatures you've probably heard about in stories," Vonawyn answered. "You'll get to meet him as soon as we reach the house."

Makilien was filled with curiosity but also a bit apprehensive. Whatever had made that noise sounded quite big.

They increased their pace. Along the way, Halandor said, "If Arphen is here from Minarald, he must have news from Lord Darand."

Vonawyn agreed.

When they came around the corner of Lord Elnauhir's house, Makilien stopped abruptly. There, in the midst of her group of friends, stood a most amazing creature. It had the body of a dark coated lion, but its head was that of an eagle. On the sides of its head, however, were feathered, but catlike ears and stretching out from its shoulders were huge wings like those of a giant eagle.

"What is he?" Makilien asked in awe.

"A griffon," Halandor answered, enjoying her reaction.

"A griffon," Makilien murmured to herself. She had indeed heard of them in stories, but they'd never been described as the stunning and majestic creature that stood before her.

His keen eyes picked her out immediately. "Well now, who is this?" Arphen spoke from his beaked mouth in a clear and most friendly voice.

Makilien gasped. "You can speak!"

The corners of the griffon's mouth turned up in a smile.

"Indeed, I can," Arphen replied in amusement.

"Arphen, this is Makilien," Halandor made introductions, explaining how she had come to be here.

"My dear, it is an honor to have you among us," Arphen said to Makilien, dipping his head politely.

Despite feeling a little intimidated, Makilien smiled. She liked him very much already. "And I cannot tell you what an honor it is for me to meet such an amazing creature as you."

Arphen's smile grew larger. "Good, then we shall be friends."
Makilien nodded eagerly.

Once their introduction had concluded, Elnauhir spoke to Halandor.

"Arphen has news from Lord Darand."

"Ah, yes, the news," Arphen said, getting back to the business at hand. "Two days ago, a man arrived in Minarald claiming to be a captain under the command of Zirtan. He swears he has turned against Zirtan and wishes to assist us."

"Does he have information concerning Zirtan and his plans?" Elnauhir questioned.

"Some, yes. He told Lord Darand that Zirtan's army is not as large as we believe it to be. He insists Zirtan only wants us to think we are vastly outnumbered, but we really stand a good chance of victory, even without assistance from Beldon."

Halandor looked thoughtfully at him. "Does Lord Darand trust what he says?"

"I do not know. I was sent straight here with the news."

"Do you trust him?"

"Personally, I do not, but it is not my place to judge a man I have only met but once," Arphen answered.

"Does Lord Darand want us in Minarald?"

"He does indeed wish to seek your counsel. And, if Lord Elnauhir is willing, Lord Darand also believes it would be wise to bring our armies together at this time and fortify the city."

"Has this former captain of Zirtan said we'll be attacked soon?" Lord Elnauhir asked.

"No, my lord, quite the opposite in fact, but Lord Darand does not want to take the risk."

Elnauhir nodded grimly. "I will gather my army and set out for Minarald within two days' time."

"And I, and whoever wishes to join me, will leave in the morning," Halandor said.

"I too will rest here overnight and leave in the morning," Arphen told them. "I will fly straight to Minarald and inform Lord Darand you are on your way. I will also see that the road ahead is free of danger."

"Thank you, Arphen."

Everyone turned to go their separate ways. Elnauhir had much to do to prepare his army, and Vonawyn and her brothers went off with Arphen to show the noble creature a place to rest and spend the night. Makilien found herself left standing with Halandor, Loron, and Torick.

"I'm going with you to Minarald," Torick informed Halandor.

"So am I," Loron said.

"Is it still all right if I come?" Makilien asked.

"If that is still what you want," Halandor answered. "Elimar is one of the safest places in Dolennar right now."

"I do want to."

With a smile, Torick said, "Well then, when we get there, we can introduce you to Meniah."

Makilien frowned. "Who is Meniah?"

"He has been advising Lord Darand," Halandor explained. "We all feel that without him, we wouldn't be nearly as prepared to face Zirtan as we are."

Makilien was interested by how both Torick and Halandor spoke of him with such reverence. If he was more responsible for preparing Eldor to face Zirtan than her king, he must surely be a great man indeed.

The sun only just reached the treetops, but Makilien had been awake for over an hour. Everyone gathered outside with Lord Elnauhir and his family. The horses were each saddled and waited only for their riders to say goodbye before beginning their journey.

"I'll see you in a few days," Vonawyn told Makilien.

"You're coming to Minarald?" she asked.

"Yes. Once fighting begins, there will be a need for those able to help the wounded."

It was a grim reality.

Shortly, Makilien and her companions mounted their horses. Arphen extended his wings and, with a couple of great flaps, he soared into the air. Makilien watched him in amazement until he disappeared. It was time now for them to leave. Halandor took the lead. Following, Makilien looked around her as they left Elimar. She hated to leave the beauty and comfort of the Elven dwelling, but Halandor had told her it was only a three day ride to Minarald and the greatness of that city was comparable to Elimar's beauty.

When they left the forest surrounding Elimar, wide open grassland spread out before them, interrupted only by a few shrubs and rocks and the road they traveled. They rode through the open plain almost non-stop throughout the day, their longest rest coming at noon, but even then they were on their way quickly.

After all day in the saddle, Makilien was relieved when their group halted as dusk fell around them.

"We'll camp here tonight," Halandor said, gesturing to a small, grassy knoll just off the well-traveled path.

Slowly, Makilien dismounted, aching all over. The only thing she wanted was to curl up under a blanket and sleep.

Tonight she would certainly miss her bed in Elimar. However, any rest would have to wait. Camp needed to be set up, and Makilien was determined to prove herself capable.

The horses were unsaddled first and picketed at the edge of camp. A fire was lit soon after and Makilien got her chance to sit down as Halandor aided Torick with supper preparations. By the time it was finished, Makilien was almost too tired to eat, but once she began, she realized her hunger. When her plate was empty, she took out her bedroll asking if she could do anything else to help, but her companions understood her weariness and told her to sleep.

Stars twinkled overhead when Makilien yawned and opened her eyes. She didn't know how long she'd been asleep or how much time it would be yet until dawn. Rolling over, she made herself comfortable and tried to fall back to sleep, but it didn't come as easily as it had previously. Her mind filled with thoughts that kept her wide awake.

For a long time, Makilien lay still, trying to quiet her mind, but at last, she gave up and looked around camp. Torick and Loron were fast asleep off to her left. Looking to her right, she saw Halandor sitting at the edge of camp on watch.

With a sigh, Makilien got up. She wanted to sleep knowing they had another tiring day of riding ahead, but it wasn't going to happen. Hoping she might sleep a bit more after a while, she walked quietly over to Halandor.

"Can't sleep?" he asked in a whisper.

Makilien shook her head. "No. There is too much on my mind."

Halandor looked at her face in the moonlight. "Is it anything you'd like to talk about?"

"It's just a lot of things. I keep thinking about my family. I've never been away from them before this. As glad as I am to be here, I still miss them."

"It's always hard to be separated from family."

Makilien nodded, knowing Halandor understood. She pulled her knees up to her chest. Staring out at the vast sea of moonlit grassland, she said, "All this is still so much to take in. Even something as familiar to you as all this open land is completely foreign to me. There is no openness like this anywhere in Reylaun." She took a deep breath. "It gives me a feeling of freedom. I wish my family could experience it."

Halandor gazed out at the open plains along with her and then looked at her thoughtfully. "You know, Makilien, you can be free no matter where you are, even if you were again a prisoner in Reylaun."

Makilien gave him a questioning look. "How?"

"If you've placed your trust in Elohim, even if you are physically imprisoned, your soul is free."

Makilien silently contemplated those words. Deep down, she did want to believe that, but she just couldn't quite understand it. Now and then she thought about the things Halandor and Torick said, but it all seemed so overwhelming to try to figure out. She did not respond, and Halandor let the subject drop for now.

"How long until dawn?" Makilien asked a little while later.

"About an hour," Halandor answered.

Makilien rose. "I think I will try to sleep a little more."

Listening to her return to her bedroll and settle down again, Halandor looked up at the vastness of the sky created by the

God he had spent his life serving. He had never once regretted a moment of it. On the contrary, Elohim always gave him strength, peace, and assurance, even during the times that had tested his faith the most. He wanted the same security for Makilien, and in the time before dawn, he prayed continuously.

:Chapter Eleven:

Minarald

When Makilien laid eyes on Minarald, all of the weariness from their journey was forgotten. The city truly was magnificent, even from a distance. A granite wall formed a huge circle around the city, one which had been built at the base of a towering mountain range that stretched as far as Makilien could see. She had been awe-stricken by the beauty of Elimar, but the splendor of Minarald was in its size. Makilien would have been content to just stare at it from their position on the crest of a hill, but her friends moved on and she followed, anxious to see the city from inside.

Within ten minutes, the foursome approached the city's main gate, and Makilien had to tip her head back to see the top of the wall, which towered an amazing sixty feet above the ground.

Two soldiers dressed in a combination of royal blue, black, and silver uniforms stood guard on either side of the open archway of the gate, and Makilien had seen soldiers patrolling the top of the wall as well. The soldiers at the gate nodded in recognition of Halandor and let them pass without a word. As soon as they were within the city wall, the dirt road they had traveled gave way to a wide stone-paved street.

They followed the street deep into the city, and Makilien gazed up at the buildings rising above them. Many were as tall as the wall surrounding them, and all were constructed of the same granite. They were made with great precision and quite beautiful. The granite used was not the typical, dreary gray stone a couple of the buildings in Reylaun had been built with, but an entirely different type of stone. It was much lighter in color, almost silvery, and seemed to reflect light. Upon questioning, Makilien learned it was a granite found only within this area of the mountains, therefore it was a city unlike any other.

Once Makilien had taken a good look at the buildings, her eyes dropped down to the street and the people walking there. They were certainly different from the people of Reylaun and Andin. Their clothing was finer, and they appeared more sophisticated in their manner.

At the halfway point of the city, they came to another wall. Though not as tall as the first, it was impressive nonetheless.

"Why are there two walls?" Makilien asked curiously.

"This is the original wall, built when the city was founded," Halandor told her. "The new wall was then constructed after the city expanded."

Fascinated with the grand city, Makilien wondered about its history. "Who founded Minarald?"

"A man named Baltar. He and a group of men and women escaping persecution in the south came north and settled here," Halandor gave her a brief history. "His son was the first king of Eldor."

Within the heart of the oldest, inner part of the city they came to a grand stable—the royal stable. They dismounted and left their mounts with the stablemen before they continued from there on foot. Shortly, they came to yet another wall, this one being only about thirty feet in height. They again passed the guards at the gate and came into an amazing open courtyard. On the far side stood the palace, the largest and most magnificent structure in the city. Rows of tall windows lined the three story building and huge granite pillars supported second and third story balconies. Makilien's three friends smiled at the look of wonder on her face.

In the middle of the courtyard, where a beautiful pond and fountain sparkled, they were met by a man. Auburn hair just reached his shoulders, and he wore the same royal blue shirt and black jerkin with a silver emblem embroidered in the middle as the other soldiers, but his attire sported more trim and military detailing leading Makilien rightly to believe he was of much higher rank. Makilien was immediately impressed by his dignified appearance and wondered for a moment if he was Meniah.

The soldier greeted Halandor, Loron, and Torick in a friendly and familiar way.

"Lord Darand will be pleased to know you have arrived," he said, his voice deep and noble. "He's been expecting you." Once he said this, his gaze shifted to Makilien, and he smiled handsomely. "You must be Makilien."

"Yes," she answered.

"I am Nirgon. Arphen told us of you and your escape from Reylaun. I am honored to meet you."

Makilien's smile came easily. "Thank you. I am very pleased to meet you as well."

To the whole group, Nirgon said, "Lord Darand is in the throne room. He will want to see you right away. I will join you shortly after I see to some business at the barracks."

Halandor nodded and led them up to the palace while Nirgon went in the opposite direction. As they approached the palace doors, Halandor told Makilien, "Nirgon is Eldor's general. He commands all the soldiers stationed here in Minarald as well as those in the outposts scattered throughout Eldor."

Makilien was once again impressed. "He's in charge of all of them?"

"Yes. The only ones with more authority are Lord Darand and his son, Prince Darian."

Makilien glanced over her shoulder, catching a last glimpse of Nirgon as he passed through the courtyard gate.

"He seems to be a very good general," Makilien remarked.

"He is," Torick confirmed. "He's said to be the finest Eldor has ever had."

Inside, the interior of the palace was as grand as it had looked from outdoors. Makilien hadn't thought any building could be larger than Lord Elnauhir's house, but the palace surely was. They walked down a large hall that made Makilien feel very small and then came to the open doors of the throne room, which were guarded on both sides. The room itself was spacious and fit for a reigning king. Colorful banners and tapestries decorated the walls and various pieces of furniture occupied the room. At the far end, sitting on a raised marble platform, was the throne itself, carved out of a deep mahogany wood. The throne was unoccupied, but a man stood at a long table, studying the several pieces of parchment lain across it.

This man looked up as soon as he heard them enter. Makilien could see he was very pleased to see her companions and came away from the table to meet them. She guessed him to be about the same age as Torick and Halandor. He had light hair and twinkling blue eyes, and though he wore no crown at this time, Makilien knew he must be Lord Darand. He had the look of a king, yet appeared very kind.

"I'm glad you're here," Darand said warmly.

It was in that moment Makilien realized how much the king valued her friends' counsel.

"Has anything changed since Arphen brought us news?" Halandor asked.

"No, but there are things I wish to discuss with you," Darand answered, yet he didn't go immediately into discussion of them. His attention went first to his new guest. "You must be Makilien," he said with the kindness of a grandfather.

"Yes, my lord," Makilien answered respectfully.

"I welcome you to Minarald."

"Thank you, my lord. I am very pleased to be here. Your city is magnificent."

Darand smiled at her and then motioned for her and the others to follow him. He brought them to a table and invited them to sit down. As soon as they were all seated, the men began their discussion with the king.

"Tell us about this captain of Zirtan's," Halandor said, anxious for more information.

"Gornath."

"Do you trust him?"

"No," Darand answered. "After speaking with him extensively, I didn't feel at all that he can be trusted. Meniah has also warned me not to trust him."

"Where is Gornath now?" Torick asked.

"I've provided him a place to stay. He does not know yet that we are suspicious, but I have men secretly keeping watch over him. If he is not here to help us, Zirtan must have sent him for a reason, and I want to know why. If he does anything suspicious, he'll be brought in and we'll try to gain truthful information from him."

"What has he told you so far?" Halandor questioned.

In the next while, Darand informed them of all Gornath had divulged. Some Arphen had already shared, and other bits and pieces Makilien didn't understand. Before Darand could finish, one of the palace guards walked in.

"My lord, I've received word your son has arrived," he announced.

"Good, thank you," Darand replied with a pleased smile. He turned back to Makilien's friends. "Darian has been visiting the villages to see how many extra men are capable and willing to fight."

They rose from the table as the king did.

"Supper will be served shortly. I will let you go to your rooms to prepare." Lord Darand called for a young woman servant and gestured to Makilien. "Take our new guest to a room and see that she has everything she needs."

"Yes, my lord."

To Makilien, Darand said, "After you have freshened up you can return here."

Makilien followed the servant through the palace. At one point, they came to a wide, very tall staircase and climbed it to the second floor. Makilien was careful to remember the way back to the throne room in case no one was around to direct her.

Finally, the servant opened a door, and Makilien stepped into a large bedroom.

"I will have warm water brought up for you to wash," the servant said.

"Thank you," Makilien replied with a smile.

While she was alone, Makilien explored the room. She was delighted to find it had a balcony. Opening the double glass doors, she stepped out. The view she had over the city was breathtaking. It was a perfect scene and a perfect place to add yet another sketch to her book.

In a few minutes, a servant returned with a pitcher of water and set it on the washstand. When she had left again, Makilien washed up. She didn't know how long she had until supper was served, and she didn't want to keep anyone waiting, so she worked quickly. Once she was clean, she re-braided her hair and left her bedroom.

Several voices came from the throne room as Makilien neared. She heard Darand's voice and others she did not recognize. Remembering the guard's announcement, she guessed one of the voices must belong to Lord Darand's son. She was curious to see what the prince would be like.

When Makilien walked in, five new men had gathered besides her three friends, and Lord Darand and General Nirgon. Makilien approached them quietly and studied the new group with interest. Halandor saw her first and motioned for her to join them. When Darand noticed she was present, he smiled.

"Makilien, come and meet my son."

He introduced her to one of the young men in the group. The prince was a handsome man with much darker hair than his father, but he possessed the same kindness in his eyes.

With a sincere smile, Darian said, "It's a pleasure to meet you, Makilien. It is good to know not everyone in the captive villages of the North have fallen for Zirtan's lies."

"I'm afraid I am one of very few who have not," Makilien replied regretfully.

"Well, perhaps someday, if we can defeat Zirtan, that will change."

"Indeed, that is our hope," Darand agreed.

Makilien had not considered before that victory against Zirtan could, in the future, mean freedom for her family and those she knew in Reylaun. It was an encouraging thought.

Now that Makilien was present, the group did not remain long in the throne room. Darand and the prince led them into the dining room where, over the course of the evening, the men spoke extensively. Makilien was quiet as she ate, listening carefully and trying to learn as much as possible.

Not long after the meal was finished, she felt the effects of the tiring journey and went to her room. After a quiet time out on the balcony watching the stars and the lights flickering throughout the city, she blew out her own candles and crawled into bed.

:Chapter Twelve:

Two Meetings

The bright sunlight streaming through the window signaled early morning was well past by the time Makilien woke. Rubbing her eyes, she sat up and noticed the small table across from the bed held a tray laden with food. The sight of it caused her empty stomach to growl.

Slipping out of bed, she walked over to the table finding a variety of fruit, as well as fresh bread and butter and a small jar of jam. She was going to sit down to eat, but found a note on the tray, which she picked up and read first.

The wardrobe contains a gift from His Majesty.

Surprised and curious, Makilien hurried over to the tall mahogany wardrobe. Inside hung several beautiful dresses. She was quite pleased with this discovery. The night before she'd felt a little out of place in her traveling clothes.

Deciding to dress after she had eaten, Makilien sat down at the table and took bites of each of the delicious food items that lay before her. In the silence of the room, she realized it was the first meal she had eaten alone since she'd met Halandor in Andin. She thought of her family and the last meals they'd shared. They had not been pleasant, and it made her regretful over the large part she'd played in that fact.

Driven by curiosity to explore and see more of the grand city, Makilien ate and dressed quickly. Her new dress was of the same style as her old traveling dress, but of much finer quality and more elegant. She'd chosen a dark blue one for her first day in Minarald since it seemed to be Eldor's symbolic color.

No one had told Makilien where to look for them in the morning so she decided to check the throne room first since it was the only room she knew for sure how to find. However, before she reached it, she met Halandor at the bottom of the stairs. With a smile, he greeted her.

"Good morning," Makilien replied happily. "I hope I have not slept too long."

Halandor shook his head. "It's good you were able to rest. The days ahead of us could be very tiring."

Makilien was glad he made it sound like she would have a part in it and not just be an afterthought.

"What are the plans for today?" she asked.

"Torick and I would like to take you to meet Meniah."

"When?"

"Right away, if you'd like."

Makilien nodded eagerly. She was anxious to finally meet the man she had already heard mentioned many times since she'd arrived.

She followed Halandor through the palace, and they met Torick near the entrance. As the three of them walked outside, Torick said, "We might as well take our horses. No use trudging all the way through the city."

Halandor agreed.

"Doesn't Meniah live in the city?" Makilien asked.

"No, he lives outside of it," Halandor answered.

Makilien thought this odd since he seemed to be so relied upon, but she didn't question it until after they'd retrieved their horses from the stable and had nearly reached the city gate.

"Why doesn't Meniah live inside the city? Couldn't Lord Darand call on him for advice much easier if he was?"

"Meniah has work to attend to," Halandor explained.

"What does he do?"

"He is a shepherd."

Makilien's eyes went to Halandor, her mouth open for a moment. "A shepherd?" she repeated incredulously. "You mean . . . of *sheep*?"

Halandor nodded with a faint smile.

A shepherd wasn't at all what Makilien had envisioned. She almost didn't believe it. A shepherd was advising the king on how to face the force threatening their very existence? It just didn't make sense or seem right. Makilien wondered if her confusion was apparent to her companions, but neither Halandor nor Torick spoke.

Some minutes later, they came to a lush, fertile meadow at the foot of the mountains. In contrast, the snowy white sheep were scattered throughout the green grass and moved out of their way as they rode toward the center of the meadow.

Rising to meet them was the shepherd. At first glance, Makilien noticed nothing out of the ordinary or significant about him, though he was younger than she'd expected. She had imagined a more aged man, but he was only in his thirties. He appeared to be as any ordinary shepherd, dressed in plain linen clothing with a staff in hand, nothing like the more sophisticated citizens living within the city. But as they dismounted and approached Meniah on foot, Makilien was quite suddenly overcome with unexpected emotions.

Despite the shepherd's plain appearance and Makilien's own pre-conceived notions about Meniah, she found herself stricken with a sense of lowliness and unworthiness. An odd sensation of awe and a little bit of fear overwhelmed her, yet she was drawn to him. She was all together confused by it, but when he smiled, a great calm settled inside of her. She didn't think she had ever been looked upon in a kindlier way.

Though it barely registered in Makilien's mind, Halandor introduced her. Still smiling at her, Meniah said gently, "I've been looking forward to meeting you, Makilien. Come, sit with me."

Makilien was eager to accept this invitation. They left their horses to graze and sat down with Meniah on the large mountain stones that dotted the meadow.

"You've come a long way, Makilien. Tell me about your journey," Meniah requested.

Makilien was more than willing to tell him everything she could remember about the last couple of weeks. She went into great detail, but she soon had a feeling he knew what she was going to say before she said it. As strange as it was, Makilien liked him more each minute she spent with him and could now understand why Lord Darand relied on him for advice. He seemed to possess untold wisdom and understanding.

For over an hour they sat in the meadow with Meniah. Makilien didn't think she could ever run out of things to talk to him about. He seemed interested in every aspect of her life. When finally Halandor mentioned leaving, Makilien hated to go, but knew she could come back and speak to Meniah again.

With plans to do that as soon as possible, she said goodbye and they returned to their horses.

On the ride back into Minarald, Makilien was quiet. She had much to think about. Noticing her silence, Torick glanced at her curiously and asked, "What did you think of him, Makilien?"

She looked at Torick and then back to the road. She didn't know how to explain how she felt. Finally, she turned back to him. "He was very different than I was expecting. I like him very much."

Torick traded smiles with Halandor, and they were silent again as they entered the city.

Once back at the palace, a man was just leaving the throne room as they entered. He glanced their way, his gaze lingering strangely on Makilien. It sent an uncomfortable chill through her body. Something very sinister lurked in his dark eyes.

Inside the throne room where Lord Darand and Darian stood with Nirgon, Torick asked the very question Makilien was wondering. "Who was that?"

The king's answer did not come as a surprise. "That was Gornath."

"What did he want?"

"He wanted to know if I'd made any new plans or preparations. I'm sure he's trying to gather information for Zirtan, but I never give him much. Just enough to satisfy him while not enough to jeopardize our safety."

"When will you have him brought in?" Halandor asked.

"Soon," Darand told him and went on to say, "Indiya arrived while you were gone."

"What news did she have?"

"She said there is still no activity along the Claron River. Emaril and Carmine are still patrolling there. Indiya will return to them in a couple of days."

As soon as Makilien had a chance to speak without interrupting, she asked, "Who is Indiya?"

Looking at Halandor and Torick, Darian asked, "Does she not know of dragons?"

"Dragons!" Makilien looked between the prince and her friends. "They are real too?"

The three of them gave affirming nods.

With a grin and a twinkle in his eye, Darian said, "Come with me. I'll take you to see Indiya."

Makilien eagerly followed him, and Halandor and Torick joined them also.

"So the creatures I've heard about in stories, are they all real?" Makilien asked as they left the palace.

"Most likely are," Halandor answered. "Although, I'm sure none of them are described accurately. Dragons for instance, are quite a bit smaller than you've probably heard, and while it is true they breathe fire, it is limited and must rebuild between each use."

Makilien was fascinated. "How many dragons are there? Lord Darand mentioned the names Emaril and Carmine. Are they dragons too?"

"Yes, they are. Dragons are rare creatures. Indiya, Emaril, and Carmine are the only three we know of, though we believe there are others. Many years ago, they began to die out rapidly because of very unfortunate attacks on them. Men killed them to sell off bits and pieces—their scales, teeth, claws, spines, anything they could get a good price for—so most fled to the mountains. Only five dragons remained in Eldor. Carmine and four others who were the parents of Indiya and Emaril."

"What happened to the four who remained with Carmine?"

"They were killed," Halandor answered regretfully.

"How?" Makilien asked, thinking the whole thing a terrible shame.

"Two were killed by Shaikes while patrolling Eldor's border and the other two were killed by Eldorian villagers who had a misguided fear of them. Lord Darand's father finally had to decree that killing a dragon would be considered murder, and since then Carmine, Indiya, and Emaril have been safe for the most part, at least within our borders."

Outside of the palace courtyard, near the royal stable, they came to a very large, barn-like structure.

"This is the aviary where the dragons and griffons stay," Darian told Makilien.

They walked in through a huge door. The open building was adequately lit by rows of windows and was empty save for one stunning creature near the middle. It was true the dragon was smaller than Makilien was first expecting, but magnificent nonetheless. She was still a very large creature, as tall as a draft horse, with a lean, almost cat-like body. Her neck and tail were long, and deep indigo scales that glinted like metal covered her skin. A charcoal colored membrane stretched across her wings, which were folded at her sides. On the top of her angular head were two black, goat-like horns, and black spikes ran down the base of her neck, along her back, and the length of her tail.

The dragon was just finishing up what appeared to be a deer carcass. As the last of it disappeared with one gulp, a little shiver tingled up Makilien's spine, and she was glad the creature was on their side.

When the dragon heard them, she looked up and gazed at them with large, sapphire blue eyes. Licking her lips like a cat who had just finished a mouse, she said in a deep, yet beautiful voice, "Pardon me, Your Highness, I was not expecting you." She dipped her head respectfully.

"That is quite all right, Indiya," Darian assured her. "I just came to introduce you to someone."

With smooth, agile movements, the dragon approached, a curious look on her face.

After Darian introduced Makilien, Indiya lowered her head to Makilien's level. "Well, hello there." Her hot breath warmed Makilien's face and made her smile. "You've certainly come a long way from Reylaun."

"Yes. I have."

Indiya peered a little closer. "Have you ever seen a dragon before?"

Makilien shook her head. "No. I didn't know dragons truly existed until today."

Indiya narrowed her eyes slyly at Darian, Halandor, and Torick. "Just what have you been teaching her if she did not know of dragons until this day?"

Darian chuckled. "We apologize, Indiya. I think we tend to forget the things that are normal to us but not to those who were born elsewhere."

The dragon smiled mischievously. "Well, I'll forgive you . . . this time."

"Thank you. You are most gracious," the prince replied with a grin.

Makilien laughed at the exchange.

"Indiya, perhaps, after you've rested, you can take Makilien for a ride," Darian suggested to Makilien's delight.

"I'd be pleased to." Indiya once again lowered her head to look at Makilien. "Would you like that?"

"Yes," Makilien answered, a little breathless at the thought.

"How about tomorrow morning?"

"All right."

"I shall see you in the morning then."

Makilien nodded, still hardly daring to believe this was happening, and she and her friends took their leave. Back at the palace, Makilien went to her bedroom. She had a strong urge to sketch. She'd seen so many things already today she barely knew where to begin. Happily, she spent the hours before and after lunch drawing one sketch after another, taking great care with the sketch of Indiya, filled with anticipation for the next day.

:Chapter Thirteen:

Poison

Makilien's stomach filled with butterflies as she and Halandor approached the aviary before breakfast the next morning. Halandor had warned against eating anything beforehand, and Makilien was glad she'd agreed.

"Have you ever ridden a dragon before?" Makilien asked, feeling a nervous excitement she hadn't experienced since she was a child.

"A few times." Smiling, Halandor added, "It's certainly not an experience you will ever forget."

A thrilling shiver raced through Makilien's body.

When they reached the aviary, Indiya stood outside, the bright morning sunlight making her sleek scales shine vibrantly in varying shades of dark blue.

"Good morning," the dragon greeted them, the tone of her voice lilting cheerfully.

Makilien and Halandor returned the greeting.

"It's a fine morning for flying," Indiya told Makilien. She crouched down. "Go ahead and climb up. It's most comfortable if you sit between the two spines just in front of my shoulders."

Halandor helped Makilien up, and she situated herself on the dragon's strong neck. She took hold of the foot-long, ivory-like spine just in front of her and drew in a deep breath.

"Now don't worry. I won't let you fall," Indiya promised. "Are you ready?"

With another quick breath, Makilien nodded. "I'm ready."

Indiya spread her massive wings and flapped hard. In a moment, they left the ground, and Makilien's breath was sucked from her lungs as the dragon ascended and the city shrank dizzyingly beneath them. It was the most awesome thing Makilien had ever experienced.

In mere seconds they were soaring high above Minarald. The view was incredible. The sun shone on the snow of the tallest mountain peaks in a dazzling white, and the buildings of the city almost sparkled in the light. It became apparent from this height just how vast the Eldorian plains were. All Makilien could see for miles was green grass, though she did notice a tiny dark spot on the horizon.

"Is that a village?" she called over the wind.

"Mm-hmm," Indiya's throat rumbled in response.

She gradually curved to the left and, looking down, Makilien spotted all the tiny white dots that were Meniah's sheep. Thinking of him down there, tending to them, brought a little smile to her face, and she planned to ask Halandor if they could visit him later.

Indiya flew around for a good long time, circling the city and then flying up into the mountains before returning to Minarald where she came to a graceful landing in front of the aviary. The dragon crouched and Makilien slid off her neck, still experiencing the rush of excitement from the ride.

"Thank you so much, Indiya. That was amazing!"

Indiya smiled. "You're welcome. I enjoyed it too."

The growling of Makilien's empty stomach cut off any more words she may have spoken. Indiya chuckled lightly.

"You better go on to the palace and get something to fill your belly."

Makilien smiled and turned from the aviary. Back at the palace, Halandor was waiting for her and brought her to the kitchen where her breakfast had been kept. After she had told him all about the ride, she asked, "Halandor, can we visit Meniah later?"

Halandor smiled at her eagerness. "Sure. It will have to be sometime after lunch. Torick, Loron, and I are meeting with Lord Darand and Nirgon about the city's defenses. They're probably about to start now."

Knowing he had to go, Makilien asked, "Can I explore the city until lunch?"

"That would be fine."

Excited to look around, Makilien finished her breakfast and left the palace right away. It was a perfect day to explore the vast city, and she couldn't wait to see what she could find. Everything was so new and foreign to her.

Makilien stuck to the main streets in the beginning, wanting to make sure she didn't get too lost. Near the center of the city, she found a market and spent most of the morning there looking at all the wondrous contraptions and goods for sale. She wished she still had some money left over from her purchases in Andin. She would have liked to buy some little things for Leiya to give her whenever she returned home.

A couple of hours after she had set out, Makilien headed back, taking a more roundabout way along side streets. She walked slowly, admiring the different architecture and getting an abundance of ideas for future sketches.

Approaching a narrow alley, a pair of low voices caught Makilien's attention. Not meaning to eavesdrop, Makilien casually approached the corner of the alley and glanced around it. Her eyes widened. One voice belonged to Gornath. Knowing he couldn't be trusted and sensing the two men were up to no good, Makilien hid herself around the corner again and listened. Her better sense told her not to stay, but she also told herself maybe she could hear something Lord Darand would want to know.

"Now that the prince has returned, I can complete the mission," Gornath said barely loud enough for Makilien to hear.

"When will you do it?" the other man asked.

"As soon as the opportunity presents itself. I am going to the palace now. I may just be finished here by tonight."

"Good. I'll have word sent. Once Eldor loses her king and her prince, the people will be devastated and leaderless. They won't be in any position to put up a fight."

Makilien's heart slammed against her chest with the realization that she'd just overheard an assassination plot— the assassinations of Lord Darand and Prince Darian! She looked around to determine the best way to leave without being detected. She stiffened when she realized the men were no longer talking. Before she could make a move, an arm came around the corner and latched onto her. Makilien cried out as she was yanked into the alley, but the sound was cut off as she was shoved roughly up against the building. Gornath held her tightly by her overdress, and the other man stood close by. Their expressions showed both surprise and anger.

"It's the girl from Reylaun," Gornath informed his friend.

"How much do you think she heard?"

"I don't know." Gornath narrowed his eyes.

"I didn't hear anything," Makilien lied.

"Who sent you to spy on us?" Gornath demanded.

"I'm just exploring the city."

"You weren't just exploring. You were standing at the corner listening. We saw your shadow."

Makilien gulped, realizing how she'd been found out.

"I really didn't hear anything." She was desperate to make them believe her.

Gornath peered at her closely and then glanced over his shoulder, telling the other man, "Go on. I'll finish this."

Swallowing hard, Makilien feared what Gornath would do as the other man strode away. To her surprise, Gornath released his hold on her but still watched her with cold eyes.

"What is your name?"

"Makilien," she answered cautiously.

"Makilien, do you know what side you're on?"

She wasn't sure what he meant, so she kept silent.

"The wrong side," Gornath declared. "You might believe your friends are on the right side, and even they believe it, but they are wrong."

His voice lowered to a persuasive tone. "Zirtan is not the enemy. He has always wanted to provide what is best for the people of Dolennar. In thanks for his care, the people have turned on him and attacked him. Your friends have brought this war on themselves. Makilien, do you really want to get caught in the bloodshed that is coming? Do you really want to fight for a lost cause, one that could have been avoided had the people only shown a little loyalty?"

Makilien swallowed again at the effect his smooth words had. Pleased with the reaction he detected in her eyes, Gornath went on, "Makilien, come with me to Zirtan. Show your loyalty and he will give you anything you desire. There are other villages and cities besides Reylaun, some far greater than

Minarald. Just ask and you and your family can live in any one of them, completely safe and completely content . . . "

Images of beautiful and peaceful cities like Minarald and Elimar overwhelmed Makilien's mind, and she thought of herself, and her family, and Aedan all living there, happily, peacefully. It was what she'd always wanted . . . *No it isn't!* the realization hit her. She'd wanted knowledge, to know the truth, and she'd wanted freedom.

Seeing her doubt, Gornath redoubled his attack, targeting the very thing that was her greatest weakness. "Zirtan can take care of and protect you and your family. That you can be sure of. Your friends are on the brink of a war they cannot win, and they are trusting in a god who cannot be seen or heard. How can you possibly know he exists? How can you be sure of any care or protection?"

Makilien's grip on what she thought was right slipped. Gornath was right. How could she possibly know or be assured of anything? In that perilous instant, Halandor's face appeared amidst all the doubts and uncertainty in her mind. Then she remembered Torick's words to her, *"Zirtan is evil . . . he is the root of all evil . . . evil itself."* Makilien looked into Gornath's eyes and saw a deep darkness there. If Zirtan was as good as this man claimed, why would he have such evil men and creatures working for him? It was all wrong.

Resisting the temptations that had been raging inside her to believe Gornath, Makilien set her jaw and said defiantly, "Zirtan is evil."

Gornath's face contorted into an ugly sneer. In a flash of movement, he reached for something on his belt. All the air rushed from Makilien's lungs. She felt like she'd been punched in the stomach, but the pain was far worse. Barely able to breathe through the horrible burning sensation spreading through her abdomen, Makilien looked down to see the hilt of a dagger protruding just below her ribs.

Gornath's once smooth voice had turned cold. "Now you can decide if you made the right choice as you die."

Makilien cried out in terrible pain as Gornath yanked the dagger from her stomach. Her knees buckled. Eyes wide with pain and fear, she looked around frantically. Where were the guards who were supposed to be watching Gornath?

The evil man's low chuckle mocked Makilien as he read her thoughts. "I know about the men who have been spying on me. They think I'm still at the house Darand *so graciously* provided me." Maliciously, he went on, "There is no one here to help you."

With a laugh of pure evil, he turned away from her, walking out of the alley and leaving Makilien completely alone and helpless. Gasping, she tried to get up, but only collapsed with a moan. She clutched tightly at her wound, but blood still seeped through her fingers. *What am I going to do?* If she didn't get help soon, she would surely die. *And Lord Darand and Prince Darian!* If they weren't warned, Gornath would kill them too. Two tears leaked from Makilien's eyes as she realized the horrible position she was in.

Lying there, more of Torick's words rang in Makilien's mind, "*. . . at the end of life, these people will realize they never knew the truth and will be separated from it forever.*" What exactly was the truth? Did she know it? How could she if she didn't even know what it was? Deep rooted fear encased her heart at the thought of dying without knowing.

In desperation, Makilien did the only thing she could think of. "I don't know if You're really there, Elohim, or if You can hear me, but please, let someone find me before it's too late."

Makilien's strength seeped away with her blood. Her head throbbed, and her heart pounded abnormally hard. An unnatural coldness spread through her limbs even as beads of sweat dampened her forehead. It grew difficult to focus and soon only pain engulfed her senses as she slipped toward unconsciousness.

Torick glanced up and down each street he passed, his pace quickening. Halandor had asked him to look for Makilien while he and Nirgon finished with Lord Darand. Their meeting with the king had extended past their planned lunchtime, but Makilien had not yet returned to the palace. Torick knew the city was large, and it was easy to lose track of time, but he couldn't shake the feeling something was wrong.

Once Torick reached the market, he asked around for Makilien. Some of the merchants had indeed seen her. One directed him down a less populated side street.

"Makilien!" he called out as he hurried along, hoping against all hope she would answer. "Help me find her, Elohim."

Torick was nearing the palace again with a growing panic when his hearing picked up the sound of a faint groan. Stopping abruptly, he looked all around. Then, down a dark alley, he spotted a figure lying motionless. His heart skipped a beat as he entered the alley and knelt beside Makilien, eyeing her blood-soaked dress. Gently, he lifted her head and her eyes opened, looking feverish. Torick put a hand to her forehead discovering it was burning hot.

"Torick," Makilien gasped, in both relief and desperation.

"Makilien, what happened?" Torick asked, moving carefully to lift her into his arms.

"Gornath," Makilien ground out, her voice weak. She groaned. "He's going to kill . . . kill Lord Darand . . . and Prince Darian! He's at the palace . . ."

With this last effort, Makilien's eyes closed, and she went limp in Torick's arms. If not for the subtle sound of her breathing, he would have feared her dead. Torick turned immediately for the palace, moving as fast as he could through streets. Time was counting down for both Makilien and the king and prince.

As soon as the courtyard gate came into view, Torick called urgently to the guards, "Lord Darand and Prince Darian are in danger! Warn the palace guards!"

They needed no further prompting. One of the guards left his post at a run toward the palace.

Inside the courtyard, Torick met Halandor and Nirgon. Already alarmed after having seen the first guard, the sight of Makilien confirmed their fears that something was terribly wrong.

Halandor rushed to Makilien's side.

"What happened?"

"I think it was Gornath. He is going to try to assassinate Lord Darand and Darian. He may be here now."

Nirgon turned instantly for the palace, but Halandor stayed, looking Makilien over with worried eyes.

"We must get her inside to the healers," Torick said.

They hurried into the palace.

"Do you know where Lord Darand and Darian are?" Torick asked along the way.

"Lord Darand is still in the throne room, but Darian left just before I did," Halandor answered, not knowing the prince's intended destination.

In the healing quarters of the palace, Halandor and Torick were both thankful when Lintar, one of the Elven healers, met them.

"She's been stabbed," Torick told him. "And she's burning up."

"Bring her in here." The dark haired Elf led them into a small room.

Torick set Makilien down on the bed and let Lintar take over. Though not nearly as old as most of the other healers, Lintar was the most skilled.

They pushed aside Makilien's dress to see the wound, not expecting what they found. The edges of the stab wound were inflamed, and dark, bluish veins were spreading out across Makilien's stomach.

"Poison," Lintar said gravely.

He went to work immediately, gathering whatever he thought he'd need, knowing he had little time to try to stop it. He had no way of knowing what kind of poison he was dealing with so Lintar had no choice but to guess what might be helpful.

Worried also for his king and the prince's safety, Torick turned to Halandor. He hated leaving Makilien, but he had to know the whereabouts of Darand and Darian.

"I am going to see if Lord Darand and Darian are safe. I'll be back as soon as I can."

Escorted by several of his guards as well as Nirgon and Loron, Lord Darand rushed upstairs to his son's chambers. His heart pounded and his stomach knotted with the intense fear only a parent could feel for their child. He'd already lost his wife—he couldn't now lose his son, the very one who reminded him so much of her. Desperate pleas to Elohim filled his mind for his son's safety.

When they reached the hall outside of the prince's rooms, their progress slowed to a stealthy pace. The door stood partially open when they reached it giving Darand a terrible feeling. Cautiously, Nirgon pushed open the door and stepped into the spacious sitting room. They found no sign of Darian at first glance, but then Nirgon pointed out a few drops of blood on the floor that made Darand fear the worst. What would they find in the next room?

Swords drawn, they hurried to the bedroom. In the doorway, they came to an abrupt halt. The king's relief was beyond words to see his son still alive, yet Darian was in great peril. Gornath stood behind him, a dagger pressed to the prince's throat.

"Do not come any closer," Gornath ordered.

"Let my son go, Gornath," Darand told him. "You are outnumbered and will have nowhere to go if you kill him."

Gornath simply laughed. "My escape does not concern me. It is Lord Zirtan's wish to see you and your son die and your country fall. I may have failed in killing you, but killing Eldor's prince will be enough."

Darand's blood ran cold at the horrible position they were in. Gornath had nothing to lose so there was no bargaining with him and no way to reach him before he killed Darian.

"Kill me instead," Darand offered suddenly. "Let my son go, and you can have me."

"Father, no!" Darian told him, but Darand would not reconsider.

The king took a step toward Gornath putting his hands up unthreateningly. "Release him and kill me. I'm sure Zirtan wants me more."

Gornath chuckled low, pleased with this turn of events.

"My lord," Nirgon murmured in uncertainty. He was torn. His deep sense of duty screamed at him to protect his king, yet it wasn't in him to condemn Darian, the only heir to the throne.

Gornath grinned wickedly as Darand took another step closer. Unknown to either of them, one person had a chance to save both Darand and his son. With a prayer for accuracy and success, Loron whipped an arrow to his bowstring. He fired at Gornath before the man even realized it. The arrow pierced his arm, bringing the dagger away from Darian's throat allowing the prince to escape his grasp.

Shouting in rage and pain, Gornath grasped his wounded arm. In an instant, he was surrounded by the guards and removed of all weapons.

"Take him to the barracks for questioning," Nirgon ordered, his voice taut over how narrowly they had avoided disaster.

His thoughts only on his son, Darand rushed to Darian's side as he praised Elohim for sparing him. "Are you all right, son?"

Darian nodded, unconcerned with the wound to his arm from the struggle with Gornath. "Yes, I'm fine," he assured his father.

"Come, let's go down to the healing quarters and have your arm looked after."

On the way out, Darian put his hand on Loron's shoulder. "Thank you for saving my life and my father's."

"Thank Elohim I was here, my lord."

Halandor was overcome with helplessness as he watched and assisted Lintar. It was a horrible feeling, one which brought back deep, painful memories of his daughter's death. *Please, Elohim, bring Makilien through this.* But Lintar's expression did not offer him hope. Finally, the Elf turned to Halandor, pausing reluctantly.

"I can't stop the poison. Nothing I've tried is effective, and the blade did much damage . . ."

"There's nothing you can do for her?"

Lintar shook his head in regret. "I've tried everything."

Halandor could hardly bear the thought of her dying, but he would not give up hope just yet.

"Do whatever you can to keep her alive," Halandor told Lintar. "I'll be back as fast as I can."

The Elf nodded, and Halandor hurried from the room with determined strides.

:Chapter Fourteen:

Lord Glorlad

Breathing deeply, Makilien returned to consciousness. As her mind cleared, she remembered what had happened and was surprised to find she was warm and comfortable. Even more surprising, no pain at all. For a moment she wondered if she had died, but opening her eyes, she found herself in bed in her room.

Makilien turned her head. In a chair at the bedside sat Meniah. As their eyes met, he smiled. Without even having to be told, Makilien knew at once he was the reason she was still alive.

"Thank you," she murmured, quiet and earnest.

"You're welcome," Meniah replied gently.

Makilien swallowed, remembering her helplessness in the alley. "I was so afraid. I thought I was going to die."

"You weren't alone," Meniah told her.

A moment later, Halandor stepped into the room. Makilien saw the immense relief in his expression. She had been unconscious, but stable for a few hours, and Halandor was comforted to see her finally awake.

"Makilien," he said softly as he came to the bedside.

She smiled, but then remembered Gornath's plans. "Are Lord Darand and Prince Darian all right?"

"Yes, they are safe. Gornath reached Darian, but he was rescued just in time."

Makilien sighed in relief. "Good. I was afraid it was too late when Torick found me."

"Did Gornath do this to you?" Halandor asked.

"Yes."

She told them of the confrontation in the alley. Meniah remained to hear most of it, but then rose to return to his sheep. Makilien was disappointed to see him go, but she was growing sleepy again.

"Was Gornath captured?" she asked.

"Yes, he's being questioned."

Makilien took a deep breath and let it out slowly. Everything had turned out well. She, the king, and the prince were alive. Her eyelids drooped and Halandor said, "Get some rest, Makilien."

With a smile, he left the room and closed the door. Makilien's eyes slid as she listened to his footsteps fade away, and she fell into a peaceful slumber.

A cheerful chirping brought Makilien out of sleep. She opened her eyes and looked toward the open door. On the railing of the balcony, a brilliant sapphire mountain bluebird sang happily. It brought a smile to Makilien's face. She stretched under the light covers and realized she must have slept through the night. Again, she was surprised to feel none of the pain she would have expected from receiving such a wound. But a sudden gnawing ache of hunger squeezed her stomach from missing both lunch and supper.

Makilien sat up, pushed back the covers, and swung her legs over the side of the bed. Since she felt fine, she could see no reason to continue lying down. She walked over to the wardrobe, chose a dress, and then started taking off her night-clothes. When she saw the bandages around her middle, she frowned, wondering what her wound looked like, and why it caused her no pain.

Knowing she really shouldn't but unable to help herself, Makilien began unwrapping the bandages. She knew she could easily bandage herself again. As the last of the bandages fell away, Makilien gasped. Where the wound from Gornath's dagger had been, only a healed scar remained. But how could it have healed so quickly? She knew without a doubt it had been Meniah. Her heart pounded. If he could heal her like that then who and what was he? Torick told her there was no such thing as magic, so what kind of power could heal?

Makilien swallowed, overwhelmed. *How?* echoed over and over in her mind. She didn't have an answer. Shaking her head, she finished dressing, but couldn't shake the questions.

Driven by hunger, Makilien left her room in search of her friends. She expected them to be near the dining room this time of morning, but as she neared it, voices came from the throne room. Stepping inside, she saw everyone she knew, including Meniah, gathered in the center of the room with Lord Darand. Makilien approached quietly, sensing their discussion to be serious, and she did not want to interrupt.

Torick noticed her first and smiled, glad to see her up and about.

"Makilien, you're awake. And looking well, I might add."

"Yes, I am very well," Makilien replied, and for a moment her eyes locked with Meniah's. The smile he gave her caused the familiar peace to fill her that she always felt in his presence.

"Makilien, I am very glad to hear this," Darand said. "We are indebted to you. If Darian and I had been killed, Eldor would not have been prepared to face Zirtan."

"But I did nothing, my lord. It was just luck I happened to overhear Gornath and survived to share the information."

"On the contrary, I believe it was meant to be," Darand said gently.

Makilien considered that for a moment. Had she been meant to go down that street and overhear Gornath? She remembered praying after she'd been stabbed, asking Elohim to help if He was really there. Had her desperate plea in the alley been heard? What were the chances of Torick finding her there just in time without some guidance?

As she was used to doing when her mind was overrun by these types of questions, Makilien pushed them away for another time. Remembering her friends and the serious conversation they were having when she walked in, she said, "I'm sorry, have I interrupted?"

"No," Darand assured her. "I think we've all come to the same decision."

"Yes," Darian said and looked at his father. "I will leave for Althilion right away."

"And we'll go with you," Torick added.

"I will have breakfast brought to the dining room immediately," Darand told them. "You can leave as soon as you have eaten and are packed."

The group moved toward the dining room, and Makilien hurried to Halandor's side.

"Are you going with Prince Darian?"

"Yes," he answered.

"What is Althilion?" Makilien remembered seeing the name on the map, but knew nothing of the place.

"It's the country just west of Beldon. It's an Elven country ruled by the Elven-lord Glorlad."

"Why is Prince Darian going there?"

"Because Althilion is our ally and will join us in our fight. Darian wants to urge Lord Glorlad to send his armies as soon as he can. Though Gornath is prepared to die before providing us with any useful information, he has told us enough to know Zirtan will not hold off his attack for much longer. Darian will also visit Beldon to speak with their king, Lord Andron. He must try to get their assistance."

"Who else is going besides you and Torick?"

"Loron is going with us. We want to travel light and fast, but also be able to protect Darian if need be."

"May I go with you?"

"You were stabbed just yesterday," Halandor reminded her.

"I am well enough to travel." Makilien looked up at him earnestly. "Really."

Halandor gave her a knowing look. "All right."

Makilien smiled, happy to be allowed to go. She desired to see as much of Dolennar as she could.

Everyone rushed through their breakfast and, once they had finished, Halandor sent Makilien up to her room to pack. She put her clothes back into the old leather pack she'd had since leaving Andin. Onto her belt she secured the dagger from Aedan and then her sword, which she determined never to wander around without again. Finally, she strapped on the Elven bow and quiver she'd received from Lord Elnauhir. Picking up her pack, she hurried out to the courtyard, not wanting to hold anyone up.

Outside, the stablemen had all the horses waiting. Halandor, Torick, and Loron were just beginning to strap their belongings to their horses' saddles when Makilien joined them.

"You're sure you're up to coming with us?" Torick asked Makilien. "We'll be doing about two weeks' worth of steady traveling in all."

"Yes, I'm up to it," Makilien answered confidently, determined she would be no hindrance to the group.

In a few minutes, Darian and Darand joined them.

"I will make sure Lord Andron knows how desperately we need his aid," Darian assured his father.

"Good. We've always been able to count on Beldon in the past. We must try to repair the situation that has arisen between them and Althilion."

Everyone mounted their horses, and Darand looked up at Darian from the ground. "Goodbye, my son. Be careful."

"I will, Father."

Encompassing the group, Darand said, "My prayers go with each of you."

After last parting words, the prince turned his horse and led them out of the courtyard. They rode through the city and soon passed through the main gate. Turning west, they followed the towering mountains on their left, Minarald shrinking behind them.

Makilien heaved the saddle up onto Antiro's back and finished saddling him, something she had become quite proficient at. When she had finished, she tipped her head back to gaze up at the white capped mountains. Turning around, her eyes saw the same sight on the other side.

For four days now they had been traveling south through a gap in the mountain range. It was not a wide gap, and quite rocky in some areas, but it was the only passable area of the Irrin Mountains. Makilien had been nervous to travel the gap at first, having heard Halandor mention robberies were not uncommon since ambush points were plentiful, but the journey had been uneventful so far, and they planned to reach the border of Althilion before nightfall.

During the journey, Makilien had learned much more information concerning Beldon, never understanding their refusal to come to Eldor's aid. It turned out it was not so much a lack of friendship with Eldor as a lack of friendship with Althilion. King Andron's father had once greedily attacked Althilion, wanting to claim it as part of Beldon. He'd lost to the Elves, and though they were willing to forgive Beldon and forget the incident, friendship was never restored and Beldon did not want to fight alongside Lord Glorlad's people.

Makilien thought it was ridiculous, as did her friends. They hoped, now that the crown had passed to Lord Andron, he would have more sense than his father and, once Darian had spoken to him, he would come to Eldor's aid.

As they continued their journey, it seemed as though the mountains were never going to come to an end, but the gap suddenly widened and before Makilien knew it, the mountains were behind them. The wide open country before them looked a lot like Eldor, but not as lush and fertile.

Early that evening they reached the bordering trees of a large forest, which made up more than half of the country of Althilion. It was here Lord Glorlad and his people dwelled. They slowed the horses to a walk as they entered the forest, and Makilien welcomed the slower pace and change in scenery.

This forest of Althilion was different from Eldinorieth. The trees were taller and wider, and the canopy of leaves above them was very thick and didn't allow much sunlight to penetrate except in some spots where shafts of golden light hit the forest floor. It was also much quieter than Eldinorieth. There was a mysteriousness about it, but at the same time, Makilien did not feel ill-at-ease. It was a more peaceful mysteriousness than dangerous.

Urging Antiro up next to Halandor, Makilien lowered her voice, feeling almost as though she shouldn't break the silence. "Where are we going?"

"To Silnar. It's a city hidden deep in the forest."

Silence overtook the travelers again. Only the muffled sound of the horses could be heard.

Little more than a mile into the forest, Makilien merely blinked and three Elves appeared, seemingly out of nowhere. Everyone pulled their horses to a stop. One of the Elves stepped forward. He was a blonde-haired Elf with clothes of dark earthy colors. Makilien thought it no wonder they could easily appear and disappear, blending in with the forest. The Elf wore a serious expression, but his face was not unkind. He approached Darian at the head of the group.

"My lord, Darian, welcome to Althilion." He bowed respectfully.

"Thank you, Gilhir."

Gilhir gazed at the rest of the group.

"*Cellomwé.*"

"*Yothaun,*" Halandor thanked him.

Finally, Gilhir's eyes fell upon Makilien.

"Gilhir, this is Makilien," Halandor made the introduction. To Makilien, he said, "Gilhir is a captain of the Elves guarding Althilion's border."

"Welcome to Althilion, Makilien," Gilhir said. The Elf's attention then turned back to Darian who spoke next.

"Gilhir, we've come to speak urgently with Lord Glorlad. We believe Zirtan's attack will come soon, and we must have all forces ready as soon as possible."

A troubled expression crossed Gilhir's face. "Lord Glorlad will be glad you have come. Things have become much more complicated since we last had contact with your father, which I'm afraid, puts us in a difficult position."

"What has happened?" Darian questioned.

"Trouble has grown between us and Beldon," Gilhir informed him regretfully, "but I will let Lord Glorlad give you the details. I will take you to him." Once again, he glanced at Makilien. "However, I'm afraid we have had to become more cautious in allowing newcomers into our city."

"Don't worry, Gilhir," Darian assured him. "We can all speak for Makilien. She has already proven her loyalty."

"Very well, my lord." The Elf turned and whistled. In a moment, a beautiful cream colored horse trotted out of the shadows. It was not saddled or bridled, but Gilhir swung onto its back and urged the horse in the direction they had been traveling. Darian and the rest of the group followed him.

They traveled more quickly now. Still being near to the mountains, the terrain was hilly and rocky in areas, but, though Makilien could not see it specifically, they seemed to be following a path, therefore riding was not difficult. The forest only grew more beautiful the farther they went. Once in a while they crossed over narrow streams where the rocks and ground were covered in soft moss. Though the forest seemed unnaturally quiet, it did not lack wildlife. Twice Makilien spotted deer that would look at them curiously for a moment before bounding off and disappearing.

Almost an hour later, Makilien finally saw Silnar, which appeared almost as suddenly as Gilhir and the other two Elves had. The Elven city was much like Elimar in that the buildings were constructed to preserve the forest, and the architecture was as graceful as the Elves themselves.

Near the center of the peaceful city, they came to a small hill where Lord Glorlad's home was built. They dismounted and Gilhir led them up to the front doors, which stood at the top of a tall flight of steps. Inside the magnificent structure, Gilhir brought them all into a large meeting hall. He invited them to sit down and made sure they were comfortable before he walked away to find Lord Glorlad.

While they waited, Torick, who had obviously been stewing over it during their ride, spoke his mind. "What do you think Beldon has done now?"

No one had an answer.

"Mark my words, they are going to be the death of Eldor. For the life of me, I don't understand how they cannot see if Eldor falls, there will be nothing stopping Zirtan from marching straight down here and conquering them as well. He doesn't just want Eldor, he wants *all* of Dolennar under his control."

"That is exactly what I am going to try to get Lord Andron to understand," Darian said.

"Unfortunately, Lord Andron doesn't seem to be open to discussion as of late," a voice sounded from the doorway.

Makilien turned. Gilhir had returned in the company of a second Elf. Blonde haired, his features were the opposite of Lord Elnauhir's, but his dignified manner was the same. He was dressed in deep green robes, and a silver crown shaped like vines encircled his head.

Makilien rose with her friends as the Elf approached them. Darian stepped forward and bowed. "Lord Glorlad."

"Prince Darian, I am very pleased you have come. I am glad to speak with you in person instead of having to send a message to your father. Please, sit."

They sat once again, and Lord Glorlad joined them.

"What brings you to Althilion, my lord?" he asked Darian first.

"We've captured one of Zirtan's men in Minarald. He was sent there with the purpose of assassinating me and my father, but thanks to Makilien," Darian gestured to her, "and Loron, that plan was foiled. We were not able to extract much information from him, but we strongly believe Zirtan will not hold off his attack for much longer. My father sent me to urge you to send your troops as soon as possible so we can fortify the city before Zirtan arrives."

Glorlad grimaced and sighed heavily. "I don't know if I can do that," he said in dismay. "I fear we are facing war with Beldon."

Makilien's friends traded worried glances.

"What has happened?" Darian asked.

"Several of the Elves patrolling our border have been attacked by Beldonian soldiers. Most of these attacks have occurred more than two leagues inside Althilion's boundaries. I've had a handful of Elves wounded and two have been killed."

Makilien sensed her friends' disbelief and disgust.

"I have sent four separate messengers to Dallorod trying to secure peace," Glorlad went on, "but all were sent away and two were even attacked and wounded." He paused for a moment, despair contorting his noble face. "Then Sirion went. He had hoped since he is half Beldonian that Lord Andron would speak to him . . . he has not returned."

Speaking in a tone of deep concern, Halandor asked, "How long ago was this?"

"Two weeks now," Glorlad responded, his voice low and sad. "So you see why I cannot spare my troops. I believe war between Althilion and Beldon is imminent. If Lord Andron refuses to discuss any kind of peaceful relationship between our countries, then these attacks we are suffering will continue, and I cannot stand for that. And if Sirion is still alive, I will not allow them to hold him captive. Even if we held off and did give you aid, I am afraid Beldon would see it as an opportunity to attack Althilion while she is left defenseless. I'm sure you can understand our position."

"Yes, of course," Darian assured him, though all could see he was considering what this news meant for them. "You must protect your people, but I fear this means defeat for Eldor."

With a deeply troubled expression, Glorlad said, "I know not what else to do."

Darian sat back in his chair as the room fell silent. Finally, he spoke with determination. "It is our plan to go to Dallorod from here because I believe we need Beldon's help as well if we are to defeat Zirtan. I will do everything in my power to convince Lord Andron of what a dire situation we are in and that making you their enemy is beyond foolish. If we do not all stand together against Zirtan, all will fall."

"I sincerely hope you can. The last thing I desire is war."

Darian went on, "And if Sirion is there, we will do whatever it takes to get him out, I promise you that. We will leave first thing in the morning."

"Thank you, my lord," Glorlad said gratefully. "You are all welcome here tonight." He instructed Gilhir, "Assist them in bedding down their horses." To the group he said, "I will have supper prepared for you."

Darian stood. "Thank you, my lord."

He and the others followed Gilhir back outside. As they were leading their horses toward the stable, Makilien looked up at Halandor.

"Who is Sirion?" She'd noticed how concerned everyone had become at the news he was missing.

"He's a good friend of ours," Halandor answered, "and he is Lord Glorlad's nephew. His mother was a Beldonian woman. His family was killed when Sirion was a young boy. Lord Glorlad took him in and raised him as a son."

Makilien felt terrible now that she knew what he meant to all of them, especially to Lord Glorlad. "Do you think . . . he's alive?"

"I pray so," Halandor answered quietly.

As soon as the horses were taken care of, Gilhir brought them back to Lord Glorlad's house where a delicious meal awaited them. Their conversation with Lord Glorlad about the situation with Beldon continued late into the night.

The quietness of early dawn surrounded Makilien as she came to consciousness. After four solid days of travel and camping out, she was reluctant to get out of bed, but she knew she must. Her friends were likely already up and would soon be ready to leave for Beldon.

She dressed, made the bed, and left the comfortable room. The house was quiet, but as she made her way down the hall, a door opened ahead of her, and Halandor appeared. They smiled at each other.

"Good morning," Halandor said. "Lord Glorlad has breakfast for us. We will leave when we are finished."

With their packs in hand, Makilien and Halandor walked into the dining room where Darian, Torick, and Loron had already gathered. In a moment, Lord Glorlad and Gilhir also arrived.

"With your permission I will send Gilhir with you," Glorlad told Darian. "I believe there should be someone to represent Althilion when you speak to Lord Andron."

Darian nodded. "We'd be glad to have him with us."

They sat down at the table and quickly ate the meal that had been prepared for them. When they were finished, they left Lord Glorlad's beautiful house. Outside, their horses were saddled and waiting for them.

"I pray your meeting with Lord Andron goes well," Glorlad told Darian just before they mounted. "If you can bring peace between our two countries, then I will not delay in leading my troops to Eldor." He paused. "But above all I have to pray that you find Sirion and he is safe. I could hardly bear to lose him too."

"You can be assured we will do everything we can to find him and to put an end to this."

The group mounted up and said farewell to the Elf-lord. Gilhir led the way from Silnar, back along the hidden forest path. In an hour, they reached the open plains and rode northeastward toward Beldon.

:Chapter Fifteen:

King of Beldon

For three days, they were surrounded by nothing but grass. In the distance, the mountains drew gradually closer and were the only indication of the miles they had traveled. The only forms of life they encountered were the birds and rabbits they would scare up. When Makilien asked where all of Beldon's people were, Halandor explained most of the villages were farther to the east and south.

At last, as afternoon closed in around them, Darian pulled his horse to a stop. The rest of the group halted beside him. Little more than a mile ahead, Makilien spotted a city. It was fortified by an outer wall like Minarald, but was only half its size, constructed not of the silvery granite but of a dark stone. Glances were traded within the group. Makilien knew from talk amongst her friends the night before that they were concerned with what would happen when Gilhir was recognized as an Elf from Althilion.

But they rode on. After several minutes they reached the gate where only one guard stood watch. The young man was surprised to see them approach. When they halted in front of him, he looked over each of them and asked, "Who are you and what is your business here?"

"I am Prince Darian, son of King Darand of Eldor," Darian told him. "We are here on urgent business to speak with Lord Andron."

The guard's brows rose over Darian's identity. Still, he hesitated. He glanced once at Gilhir and then said with reluctance, "I am sorry, my lord, but Lord Andron has ordered that our enemy and any who are friends of theirs are not to pass through this gate."

With firm confidence, Darian replied, "I don't think Lord Andron was expecting me when he gave that order."

The young guard shifted, conflict in his eyes, but before he could speak, a second man, a little older, joined him. He too wore the uniform of a soldier, though one of higher rank.

"Is there a problem, Bornil?" he asked in a kindly voice.

"This is Prince Darian, son of King Darand. He wishes to speak with Lord Andron," Bornil explained.

The other man examined the group, and when he saw Gilhir, he immediately realized the trouble. Stepping forward, he addressed Darian. "My lord, I am Eredan. I will take you to the king."

Bornil's eyebrows shot up incredulously.

"I will take the blame for this," Eredan assured him.

But Bornil wasn't comforted. His friend would surely be disciplined, or worse.

"What of you then?"

Eredan did not speak, his mind set.

Darian dismounted, and the rest of them did the same.

"Follow me, my lord," Eredan said, and he led them all through the gate.

No one spoke as they traveled through the city. It seemed a dreary place to Makilien, reminding her a little too much of

Reylaun. She felt as though not all was right here, and it made her apprehensive.

When they reached a great stone palace, Eredan called for a couple of the servants nearby to watch the horses and then led everyone up the palace steps. Pausing, he turned to Darian.

"If you will wait here, my lord, I will go in and announce your arrival."

Darian nodded, and Eredan went inside, but in a very short time, he returned and did not look pleased.

"Lord Andron will see you," he said.

Silently, Eredan led them inside and down a long, open hall to a large double-door, which opened into the throne room. Lord Andron sat on the throne at the far end. Straight, light brown hair fell to his shoulders. A silver crown rested on his brow above steel-blue eyes. He was barely older than Darian. Though he appeared displeased, he didn't have the face of a cruel-hearted man, and Makilien wondered his reason for causing the Elves so much grief.

A good many men and guards were also gathered in the throne room with the king, standing at various positions. Makilien glanced at some of them and realized she and her friends received cold stares, especially Gilhir and Loron. One man in particular who stood near the throne caught her eye. He reminded her eerily of Gornath, and the way he leered at them made her shiver.

As Eredan approached Andron, the king's scrutiny followed him, his eyes slightly narrowed. When they were near to the throne, Eredan stepped aside, and Darian halted before the king.

Lord Andron finally turned his eyes to the prince. "Lord Darian."

"Your Majesty," Darian replied with a bow.

All was quiet for a moment. Makilien held her breath in anticipation. Who knew what could befall them in the midst of these hostile men.

Finally, Lord Andron asked, "What business do you have in Beldon, my lord?"

"My father sent me, feeling it necessary to inform you of the gravity of the situation in Eldor."

Andron settled back in his throne but said nothing. With his silence, Darian continued.

"An attack on our country by Zirtan is very near. We are outnumbered and face defeat if we cannot gather the aid we require. If you would join us in this fight, I believe we have hope of defeating Zirtan." After a brief pause, the prince went on, "I have also come on behalf of Lord Glorlad and the people of Althilion."

Andron's face contorted with disdain. "I do not wish to discuss Althilion any more than I would wish to have any of her people in my palace." Tension and anger rose within the group as Andron finished, "I'm sure you have all the help you need from your Elven friends."

"That is not true," Darian replied firmly. "We are in desperate need of all help we are able to receive. Furthermore, Lord Glorlad is not free to give us his aid at this time because he fears war with you after the unprovoked attacks on his country and your refusal to discuss peace. Without their help we will not be able to stand against Zirtan. My lord, I implore you to put aside your ill-feelings toward Althilion. Lord Glorlad has ever been willing to forget the hostility that has been directed toward his people. Restore the alliance your countries once shared and take a stand with us."

For the briefest moment they had hope as Lord Andron appeared to consider it, but then his expression hardened stubbornly.

"We will not fight alongside Althilion."

The muscles in Darian's jaw tightened as he stared at the king.

"If I may," Torick said, boldly stepping forward. "We are not concerned only with our own self-preservation, but yours as well. Eldor is the only thing standing between you and Zirtan. If we are defeated, there will be nothing stopping him from marching straight down here and overtaking you as well."

The guard who had reminded Makilien of Gornath scoffed and addressed Lord Andron. "My lord, why would Zirtan bother? We have nothing of any value to him."

Torick glared at the man. "That is where you are gravely mistaken. You have a country, you have land. Zirtan wants *all* of Dolennar under his power, and he will not stop until he has accomplished that. This war about to be waged in Eldor is our one and only chance of stopping him. If we fail now, he will take control of Dolennar."

Still, Andron shook his head. "I cannot help you."

"Will you at least make peace with Althilion so Lord Glorlad can help us?" Darian implored.

Gilhir entered the conversation then, speaking carefully and with due respect, "Your Majesty, we have no quarrel with you. We want only peace and friendship."

Andron looked at Gilhir once, but would not hold his gaze. "No, I cannot do that."

"Then, my lord," Darian spoke decisively, bringing the king's eyes back to him, "this regrettably brings an end to the alliance between Eldor and Beldon—both by your unwillingness to come to our aid as well as your unwillingness to make peace with Althilion."

Shock colored Andron's face, and he appeared truly regretful. In spite of this, he made no attempt to make amends.

"My companions and I will take our leave," Darian said, "but first I must inquire after a messenger who came here from Althilion about two weeks ago. A man named Sirion, half Elf and half Beldonian. He came seeking to bring peace and has not returned home to Althilion. Do you know of whom I speak?"

Andron shifted on his throne and cast a quick glance at his guard. "No."

"He did not come here?"

"No," Andron answered again.

Darian narrowed his eyes a little, not believing the king's answer to be truthful. "This man is a close friend of mine, my lord. I would hope if anyone here knew of his whereabouts you would tell me."

"I know nothing of what happened to him," Andron insisted.

For a long moment, Darian stood in silent frustration, knowing he had exhausted his effort to convince the stubborn young king to cooperate. Finally, he bowed curtly.

"Your Majesty."

He and the rest of the group turned to leave, yet before they had gone far, Darian paused for a moment and turned back to Andron.

"If, by the power of Elohim, we are victorious in the coming battle, know that Eldor will offer Althilion any aid she may require for whatever reason," he warned.

As they continued on their way out of the throne room, they heard Eredan tell Andron, "I will escort them back to the gate."

"And then you will return here," Andron commanded shortly.

"Yes, my lord." Eredan sighed. Things did not bode well for him at the moment.

Outside, the group retrieved their horses and followed Eredan back to the gate. As they neared it, Torick wasn't shy in saying, "I think he was lying to us. I think he knows exactly what happened to Sirion."

No one replied, and Makilien wondered what they would do now that things seemed so hopeless. Once outside the city, they all turned to Darian to see what he would decide to do. Before anyone could speak, Eredan approached them.

"You are right. Lord Andron was lying to you."

"Eredan!" Bornil cried in astonishment from his position at the gate. He looked around worriedly for anyone else who may have overheard.

"Your friend Sirion is being held at the prison," Eredan went on unconcerned. "Lord Andron has been trying to gain information from him for an attack on Althilion."

Eyes widened at this information, and Darian asked, "Has he been harmed?"

"He has not been treated well," Eredan answered in regret. "Thardon, the man you saw inside, is responsible for this. Despite what you have seen, Lord Andron is a good man, but he is too concerned with wanting to be as great a king as his father. Thardon is taking advantage of that and persuading Lord Andron to do things he would never normally do, convincing him it is what his father would have done. Thardon is really the one who is driving the war against Althilion, though I do not know why."

"Is there any way to stop him?" Darian asked.

Eredan shook his head. "No. Lord Andron and I are old friends, and I've tried speaking to him, but he won't even listen to me."

"What do you suggest we do about Sirion? We will *not* leave here without him."

"There is a small gate at the southern end of the city. Meet me there after dark, and I will help you free him. Ride away from the city and stay out of sight until then."

Darian touched Eredan gratefully on the shoulder.

"Thank you."

They mounted their horses and rode away from the city. After riding for a distance of three miles, they stopped again.

"We should be far enough now," Darian said. "We'll remain here until nightfall."

They set up a small camp, but kept the horses saddled in case they had reason to leave in a hurry. Halandor and Torick built a small fire and prepared supper.

"Well, that didn't go at all the way I had hoped," Torick spoke for everyone. "I cannot believe Lord Andron still refuses to help us or to make peace. Somewhere inside he must know how foolish this is."

Darian shook his head in frustration. "As Eredan said, that man Thardon seemed to have a powerful influence over him."

"A king should not be so easily influenced." Torick sounded harsher than usual, but the deep, drawn out sigh that followed told Makilien he wasn't so much angry as he was worried.

She looked around at her friends. Disappointment and concern colored their faces. She too let out a sigh as she thought of Zirtan and being defeated by him. How could Lord Darand's and Lord Elnauhir's armies defeat such evil alone? Makilien shuddered to think of everyone she knew being killed or imprisoned by Zirtan. It was bad enough to think of being imprisoned again herself.

Torick spoke again, drawing Makilien out of her despairing thoughts. This time he was more subdued.

"I hate to think of Sirion having been in their hands for all this time. That Thardon has probably been torturing him for information."

"He would never talk," Halandor said with complete confidence.

Torick sighed. "All the worse for him, I'm afraid."

"I just pray he was spared some of what he might have endured and we'll be able to get in easily and get him out."

"Yes. Thank Elohim for Eredan otherwise we may never have known what happened to Sirion."

Restlessly, Eredan paced what dry area was left of his prison cell. He'd been prepared for some penalty after disobeying Andron's orders, but he truly hadn't expected his king to go this far. *Ah, but it's not Lord Andron.* It was Thardon. Every poor decision came from his conniving.

Eredan glanced at the small barred window high above his head on the opposite side of the cell. No hint of light showed through anymore. Now rain spat in from the downpour outside.

He sighed and ceased his pacing as he leaned against the bars at his back. He'd just sent Bornil to the city's southern gate to meet Prince Darian and the others now that he was incapable of doing so himself. He hated involving his friend, especially now that Lord Andron was no longer influenced by loyalties, but Bornil was the only one Eredan could trust.

Eredan's head bowed. *Elohim, please bring Bornil, Lord Darian, and the others here safely and undetected, and show me how to remove any blame from Bornil.*

His prayer came to an abrupt end when the sound of footsteps approached his cell. It seemed too soon, but he hoped it was Bornil returning with the prince. As Eredan looked eagerly down the hall, a torch appeared from around the corner. Disappointment smothered his hope when he saw the torchlight illuminating Thardon's menacing form.

He stared hard at the man, straining against his present state of helplessness. Then he noticed more than one dark figure followed Thardon. Some were too short to be men, yet others were very much taller.

Eredan frowned as they neared, but then gasped when they were close enough for him to clearly distinguish their hideous faces. *Goblins!* He'd seen a goblin only once before in his lifetime, when he was a boy. A rogue goblin had been killed after leaving its hiding place in the mountains to steal sheep. The other tall, monstrous creatures he'd never laid eyes, but he had heard of them. Shaikes.

Seeing the foul creatures left him with only one question— what were they doing here? They must surely be in league with Zirtan, and if Thardon was in their group, it could only mean he had an allegiance to Zirtan as well. Eredan did not find himself surprised. It was no wonder the other man continually advised Lord Andron to go to war with Althilion and encouraged him to refuse help to Eldor. Anger burned inside Eredan that the man would betray his country and associate with such evil.

"How dare you bring such foul creatures into the city!" Eredan said when Thardon reached his cell.

The sinister group paused at the door. The Shaikes growled and the goblins hissed at him, bearing their pointed teeth as their large, hateful eyes glinted. The only thing preventing them from killing him right then were the bars keeping him in his cell.

Grinning cruelly, Thardon took great pleasure in saying, "These *foul* creatures will soon be keeping you company . . . the last company you will ever have."

The goblins sneered viciously and fingered their jagged swords with anticipation.

"This way," Thardon ordered, and the group continued down the hall.

"What are you up to, Thardon?" Eredan called after him, but no answer came back, as they disappeared around another corner.

Once they were gone, Eredan searched his cell for some way of escape, but the dying torch across the hall was of little help. If only Bornil would return with Prince Darian. They were seven strong, and if they could free him, it would be eight. Besides Thardon, Eredan had counted only four Shaikes and six goblins.

Realizing he could do nothing but wait, Eredan finally gave up his search to pray. It was not long before, the sound of Thardon's return echoed through the hall. This time their group had gained a member.

As they drew closer, he realized it was Sirion, though the young man did not come willingly. The goblins and Shaikes shoved him from behind, the chains clanking from his wrists confirming he was still a prisoner.

"Where are you taking him?" Eredan asked, wondering what the Half-Elf had to do with Thardon's evil schemes. Hadn't Thardon caused the young man enough pain and hardship?

Thardon ignored Eredan, sparing him not even a glance.

Sirion, however, caught Eredan's gaze, his serious, dark brown eyes communicating the gravity of the situation as he tried to warn Eredan.

"They are taking me to the pala—"

One of the Shaikes drove its rock hard fist into Sirion's ribs. The young man groaned and stumbled, but the iron grip of the Shaikes kept him upright and forced him onward. Eredan could only watch, unable to do anything to intervene. His mind raced with unanswered questions. What purpose did Thardon have in taking Sirion to the palace? And more importantly, did Lord Andron know of Thardon's dealings with Zirtan? Could he be in on it as well? Eredan didn't want to believe such a thing.

:Chapter Sixteen:

The Plot

Makilien felt as though she were riding through ink as they made their way back to Dallorod. The rain had long since soaked them to the skin, and Makilien could barely see a thing. She only hoped Antiro could see better in the dark and not stray too far from the group. She'd given up all attempts to direct him, deciding it better to let him follow the others on his own. Makilien desperately wished to get dry and sit by a fire, but she had no hope of such comfort any time soon.

Suddenly, Antiro stopped. Makilien couldn't hear the other horses, but Loron's voice penetrated the rushing of the rain.

"This is the gate."

He and Gilhir were likely the only two able to find their way in the darkness. Everyone dismounted and followed the Elves to a small gate in the city wall. As they approached, the door opened, and they were offered dim light from a lantern down the street. Bornil stood in the archway of the gate. They huddled around him, pulling their soaking cloaks closer though it was of little comfort.

"Where's Eredan?" Darian asked.

"He was arrested after he returned to the palace," Bornil explained. "He sent me here to bring you to the prison."

He closed the gate and led them through the city. The streets were deserted, lit only by an occasional lantern, and running with rivers of water fed by the unrelenting downpour.

They walked until a building loomed menacingly in front of them. Bornil took them into a dark alley and unlocked the side door to the prison, which opened into a storeroom. A torch in the hall gave them enough light to see by, and Bornil led them deeper into the structure.

After navigating a couple of halls, they came to a long corridor lined on one side with dreary, damp cells. In one, Makilien spotted Eredan. He beckoned them closer.

"Let me out, Bornil," he said urgently. As the younger man unlocked the cell, Eredan went on. "Just a short time ago, Thardon was here. He had a group of goblins and Shaikes with him, and they took Sirion to the palace. We must find out what is going on."

Makilien's friends glanced at each other.

"If you saw goblins and Shaikes, Zirtan must be up to some sort of mischief here," Torick said.

"Yes, and we have to stop it."

Eredan stepped from his cell and took the lead. He went first to the armory where he retrieved his confiscated weapons and led everyone back out the side door where they had entered.

Using the darkest streets as cover, they rushed toward the palace. Thinking of the goblins and Shaikes Eredan had seen, Makilien wondered what danger they might come to face. She touched the cold, wet hilt of her sword for reassurance as she followed the darkened forms of her companions.

When the palace came within sight, they paused in the shadows of a nearby building. The entrance of the palace was lit up with lanterns and four palace guards patrolled it as usual. All appeared normal, belying whatever was happening inside.

"Do you think the guards are in on it?" Bornil asked.

Eredan shook his head. "I don't know . . ." He scanned the entire building before pointing down farther. "Bornil, does that window look like it's open to you?"

"It does, yes."

Knowing the palace windows could only be opened from the inside and would not be left open on a night like this, Eredan narrowed his eyes in suspicion.

"Come," he said, his voice only slightly raised above the rain.

Avoiding all light, they snuck along the side of the palace and cautiously approached the open window. Eredan peeked in and climbed through the window before turning back to help the others. Once inside, Makilien looked around. Though it was dark, she could tell the room was very large, and the walls were lined with tall shelves filled with books.

"We'll check the throne room first," Eredan whispered when everyone was inside.

They crossed the room as quietly as possible though their soggy footsteps echoed a little in the cavern-like space. When they reached the door, Eredan eased it open and led them toward the throne room.

Sirion tried to shrug off the two Shaikes on either side of him, but the beasts just growled and tightened their grip. He winced as pain, caused by the Shaike's blow to his ribs, radiated from his side, but it was the least of his concerns.

Another man shoved Lord Andron forward. The normally dignified king was clad only in his nightclothes, and heavy chains were clamped around his wrists. He glared at Thardon as two of his men pushed him closer.

"What is the meaning of this?" Andron tried to sound as commanding as possible in spite of his situation. "I demand to be told what is going on and what you are doing associating with these monsters."

This earned the king hisses and sneers from the ill-tempered goblins, and Thardon yanked out his sword. Placing the sharp tip against Andron's throat, he glared back at the king.

"You will be making no more demands of me," he spat. Lowering his sword to Andron's chest, a smirk grew on his face. "Yet, I will share my plans so you know before you die what a fool you are." He drew himself up arrogantly. "You are looking at Lord Zirtan's newly appointed king of Beldon."

Andron's eyes grew wide in horror. "You're working with Zirtan?"

In answer, Thardon chuckled low and menacing. Andron's eyes narrowed and his chest rose and fell heavily as anger ignited within him. He did indeed think himself to be a fool for listening to this man.

"You won't get away with this. The people are loyal to me. You won't be able to stay on the throne once they know you've killed me."

Thardon scoffed, thinking his so called *king* the epitome of stupidity. "No one but those in this room will ever be aware of that. Everyone will believe he . . ." Thardon swung his sword around and pointed it in Sirion's face, "is the guilty one. No, I won't be the one to have killed you. I'll be just in time to see this Half-Elf murder you, and then I'll have managed to kill him as he tried to escape. The people will be enraged with Althilion. All hesitancy to go to war with them will die with you.

"And while I keep the Elves busy, Lord Zirtan will crush Eldor and send an army down here to stomp out any remaining resistance. I will take my place as leader of this country and Althilion, and no one will dare defy me."

Andron hung his head in despair. The responsibility of this entire calamity rested upon his shoulders. He was to blame for dooming his country, for dooming Dolennar to Zirtan's rule.

Miserable with guilt and helplessness, Andron was surprised by the sudden determined ring of Sirion's voice.

"Zirtan would."

Andron looked up and saw deep resolve in the young man's eyes. He had not yet given up and weakness jabbed at Andron for doing so himself.

Thardon spun around to face Sirion. "What?"

"Zirtan would defy you without so much as a thought. He does nothing which does not benefit him. You may think he will give you lordship over these countries, but there are men who work closer to him than you do. I'm sure they will also have an interest in ruling Beldon and Althilion. Zirtan will think nothing of allowing them to take it from you."

"Shut up, mongrel! Or I'll cut out your tongue to keep you silent until I kill you," Thardon warned darkly.

"Leave him be."

Thardon looked over his shoulder at Andron and chuckled as he turned back to the king. "First you allow me to imprison and do whatever necessary to withdraw information from him, but now you're defending him?"

Overwhelming guilt filled Andron's heart. He was a proud man, like his father, and now that pride had placed him here. Swallowing all that was left of his pride, he glanced remorsefully at Sirion and said to Thardon, "I was wrong to allow you to lay a hand on him."

Thardon smirked at the king's sudden empathy for the Half-Elf.

In disgust, Andron shook his head. "How can you betray your people and your country?"

"This country has done nothing for me." To punctuate his words, Thardon spit on the floor near Andron's feet.

Andron's anger flared again. "I made you general, even over Eredan!"

But Thardon scoffed mockingly. "Your first mistake."

He raised his sword again to Andron's chest. The king drew himself up and locked eyes with his enemy. At least he could die bravely. He wouldn't beg for his life.

With only moments before the assassination of Beldon's king, Sirion's eyes searched for a way to intervene. At last they fell on the hilt of a sword hanging from the belt of one of Thardon's men, not three feet away. It would be an easy reach if he were free of the Shaikes. He noticed the creatures' grasps had loosened since arriving. If he was going to make a move, it had to be now. Adrenaline surged through his body. *Elohim, You are the only chance I have of this working.*

The very second before Thardon would have run his sword through Andron's heart, Sirion ripped himself away from the Shaikes. In an Elven fast movement, he grabbed the other man's sword and whipped it out of the scabbard as he spun around. The blade crashed into Thardon's, knocking it away from Andron. Thardon stumbled back in surprise, and Sirion took a stand between the king and his enemies.

The shock over his actions lasted for only a brief moment, and looks of anger grew on every face. The ringing of swords exiting their scabbards echoed in the room. Deep growls and high-pitched shrieks followed. At least twenty goblins, Shaikes, and men closed in around him.

Thardon sneered. "What are you going to do now, mongrel?"

Sirion had no plan from here. He knew he could not last long on his own. His only hope was to last just long enough, even if it ended up costing him his life, for the palace guards to be alerted to the danger their king was in.

Everything was silent making the low sounds of their breathing and their cautious footsteps seem undesirably loud. Makilien didn't know where they were in the palace or how far they were from the throne room when the resonating clang of metal against metal broke the stillness and echoed toward them. The sound made them pause, but then they rushed on, forgetting stealth. A moment of silence followed the first clash, followed shortly by more clashes that came in rapid succession.

Finally, they burst into the throne room, drawing their swords as they came upon the fight taking place. Makilien caught a quick glimpse of a young man in the middle of the room single-handedly fending off more than a dozen enemies. He was doing an incredible job but would not be able to hold them off for much longer.

Makilien's friends raced forward, but Makilien hesitated. She was suddenly terrified of having to put the skills Halandor had taught her to the test. Scolding herself, she faced the fear and ran forward, her sword ready.

The goblins and Shaikes alerted to their presence turned to engage them. Makilien raised her sword. It came crashing against the sword of a goblin, halting all forward momentum, and sending an almost painful jolt through her hands. Not waiting for the goblin to try to attack, she swung her sword, throwing all her weight into it. The goblin's sword flew to the left. Raising her sword again, Makilien swung downward, and her blade slashed into the goblin's chest. With an ear-piercing shriek, it dropped at her feet.

Raising her eyes from its body to meet her next foe, they landed on Sirion fighting just a couple of yards away. His back was turned so she knew he could not see the goblin slinking up behind him, just about to raise its wicked blade.

Without taking time to think, Makilien dashed forward and swung her sword, bringing it across the goblin's back. It too shrieked loudly as it toppled to the floor writhing. At the sound, Sirion spun around. First his eyes landed on the dying goblin, but then they lifted to Makilien.

"Thank you," he gasped.

Makilien barely had a chance to nod her head before Sirion's eyes swung past her. His expression turned from surprise to alarm.

"Look out!" he yelled.

Makilien had no time to react or move, but Sirion reached out, grabbing her arm and pulling her to the side. He raised his sword just in time to block the blade of an advancing Shaike. Now it was Makilien's turn to stand in surprise as she watched him fight the huge beast. His fighting style, though similar to Halandor and Torick's, held hints of Elven grace and speed making him a truly formidable opponent.

Just after the Shaike collapsed, following an unsuccessful attempt to block one of Sirion's attacks, commotion at the door drew everyone's attention. Palace guards rushed into the throne room. Makilien was very relieved when they proved to be on their side by attacking the goblins and Shaikes. With the added men, the battle came to a swift end. All goblins and Shaikes lay dead on the floor, and the small handful of men, including Thardon, who had not been killed were apprehended and disarmed.

Safe now from any surprise attack, Makilien looked over each of her friends with concern. Though almost all of them had some splattering of blood on their clothes, some of their own and some from their foes, no one appeared to be seriously injured. Eredan, however, did have a large splotch of blood staining the sleeve of his shirt from his shoulder to his elbow from a wound sustained in a vicious battle with Thardon.

Once the guards had unchained their king, Andron ordered for Thardon and his men to be taken away. Thardon was dragged out of the room, hurling curses and insults back at them, which did not die away until they were far down the hall. The remaining guards removed the dead from the throne room and searched the palace for any goblins or Shaikes that may still be hiding there.

After instructing his men, Andron turned to his rescuers. He knew not how Eredan had escaped the prison, nor how Prince Darian and his companions had shown up here, but he was in their debt. Noticing those who were injured and that all were soaking wet, he ordered a nearby guard, "Send for the servants and physicians."

"Yes, my lord."

As the guard hurried away, Andron said to Darian and the others, "Please, come with me." He led them to a large sitting room with a massive fireplace. "I will have a fire built as soon as the servants arrive so you may dry and warm yourselves, and the physicians will tend to your injuries."

"Thank you, my lord," Darian said gratefully.

Andron turned to face them. Makilien saw nothing of the arrogant and stubborn young man they had met earlier in the day. All pride had left him, and only remorse remained in his eyes.

"If I may," he spoke hesitantly to Darian, "how did you get here?"

"It is my doing, my lord," Eredan answered, stepping forward and hoping to take any blame away from Bornil. "I told them you had Sirion imprisoned, and I planned to help them release him. After I was imprisoned, I sent Bornil to do it. While I was waiting for them, I saw Thardon come and take Sirion. He told me they were bringing him here so when Bornil arrived with Lord Darian, I ordered him to free me, and we came here knowing Thardon must have an allegiance to Zirtan. My lord, you have my deepest apologies for acting behind your back, but I felt they were actions I must take. I am willing to accept any consequences."

"No," Andron said, shaking his head. "There will be no consequences. My own actions of late have been beyond foolish. I should have heeded your counsel and warnings about Thardon. My pride and stubbornness nearly doomed our people and all of Dolennar to Zirtan's rule."

His gaze shifted from Eredan to the rest of the group. "I am indebted to you all. I did not deserve rescue, especially not from you." His eyes stopped on Sirion. "You could easily have fled when you escaped from the Shaikes, but you remained, at great peril to your own life, to protect me when you had every reason to let me die. What can I do to show my gratitude?"

"My lord, I came here wanting nothing more than to bring peace between Althilion and Beldon. That is what I still seek," Sirion said with quiet and noble sincerity.

"And peace there shall be. The hostility my father created has lasted too long, and I was a fool to let it continue. I will be honored to bring an end to it."

The feelings of despair that had been present among Makilien's friends lifted. Now Lord Glorlad would be free to bring his warriors to Eldor's aid. Relief flooded Makilien with this knowledge.

Casting his attention once again on Darian, Andron said, "If it can be done, it is also my hope to restore the alliance between Eldor and Beldon. I will gladly lead my soldiers to Eldor to take a stand against Zirtan."

Darian's weary face broke into a grin. "Of course, Your Majesty. Our alliance is restored."

Andron also smiled.

A group of servants rushed into the room. All had received word of Andron's near assassination and were eager to offer their assistance to their king and his rescuers. Andron ordered a fire built first. As a couple of the men started the blaze, Makilien and her friends shed some of their wet clothing. Makilien unclasped her waterlogged cloak and pulled off her heavy, leather overdress. Once down to only her dress and pants, she stood at the fireplace and extended her hands toward the flames.

181

She wasn't the only one to take advantage of the warmth. Halandor and Loron came to stand there as well, soon joined by Gilhir and Sirion.

While they warmed themselves, Makilien glanced at Sirion, intrigued. He was different from any of the other people she had met on her journey. His appearance was more Elven than Halandor's, despite their shared half Human, half Elf heritage. Although Sirion's dark hair was shorter than all Elves Makilien had met—a little shorter even than Halandor's—his handsome face bore no facial hair in the fashion of an Elf.

When Makilien's hands and face had been warmed, she turned her back to the fire and watched the physicians. Only Eredan had any true injuries although they were not serious. Though Sirion didn't appear to have any outward sign of injury aside from an old wound above his brow, Andron approached him.

"If you would permit me, I would like to have my physician examine you." An expression of deep shame contorted Andron's face.

Sirion did not speak but nodded and walked over to the physician. Slowly, he pulled off his shirt. Makilien winced, and her throat squeezed a little when she spied what was underneath. Sirion's exposed torso was bruised with the signs of multiple beatings. Makilien also caught a glimpse of a laceration across Sirion's shoulder. She'd seen the effect of beatings in Reylaun and easily distinguished the wound as a result from a whip. It affected Makilien deeply to see what Sirion had endured for the sake of his country at the hands of men who could also be called his countrymen. And even so, he had risked his life for the man responsible.

Struggling with his conscience, Andron ordered a couple of servants to bring food and hot beverages.

"Your Majesty," Darian said, approaching him, "Our horses were left by the southern gate of the city. I hate to leave them in the elements any longer than necessary."

Andron nodded and called to another servant. "Tell the stablemen that Prince Darian and their companions have their horses at the southern gate. See they are brought in and bedded down comfortably. Also see that everyone's belongings are brought inside."

In the next while, the food was brought and everyone ate hungrily, but weariness from the day and late hour was overtaking them. As soon as they were finished, Andron's servants led everyone upstairs. The young, bright-eyed woman who had carried Makilien's bag stopped in the middle of a long hall and motioned Makilien into a bedroom. Makilien glanced at her friends who were directed into rooms around hers. She was uneasy about sleeping alone in a strange palace, which only hours ago had not welcomed them. But she knew Halandor would never leave her in a dangerous position so she walked into the room.

The young servant lit a couple of candles, and the room was bathed in a warm glow. She turned to Makilien after she'd set her pack near the bed.

"I will go find you a pair of dry nightclothes and return shortly," she said.

Makilien nodded and was left alone. When the door had closed, she turned in a circle to take in her surroundings. The room was a little smaller than her room at the palace in Minarald, but similar. Finally, her eyes rested on her pack, which looked soaked though she hoped since it was leather the inside would be dry. She knelt next to it and dug through her extra dresses. They were a bit damp so she pulled them out. In doing so, she found what she'd been looking for— her sketchbook. The pages were slightly crinkled from the dampness, but none of her sketches were ruined.

Makilien rose and laid the book and dresses on the bed. Tiredly, she unbuckled her belt, glad to be rid of the weight of her sword. She propped the scabbard up against the nightstand so the sword's hilt would be within easy reach while she slept. Makilien had to smile to herself. A few weeks ago, she may not have thought of something so obvious, but thanks to Halandor and Torick and the rest of her friends, she was learning quickly how to always be on guard in this dangerous world.

Makilien proceeded to lay her dampened clothes across the small table and two chairs at the one side of the bed for them to dry overnight.

When the servant returned, she had a linen nightgown in her hands. "This nightgown is one of mine. I couldn't find any other. It's not fancy, but it's dry."

Makilien smiled, thinking of the rather poor family she came from. This servant's nightgown was likely better than any she'd had at home.

"It will be just fine, thank you," Makilien told her.

"Is there anything else I can get you?"

Makilien said no and thanked her again. When the young woman had left, Makilien locked the door and changed into the nightgown. She laid out her dress and pants and blew out all the candles. Getting into bed, she touched her sword once in the darkness and snuggled down under the covers.

:Chapter Seventeen:

Ambush

Makilien's eyes fluttered open, and she put a hand to her mouth to stifle a yawn. Warm shafts of sunlight fell across the end of her bed. Everything was comfortable and peaceful, and the last thing she wanted was to get up. She knew time was too short for them to spend another night, and they would start back to Minarald right away, so it would be days before she saw another bed. Yet, she must rise or keep her friends waiting.

With a sigh, Makilien pushed back the blankets and slid out of bed. She stretched her arms, pleased that she felt no aches from using her sword, and walked over to the table where she'd laid out her dresses. All had dried out overnight. Choosing one, she changed from her nightgown and laced up her overdress. After braiding her hair, she packed the rest of her clothes and sketchbook and left the room. Outside in the hall, Makilien found Halandor waiting for her with a smile.

"I hope you haven't been waiting long," Makilien said.

"No, not long. Everyone has just started gathering in the dining room for breakfast."

They walked side by side down the hall.

"Thank you, Halandor," Makilien said suddenly.

He looked down at her. "For?"

"For taking care of me. I hate being a burden, but I really appreciate everything you've done."

Halandor smiled. "You're no burden at all."

When the two of them entered the dining room, Makilien happily took in the sight of her friends gathered together. Torick turned at the sound of their entrance.

"Ah, Makilien, you're awake. Come. We were just realizing we have not yet properly introduced you to Sirion."

Makilien and Halandor joined their friends, and Sirion smiled kindly. Makilien found herself wondering how old he was. Being Half-Elf, he could be quite a bit older than she expected, but he still had a slightly boyish appearance and appeared no more than a couple of years older than herself.

"Makilien, I am pleased to meet you formally and to thank you. When you killed the goblin last night, you no doubt saved my life. I don't think I would have noticed it in time."

With a smile in return, Makilien said, "I'm glad I did notice. I didn't have time to think, I just acted."

"You fought well, Makilien, for your first battle with goblins," Torick commended her.

She shrugged and turned her attention back to Sirion.

"I have reason to thank you as well. You saved me from the Shaike. I never realized it was behind me, nor do I think I could have successfully fought it even if I had."

"I am happy I could assist you," Sirion said as they shared another smile.

With everyone now present, they were served a filling breakfast, which they all enjoyed, but they did not linger. Time was against them, and every day brought them ever closer to the coming battle. As soon as they were finished, a servant showed them into the throne room where Andron, who had not joined them for breakfast, waited.

Wearing more kingly attire than he had been found in the night before, Andron stood near the throne, surrounded by his men, some in black and green soldiers' uniforms, including Eredan.

"Good morning," he said when they walked in. "I hope you all slept comfortably."

"Yes, my lord, thank you," Darian replied.

"Good. I apologize for not joining you at breakfast, but I had much I needed to discuss with my men. I assume you will be leaving today?"

"Yes. I want to get back to Minarald and my father as soon as possible."

"And I will send my troops as soon as they are all gathered and prepared," Andron told them. "I've made Eredan my general, as I should have from the beginning. He will oversee the army. I, myself, am taking two of my men and riding to Althilion to speak with Lord Glorlad. I personally want to assure him we want peace and are joining the fight against Zirtan."

"My lord," Gilhir stepped up. "I will be traveling home to Althilion. If it pleases you, I could join you and lead you to Silnar."

"I would be honored, Gilhir, for you to lead me to your city."

Dallorod seemed to have taken on new life. People crowded the streets, mostly soldiers preparing for the long march to

Eldor. The men were eager to defend their homeland from Zirtan's rule.

Working amidst the commotion, Makilien and her friends attached their replenished supplies to the saddles of their waiting horses. Looking up, Makilien spotted Eredan near the king, now wearing the uniform of a general as he spoke to Sirion. Though she couldn't hear what was said, she watched Eredan put his hand on Sirion's shoulder and smile kindly. Sirion said a few words and then turned toward their group. Coming to Darian, he said, "I will ride with you to Eldor. I want to be there should fighting begin before my uncle and Lord Andron arrive."

"You are most welcome to join us, Sirion," Darian replied.

Sirion turned to Gilhir. "Tell my uncle I am fine and I will see him in Minarald."

"I will do that," Gilhir assured him. The Elf looked to Darian. "Lord Glorlad will make great haste with our warriors."

"We will be watching for your arrival."

After farewells, Makilien and her party left Dallorod, riding west along the mountains, eagerly looking ahead to their planned arrival back at Minarald five days from now. They had been gone for a week, and it would be nearly two by the time they arrived. Anything could have happened in that time.

The first day of travel passed better than expected. They'd worried after the night's rain the way would be muddy, but a warm southern wind dried the ground and they traveled fast, camping that night at the mouth of the gap in the mountains.

They built a fire just as darkness fell and gathered around while supper was prepared.

As he worked, Torick looked across the fire at Sirion who was giving his sword a sharper edge.

"Do you want to tell us what happened in Dallorod? Did you go alone?"

Sirion glanced at him. "Yes, I was alone."

"Were you allowed to see Lord Andron or were you imprisoned right away?"

"I was brought before Lord Andron, but Thardon did most of the talking. He convinced Lord Andron that I could be used to gain information about Althilion and Silnar."

Sirion paused here, taking time to put his whetstone into a small pouch and return his sword to its scabbard.

Finally, he looked up at Torick. "Once they realized I would not tell them anything, Thardon persuaded Lord Andron to allow him to do whatever he deemed necessary. I was put in a windowless cell at the prison with no light and left without food or water. I'm not sure how much time passed, but Thardon came to question me at least once a day, trying to get me to talk. This went on for maybe two or three days and then Eredan came to my cell. He brought me food, water, and a couple of candles. He did this whenever he could without Thardon's knowledge."

Makilien couldn't imagine going through what Sirion had faced. It gave her great admiration for him. She also admired what Eredan had done.

"He's a good man," Halandor commended Eredan's actions.

"Yes," Sirion agreed and added, "An answer to prayer."

"Tomorrow evening we'll reach Minarald," Halandor said during their lunch break four days after leaving Dallorod.

The journey had gone well, but the thought of sleeping in a warm bed again made Makilien anxious to put an end to traveling for however long it would last.

While packing up their supplies once they had finished eating, Makilien noticed Antiro raise his head suddenly and stare off toward the mountains, his ears pointed forward and alert.

"What is it, Antiro?"

Makilien walked around him and looked up. Only fifty feet away and about thirty feet above them, she spotted an enormous bird, bigger than any she'd ever seen. Clearly some sort of vulture, its feathers were jet black and spiked around its neck, but its head was a featherless, sickly pink flesh. It had a sharp, gray beak and evil red eyes. Most alarming, it appeared just big enough to be able to pick Makilien up and fly away with her. The way it peered at her through its wide, unblinking eyes was most unnerving.

Antiro stomped his foot and snorted.

"Halandor," Makilien called nervously.

As he came to her side, the bird moved its head up and down once and made a garbled sound in its throat before flying off.

"What was that?" Makilien asked, glad it was gone, but still unsettled.

"We call them death vultures." Concern tinged Halandor's voice. "They are a type of hybrid vulture bred by Zirtan and used as spies, but we rarely see them." He glanced at the others who had gathered around. "Zirtan's presence is growing."

"We should be on our way," Darian said. "The sooner we reach Minarald the better."

They rode on with a growing apprehension. Makilien frequently glanced up the sides of the mountains and into the sky, afraid the death vulture would reappear. However, the evil bird did not show itself again.

As the sun sank below the mountain peaks, filling the gap with dark shadows, Makilien and her companions slowed their horses to a walk in order to pass through a narrow and rocky section. The gap was eerily silent at dusk, and the horses' hooves echoed loudly on the rocky ground.

Just as the gap widened again, the horses in the lead, stopped abruptly, forcing the others to halt. They tossed their heads and stomped their feet, their nostrils flaring. Unease gripping everyone, they looked around for what had spooked their mounts, but no one saw or heard anything. They had no choice except to urge the horses on, who faithfully but reluctantly obeyed.

Tingles of fear crawled up Makilien's back, causing her to shiver. She peered all around, thinking of the robbers Halandor had mentioned when they'd begun their trip. She hoped their numbers would dissuade any attackers.

After long, tense minutes, Makilien thought she caught movement out of the corner of her eye, but when she looked, she saw only dark shadows. Maybe her apprehensive mind was playing tricks on her. She tried to make herself believe that, but then Loron pulled his horse to a stop. "We're being followed."

Sirion affirmed it.

"Did you see something?" Darian asked, keeping his voice low.

Loron shook his head. "No, but I can hear something behind us and in the rocks on either side."

Makilien's mouth went dry. Her heart rate increased, her eyes darting from rock to rock as she wondered what could be hiding behind them.

"Do you know how many?"

"No."

Darian took a moment to consider what should be done and drew his sword. The rest of the group followed his example and armed themselves with their weapons of choice. Makilien withdrew her bow, hoping to shoot any enemies before they could get close enough to her and Antiro for her to have to use her sword.

"Whoever is out there, we know you are there," Darian called out, his voice echoing through the gap. "Show yourselves."

His call was met with silence for several moments, but then the darkest shadows around them seemed to morph into solid shapes. One by one, four large, black mountain wolves appeared on both sides of them and five up ahead. Makilien knew there must be some behind as well, but couldn't take her eyes away from the ones straight ahead. On either side of each wolf, two goblins held chains attached to spiked collars around the neck of each beast, though how they might actually control the giant wolves was a mystery.

"It's an ambush," Darian murmured.

Vicious snarls echoed around them as the wolves bared their teeth. The goblins joined in with their hissing and shrieking.

Makilien gripped her bow so tightly her fingers ached. She took a couple deep breaths, trying to calm all the nerves that urged her to panic. If she wasn't calm and alert, she might not react as quickly as she needed to. The main purpose of their group was to protect Darian. This gave her a sense of duty that managed to outpace her fear.

Suddenly, one of the goblins gave a bloodcurdling scream.

"Attack!"

The mountain wolves lunged forward, dragging their chains, and the goblins charged behind them. Makilien yanked out an arrow and aimed at the closest wolf off to her right. Holding her breath to steady her shot, she released the arrow and it hit the wolf squarely in the forehead. It fell instantly and tumbled along the rocky ground. Makilien grabbed another arrow to bring down a second wolf. She glanced once at Darian to make sure he was all right and saw that Loron and the rest of her friends were careful to protect the prince.

After one final successful shot, Makilien was forced to drop her bow and draw her sword as a wolf sprang toward her and Antiro. The wolf snapped at Antiro's foreleg, but Makilien swung her sword down across its muzzle. It bounded away howling. Another wolf crept up behind Antiro and tried to jump onto him but got one of Antiro's large hooves in its gut and went flying.

By now, the goblins had reached the group. Two grabbed at Makilien's dress to pull her from Antiro's back. Makilien slipped her foot from the stirrup and kicked one of the ugly creatures in the face, swinging her sword at the other.

Distracted, she did not realize the wolf Antiro had kicked had crept around to the other side of them. Lunging, it grabbed a mouthful of her dress and yanked. With a cry, Makilien toppled over and fell hard on her side. Antiro whinnied angrily and spun around. He reared up, forcing the wolf back just before it would have pounced. This gave Makilien time to scramble to her feet. Catching the wolf off guard, she thrust her sword into its shoulder. It yelped and limped off, disappearing into the shadows.

Holding her sword defensively, Makilien turned, searching for any more attackers, but she realized all the wolves and goblins were either dead or retreating. Breathing heavily, she lowered her sword and let her muscles relax. With one hand, she rubbed her aching hip, but was too pleased with the outcome of the fight to really notice the pain. No one else was injured, and she had survived another, more dangerous fight against Zirtan's minions.

Dismounting, Halandor came to her side. "Are you all right?"

"Yes, I am. A few bumps, but nothing to worry about."

Halandor bent down to pick up her bow and handed it to her.

"Thank you." Makilien strapped it back to her quiver.

"We need to find a place to camp before dark," Torick said.

"There's that small hill ahead," Halandor suggested. "It would be a good place to defend ourselves should there be another attack."

Darian agreed. "We'll camp there."

Makilien stepped up to Antiro, limping just a little, as they prepared to ride on. She pulled herself up into the saddle. Turning Antiro around, she noticed Sirion move his white and gray paint mare next to her.

"You're sure you are all right?" he asked, noticing her limp.

"Yes. Just a little sore from falling," she said, appreciative of his concern.

The two were slowly becoming good friends. Sirion was a quiet young man, almost reserved at times. Though he was always concerned with the wellbeing of their group, he didn't divulge much about himself, and his youthful appearance contradicted the wealth of wisdom and experience Makilien saw in his eyes. In a way, he reminded her of Aedan, and she liked that.

Just as the last bit of sunlight faded away, they stopped on a small hill in the middle of the gap, which they had passed earlier in their journey. They had just enough room at the top to set up camp. A fire was made quickly, for which Makilien was thankful. She hated being in the dark and not knowing what had become of the surviving goblins and mountain wolves.

Supper was prepared and everyone talked idly around the fire.

"You fought well again, Makilien," Torick said. "You've learned to handle a sword fast. Your skills with a bow have also impressed me once again."

Makilien smiled contentedly.

"Where did you learn to use a bow?" Sirion asked.

She looked at him across the fire. "My father taught me so I could go hunting with him. Though we never did get to go, I practiced almost every day until it became something I did just to pass the time. Still, I'm not nearly as skilled as an Elf."

"I wouldn't say that."

"Well, maybe my aim can compare, but I'll never have the speed of an Elf."

A howl in the distance ended the conversation. Others joined in. The horses snorted and shifted nervously, and the hair on Makilien's arms rose at the terrible sound. She rubbed the scars from her last nighttime encounter with mountain wolves. It was one thing fighting them when she could see them clearly, but altogether different having them attack in the dark.

"I think it would be wise to set up double watches tonight," Halandor advised.

"Yes," Darian agreed. "Halandor, you and Makilien can take first watch. Torick and Sirion take second, and Loron and I will take third."

As they ate their supper, the howls continued, each one drawing closer. Later in the night, no one had yet fallen asleep, finding themselves restless and preoccupied by the dry grass crunching at the bottom of the hill. Makilien ran her anxious fingers up and down the hilt of her sword and wished she could see better in the dark.

This went on for quite a time until Loron stood and peered down the hill into the darkness. He put an arrow to his bowstring and drew it back. When he released it, a yelp echoed, and they heard the sound of the wolves running off. The only sound that remained was the crackling of their fire. Makilien breathed a sigh of relief, hoping the wolves would not return.

By now, the watch she would have shared with Halandor had passed, though no one had slept. As Torick and Sirion prepared to keep watch, Halandor told Makilien to get some rest. She lay down on her bedroll, as did the others, but she was restless, and despite her fatigue, could not fall asleep.

A cool breeze blew down from the mountains causing Makilien to shiver. With it came unwanted doubts, which crowded into her heart. They were doubts she'd been plagued by for weeks and always ignored. But, for the past few days, she found them intensifying. She didn't feel like she was truly a part of her group of friends. They were each the closest friends she had besides Aedan, yet still she felt like an outsider. A painful and empty loneliness settled in her heart even with all of them around. Tears pricked her eyes, and she closed them tight, trying to force the unpleasantness away, but it just seemed to increase the harder she tried.

:Chapter Eighteen:

Preparing for War

Even in the dark, Minarald's iron gate was the most welcome sight Makilien had seen in a long time. After leaving their camp at dawn and riding almost nonstop, she couldn't wait to reach the safety and comfort inside.

The gatekeepers were swift to open the gate after Darian announced their arrival, and the stablemen were glad to care for their horses. They trudged wearily to the palace where Darand was waiting for them in the throne room, having received word of their arrival. Lord Elnauhir was also present when they entered. Both were anxious for information.

"Welcome back," Darand greeted them. "I am very thankful to see all of you are safe. And Sirion, it is good to see you."

"And you, my lord," Sirion replied.

Focusing hopeful eyes on his son, Darand asked, "What news do you have?"

Darian smiled. "Lord Glorlad and Lord Andron are on their way as we speak."

Darand and Elnauhir sighed with the immensity of their relief.

"Good," Darand breathed. "Very good. Was it difficult to convince Lord Andron?"

"You could say that," Darian said in amusement, and he gave a brief account of their journey and adventures and how peace had been restored between Althilion and Beldon.

Soon after they had returned, Makilien was happy to see Vonawyn and the rest of her family enter the throne room.

Elmorhirian elbowed his brother in the ribs and said, "I told you they were back."

Not to be outdone, Elandir hurried forward, tossing over his shoulder, "And I told you they would have Sirion with them."

Joining the group, he clapped Sirion on the back as he greeted him. Makilien noticed the slightest wince of pain cross Sirion's face. Apparently, so did Torick.

"Can't you two be a bit less enthusiastic?" he scolded. "Do you want to injure him further?"

Elandir and Elmorhirian's faces sobered immediately, almost comically so.

"You're injured?" Elandir asked Sirion.

"I'm fine," Sirion assured them.

"What happened?"

"Who needs a beating?" Elmorhirian quickly joined in.

Makilien had to chuckle to herself at the way the two Elves treated Sirion like their little brother. Sirion glanced at her and, by his expression, she was sure he was a bit embarrassed by their fussing.

"No one. It's all been resolved," he tried to tell them.

"Oh, don't give us that," Elandir said.

Sirion crossed his arms and insisted, "I am perfectly capable of taking care of myself."

"We will find out eventually," Elmorhirian persisted.

"Perhaps," Torick cut in, "but tonight Sirion and the rest of us need sleep. We were ambushed by goblins and mountain wolves before making camp last night and, needless to say, barely slept."

To Elandir and Elmorhirian's dismay, Lord Darand agreed and called for servants to show Sirion to a room. The rest of the group gladly went to their own bedrooms.

Makilien hummed happily as she descended the stairs on her way to the dining room in the morning. A comfortable night of sleep had helped dispel the gloomy mood she kept finding herself in.

Entering the dining room, she caught Torick saying, ". . . precisely why he didn't tell you last night. What do you two plan to do? Attack Lord Andron when he arrives?"

Elandir and Elmorhirian sat at the table with Sirion and Torick, and Makilien was just in time to see Elmorhirian grin mischievously in reaction to Torick's question. Torick narrowed his eyes as the Elf's grin widened.

"I'm not going to have to have Lord Darand assign a guard to you, am I?"

Elmorhirian gave him a look that suggested Torick would have to do just that.

"I'll keep an eye on him, Torick."

The voice came from behind Makilien. She looked over her shoulder and smiled at Vonawyn.

"At least one of Lord Elnauhir's children is responsible," Torick muttered.

"It's fun to be irresponsible sometimes," Elmorhirian teased impishly. "You should try it."

The younger people all laughed, and Torick had more than a hint of a smile on his face. It amused Makilien to see Elmorhirian and his brother were the same here as at home.

As Makilien and Vonawyn took their seats at the table, Elandir looked across at Makilien and said, "We heard you were stabbed."

"And almost died," Elmorhirian chimed in.

"Yes," Makilien acknowledged, "but luckily Torick found me, and Meniah saved my life."

"The information she learned and lived to tell saved Lord Darand and Darian," Torick told them. "Gornath would have killed them and disappeared before we ever knew what happened if Makilien hadn't overheard his plans."

"It seems you have a talent for saving people," Sirion murmured with a sparkling smile.

Makilien found herself blushing a little and didn't know what to say as Halandor entered the room, followed closely by Lord Darand and the rest of their friends. Once everyone was present, Darand prayed and their breakfast was served.

It was a lively meal, thanks to Lord Elnauhir's sons, with much laughing and tale telling. Because of this merry atmosphere, it was especially alarming when one of the palace guards rushed into the room.

"My lord, Indiya has returned, and Emaril and Carmine are with her."

For a moment, complete silence and dread settled over the table. The arrival of all three dragons from their patrol along river could only mean one thing—Zirtan's army was on its way.

Darand pushed back his chair and rose as did the others.

"Where are they?" the king asked on his way to the door.

"The courtyard, my lord."

Exiting the palace, Makilien was greeted by a magnificent sight. Indiya stood with two other, slightly larger male dragons. One was covered by dark green scales the color of emeralds while the other was a deep scarlet like red maple leaves.

As Darand and the group neared, the red dragon stepped forward and bowed his head.

"Your Majesty," he said in a deep, resonating voice.

"What news do you bring, Carmine?"

The dragon's voice brimmed with urgency. "We've spotted Zirtan's troops. They are traveling swiftly and crossed the Claron River a day and a half ago."

"When do you believe they will arrive here?"

"No more than four days."

Only four days. So little time before the enemy was at their door.

With some hesitancy Darand asked, "How large a force is it?"

"At least seventy-thousand."

The grave look on Darand's face put a terrible churning in Makilien's stomach. She did not know how large a force Eldor possessed, but clearly it was not a match for Zirtan's. However, determination hardened Darand's features as he went on questioning the dragon.

"What do they have for siege weapons?"

"Battering rams and catapults, my lord."

"No siege towers?"

"We did not spot any, but they may just be farther behind."

Darand nodded and gave orders to the men around him. "Send for Nirgon. We must begin evacuating the outer city immediately. I also want to speak to Arphen and the other griffons."

He turned back to the dragons. "Do you need rest or can you still fly?"

"We are ready to fly wherever you need us to, my lord," Carmine answered.

"Good. Indiya, Emaril, I want you two to fly to the gap. Lord Glorlad and Lord Andron are on their way here. Find out how soon they will arrive and warn them Zirtan's army is on its way."

"We will leave immediately," Emaril replied, his voice younger and not quite as deep as Carmine's.

He and Indiya spread their wings and launched into the sky, flying straight southwest.

When they were out of sight, Darand told Carmine, "I want you, Arphen, and the other griffons to warn the people in the villages that will be in Zirtan's path. If they do not leave right away, they will not get out in time."

"Yes, my lord. We were able to warn some of the villages along the way, but not all."

Soon, Arphen and seven other griffons flew into the courtyard and Nirgon arrived. Carmine informed them of what he and the other two dragons had seen. Once the griffons had been given their instructions to warn the villages, they and Carmine flew away, traveling east, and only men and Elves remained in the courtyard.

"We must start the outer city evacuation and gather all the provisions into the inner city," Darand told Nirgon. "Four days is not much time."

Nirgon nodded. "I will inform my men and have them begin."

As the general turned to leave, Torick said, "We can help move provisions."

"Yes," Darand said, "store them wherever you can find room."

Everyone seemed to be heading off in the direction Nirgon had just gone. Feeling lost in the commotion, Makilien hurried up beside Halandor and walked along with him.

"Why are they evacuating the outer part of the city?" she asked.

"Lord Darand wants everyone behind the inner wall in case the worst should happen and Zirtan's army breaches the outer wall," Halandor explained. "He wants all provisions within the inner city in case of a prolonged siege."

Makilien nodded in understanding.

"Can I help move provisions?"

"Certainly."

For a moment nothing more was said, but then Makilien asked, "Why is Zirtan coming from the east? I thought he would be coming from the north."

"He has long had control over the North, but has more recently taken over all the lands east of the Dûbar Mountains. Now he has a fortress on the eastern border of the country of Rhûnland. That is where he has gathered his army. It gives him a more open and direct route to Eldor."

The city was in chaos as word of Zirtan's army and the order to evacuate spread. The soldiers, however, worked to keep things orderly, but Makilien sensed nervousness and fear from the people as they left their homes, carrying only what belongings they truly needed. The people of the inner city were very generous, making room in their houses for all their friends and neighbors as families streamed in through the inner gate. Besides these people, a slower, but steady stream from outside the city. These were the people of the villages, all seeking safety within the city walls.

Makilien worked alongside her friends at one of the storehouses, loading food into wagons loaned by the people. Crates of fruits and vegetables, sacks of grain and flour, kegs of fish—all were loaded into the wagons. It was tiring work, which left little time for communicating. Makilien was left entirely to her own thoughts and speculations of the impending doom marching their way. The expression on Lord Darand's face when he had received the number of Zirtan's troops kept replaying in her mind. Would all this turn out to be a hopeless struggle? Makilien wanted to believe it wouldn't, but hope seemed to be waning throughout every part of the city.

With her energy and spirits drooping by the hour, it was a great relief to Makilien when they returned to the palace for supper. Everyone was tired and quiet, and no one seemed to notice her despondency.

Drained and quite hopeless, Makilien went straight to her room after she was finished. Though it was still early in the evening, she dressed in her nightclothes and got into bed. For a long time, she tried to talk herself out of her gloomy mood, but sleep took her before she was successful.

:Chapter Nineteen:

A Strange Thing

Rolling onto her back, Makilien rubbed her forehead. She'd woken in the night with a terrible headache, and even after returning to sleep it lingered. She sat up, wincing at how sore her shoulders were after the work she'd done, and looked out the window. The sky was gray, making it difficult to tell what time it might be.

Makilien slid out of bed and dressed. She sighed, feeling reserved this morning and alone inside.

Downstairs, she stopped in the doorway of the throne room where the men were speaking. Darand and Darian had gathered with Nirgon and Meniah, and most of her friends. Several soldiers, captains by the look of their uniforms, also stood with them talking strategy. Not wanting to disturb them, Makilien turned away, deciding to look around the palace until breakfast was served.

Passing the dining room, she found the ballroom, a magnificent open space. The blue tinted marble floor was glossy smooth and gleamed from the light shining in through a wall of tall windows. It brought a smile to her face to imagine what a dance might look like. They occasionally had dances in the town square in Reylaun for weddings and such, but Makilien knew they would never compare to a dance here at the palace. But her smile soon faded. Would there ever be a chance for celebration to fill the room once Zirtan attacked?

From the ballroom, Makilien explored on, finding a couple of smaller sitting rooms and a study. Finally, she came to the library, bigger than what she'd seen in the dark at Lord Andron's palace. Too many books and scrolls to count filled the shelves. If only she could read them all and obtain their knowledge.

Quietly circling the room, she came to the large fireplace at the far end, and her eyes were drawn up to the artwork hanging above the mantle. It was a beautiful painting of a magnificent lion. On the lion's head sat a golden crown. Seven silver, eight-pointed stars formed a perfect arch above the lion. Dropping her eyes lower, Makilien noticed under the lion's two front paws was a staff—a shepherd's staff.

She gazed at the painting, mesmerized. Something was familiar about it. Then she realized it was the emblem on the uniforms of Eldor's soldiers and on their city's flags. But what was its meaning and importance to the country? That was what Makilien wished to know.

When she moved on, her thoughts lingered on the painting for a long time after. It struck her as something of great significance.

A short while later, Makilien's name sounded from down the hall. Turning, she spotted Vonawyn.

"Good morning," the Elf said brightly.

Makilien greeted her with an admittedly weak smile.

Vonawyn's expression turned to one of concern. "Are you all right?"

"Yes." Makilien shrugged. "I think I'm still tired from the journey and a little overwhelmed by what's been happening."

"I understand," Vonawyn comforted. Her smile returned. "I came to find you and let you know breakfast will soon be served."

The two of them walked together toward the dining room.

"Vonawyn," Makilien said along the way, "you told me you are almost seventy-two years old. Has anything like this happened before in your lifetime?"

Vonawyn nodded. "Eldor has been attacked once before since I was born, though not quite like this. Many have tried to conquer us, but never Zirtan himself."

That didn't give Makilien a lot of confidence in her weakened emotional state. Trying to take her mind off it, she said, "I was looking around the library this morning. I saw the painting there, the one of the lion, and realized it was the emblem on Eldor's flags and soldiers' uniforms . . ." She paused and Vonawyn nodded in affirmation. "I was wondering what it is . . . I mean, what is so important about the lion that it would be Eldor's emblem?"

"A lion is a symbol of Elohim," Vonawyn explained. "That is why the lion is wearing a crown. Elohim is the King of kings."

"What do the seven stars mean?"

"They represent the seven people who first came here. They journeyed to find a land where they could serve Elohim and not be persecuted for it."

All of it made sense to Makilien except for one thing. "What about the shepherd's staff?"

"Elohim is also seen as the shepherd of His people."

This turned Makilien's mind immediately to Meniah and the gentle way he cared for his flocks. Could it really be the same with Elohim and people?

Contemplating this, Makilien followed Vonawyn through the door of the dining room where they took seats among their friends.

Breakfast was nothing like the day before. Everyone was serious and subdued. Even Elandir and Elmorhirian were not their mischievous selves. No joking, no teasing Torick, and no laughing. Mostly the men spoke, still discussing the city's defenses.

After eating, Makilien and her friends left the palace once again. They still had much to do to get the outer city evacuated and supplies moved.

Makilien passed through the city gate, leaving behind the quiet, almost deserted streets. She was exhausted after many long hours of work and welcomed the cool evening breeze blowing across the plains. She needed a break away from the grim atmosphere of war preparations, so she'd left the city, upon Halandor's gentle urging, to visit Meniah.

Turning west, she soon came upon the meadow and found him. As she approached, he turned to face her, a small lamb in his arms. One of the lamb's front legs was streaked with blood.

"What happened?" Makilien asked.

"This little one cut herself on a rock," Meniah answered. "I was just about to bandage it. Would you like to help?"

Makilien nodded and came closer.

"You can hold her while I clean the wound." Meniah transferred the little creature into her arms. Makilien held her close, feeling the warmth and the steady rise and fall of the lamb's sides. Despite being wounded, the lamb was perfectly calm.

Meniah wet a cloth with his waterskin and cleaned the cut. As he wrapped a bandage around it, Makilien said, "She's so small compared to the other lambs. Do you think she'll make it?"

She remembered several occasions where some of the smallest lambs her family raised had died or been rejected by their mothers. It made her unusually sad to think of this little one meeting the same fate.

"She'll be all right," Meniah assured her. "With care and nurturing, she'll grow and become stronger. I won't overlook or discard her because she's smaller or weaker."

Makilien looked up, meeting his eyes. At that moment, those words didn't seem to be for the lamb, but spoken right into her heart.

"You won't?"

Meniah gave her a smile full of gentleness and love. "No."

His eyes switched back to the lamb, and he pet it gently on the head. Makilien set the lamb down, and they watched it scamper off. Suddenly, Makilien didn't feel quite so burdened by the cares of the day and the future.

"Would you like to help me count the sheep?" Meniah asked. "I count them every morning and every evening."

Makilien smiled at him. "I'd love to."

"Why don't you start on that side of the meadow," he told her, gesturing.

Thankful for this diversion, Makilien crossed the meadow and counted each sheep and lamb. She loved it out in this quiet and peaceful openness.

A short time later, she met up again with Meniah.

"How many did you count?" he asked.

"Seventy-three."

Meniah was pleased. "Good. Two-hundred thirty-four in total. That is all of them."

The two of them began walking toward one of the large boulders.

"What happens if one is missing?" Makilien asked. "Would you go look for it?"

"Always."

"Even for just one?"

Meniah nodded. "Even for just one."

At the boulder, they sat and Makilien looked off toward the city. She felt protected here, next to Meniah, as if surrounded by an invisible shield. She wanted to stay here, away from what was coming.

"Why does there have to be war?"

Meniah leaned forward a little, resting on his staff as he too looked at the city. "Everyone has it inside themselves to be selfish and greedy, to try to please themselves and want more than what Elohim has given them. Not all give in to that, but it is what fuels those who follow Zirtan. They are driven by a hunger for power and pleasure for themselves."

Makilien sighed and shook her head. "I still don't understand why Elohim would allow evil like that. Why can't He just make people good?"

"Because He has given people the freedom of choice—to either choose Him and what is right, or to choose to be against Him. If He controlled the way people believe and act and love Him, would that truly be love?"

Makilien thought this over for a long moment. "No, I guess it wouldn't be."

"And that is exactly why, Makilien. He wants true love from His people, not forced love."

Still thinking on this, Makilien realized it was growing dark. She should get back to the city, but she was reluctant. The empty streets would be eerie now in shadows, especially walking alone. She wished she would have thought to go sooner.

Beside her, Meniah rose. "It's getting late. Come, I'll take you back to the palace."

Makilien looked up at him in wonder. Could he know what she had just been thinking? But it didn't matter. She welcomed the invitation.

"Thank you."

Early the next morning, Indiya and Emaril returned. All hoped for good news from Lord Glorlad and Lord Andron as they met in the courtyard.

"How close are they?" Darand asked.

"They are about a day behind Zirtan's army," Emaril answered. "Lord Glorlad and Lord Andron said they would travel into the night to try to make up time. They may arrive here shortly after Zirtan, but not before."

Darand nodded slowly. "We will just have to hold out until then."

"How are preparations coming along?" Indiya asked. "It looks like you have the outer city evacuated."

"Yes, we finished last night, though some people may still be on their way from the villages. I sent Carmine and the griffons to warn those in Zirtan's path."

"If there is anything more we can do to help, my lord, we are willing," Emaril said.

"You and Indiya should get some rest. We will all need it," Darand replied grimly. "All we can do now is wait."

"They will arrive tomorrow."

Silence followed Carmine's report. It was just what they'd expected, yet the short time before the enemy would arrive was sobering.

However, Darand gave a strong nod. "We'll be ready for them."

"There is a strange thing, my lord," Carmine went on with a tone of uncertainty.

"What is that?"

"It seemed most of the army was pulling back, sending only a small force on toward the city."

"How small?"

"About a thousand goblins and Shaikes."

Darand lowered his brow in confusion. "With seventy-thousand on their side, why would they only send a thousand?"

"It is a mystery to me as well, my lord," Carmine said. "I could find no reason for it."

Turning to a nearby guard, Darand said, "Send for Meniah, Nirgon, and the captains."

The guard nodded and hurried off while Darand turned back to the dragon. "Now, Carmine, you should get some rest. Let Indiya and Emaril know I may call upon them later to check the progress of Zirtan's force."

"Yes, my lord."

Carmine flew off to the aviary and everyone went inside to the throne room. Curious to know what would be decided about the small force marching their way, Makilien and Vonawyn stood off to the side to listen. When everyone Darand had summoned arrived, he informed them of Carmine's report and asked for their thoughts.

"It is strange for them to send so few when they clearly have the advantage in numbers," Nirgon agreed. "Surely they know we are better prepared than to be defeated by so small a force."

"If not, then let's show them," one of the younger captains spoke up eagerly. "Six hundred riders could easily defeat them."

Nirgon dismissed him with a shake of his head. "We could just as easily defeat them from the safety of the city with less risk of casualties."

"But that would look weak and cowardly," the captain argued. "Let's ride out boldly and show Zirtan we are not going to just sit here and let him walk in."

"I don't advise it," Meniah said calmly. "Zirtan is a deceiver. He will use all form of trickery and deception to accomplish his purpose. This could easily be a trap."

"If I may speak freely," the captain said with an edge to his voice and an air of arrogance. "Are we all going to listen to a man with no military experience?"

"Rollan!" Nirgon snapped. "Your words are those of a fool."

Rollan hung his head embarrassed by the rebuke, but a bitter look smoldered on his face. Makilien glanced at Meniah. His expression had not changed, but the sorrowful look in his eyes concerned and disturbed her.

"We will not march out against this army," Nirgon declared firmly. "Whatever its intent, we will face it here."

Darand agreed. "Now, we must make sure the men are armed. That army could be here by tomorrow morning."

"My soldiers are ready," Nirgon informed him, "but the men we have recruited from the villages are not."

"Then we must prepare them. Take them to the armory and make sure they are properly equipped."

Nirgon nodded, and he and his captains turned to leave. As the group thinned, Makilien worked her way to Halandor's side.

"Halandor," she said, a little uncertain at first.

He turned to face her. "Yes?"

"I've been giving this much thought lately and . . . I want to help fight," she told him. "I know I don't have as much experience as any of you, but I've gone through so much since I left Reylaun, and I didn't come this far just to sit and wait to learn the outcome of this battle."

Halandor's eyes narrowed a little, in conflict and reluctance. "Are you sure?" Makilien knew he was afraid for her. "It will be unlike anything you can imagine." He warned her. "It will be terrible, and it will be very difficult to stay alive."

Makilien did hesitate, but then nodded firmly. "Yes, I'm sure."

"All right." Halandor called for Vonawyn to join them and said to her, "Makilien is going to fight. Will you help her prepare?"

Vonawyn nodded and motioned for Makilien to follow her. They walked over to Elandir and Elmorhirian.

"Will you two get the trunk I brought with me and bring it to Makilien's room?"

Upstairs, inside Makilien's bedroom, the two Elf brothers set a small trunk on the floor. Vonawyn opened the lid and reached in to lift something out.

"This was made for me, but I've never used it. I suspected you might want to fight so I brought it along because I knew you'd put it to good use."

Hanging from the Elf's hands was a shiny, silver chain-mail dress. Makilien marveled over the expert craftsmanship of the piece.

"It's amazing," she breathed. "Are you sure you want me to use it?"

Vonawyn smiled. "Of course. I want you to still be alive at the end of this battle."

Makilien smiled in return.

"You should try it on to make sure it fits properly," Vonawyn suggested.

Makilien took off her overdress and slipped her arms through the sleeves of the chain-mail. Vonawyn laced up the back with leather lacing. The chain-mail dress was much like her regular dress in its shape. It had a close fitting bodice and the skirt was split into four separate panels. The only real difference was the sleeves were only half-sleeves.

Moving her arms to get the feel of it, Makilien was surprised the dress was lighter than she was expecting.

"Does it fit well?" Vonawyn asked.

"Yes," Makilien answered. "It's not as heavy as I thought it would be."

"We Elves have a special way of constructing the rings that makes them lighter than normal chain-mail," Vonawyn explained.

Makilien took the chain-mail off again, and Vonawyn laid it on the bed. Reaching back into the trunk, she pulled out a pair of black leather vambraces. A beautiful Elven leaf design was tooled into them. Vonawyn also withdrew a pair of matching greaves to fit over Makilien's boots and protect her shins.

After each of these items were laid out in preparation, Vonawyn looked Makilien in the eyes, and her voice lowered solemnly. "These will all do well to protect you, but your best defense will be your sword."

:Chapter Twenty:

The Sacrifice

Darkness had fallen well over an hour ago. The palace was quiet and Makilien knew she should sleep, but she was wide awake. She looked absently through her sketchbook, nearly full now. Only a few more sketches would fit. She turned to the sketches at the beginning—sketches she'd drawn before she left Reylaun, of her family and Aedan. She smiled wistfully, missing them tonight especially. It pained her that she'd only been able to say goodbye to Aedan and Leiya.

Finally, Makilien closed the book and set it on the nightstand, but her restlessness did not diminish so she got up. Quietly, she left her room, careful not to disturb anyone who might have been able to find sleep. Wandering the quiet palace was better than sitting idly and alone in her room.

As she neared the stairs, Makilien noticed the door to one of the large second story balconies was open and someone stood at the rail. Stepping closer, she realized it was Meniah. She knew he was staying at the palace, but she had not expected to find him here. Before she could speak, he turned to her and smiled.

"Makilien."

"I'm sorry if I disturbed you," she apologized.

"No, not at all," Meniah assured her. "Please, come join me."

Eagerly, Makilien walked out. "I'm having trouble sleeping tonight," she admitted.

She looked out at the city. A couple lights twinkled nearby, but the city was mostly dark. Looking up at the sky, she saw no stars. The dampness of rain was thick in the air and sent a shiver across her arms and down her back. She sighed, thinking of one of the things, or maybe the one thing, that had kept her awake.

"I want to fight, but . . . I'm afraid, when the time comes, I won't have the courage to really do it."

"You are a brave young woman, Makilien," Meniah comforted. "It took courage to leave your home when you had no idea what you would find. You will find the courage to fight your battles."

Makilien hoped he was right. She looked up at him when he said, "Elohim has great plans for you, Makilien."

She blinked in surprise. "For me?"

Meniah nodded, but Makilien hung her head.

"I don't think I have the faith to believe in Elohim."

"But He always believes in you."

Makilien sighed. "Even if that is true, why would Elohim use me? I'm so small, and I don't even know if I can believe in Him. I'm not great like General Nirgon or any of my friends."

"Elohim often uses the smallest and weakest people to do His greatest works, to show with Him, you can do anything. Consider that."

"All right," Makilien said quietly.

For a long time they did not speak, but they didn't need to. Just being near Meniah seemed to relieve the fears and uncertainties that had kept Makilien up. She also had a lot to think about. She couldn't imagine Elohim wanting to use her in any way at all, let alone a great one. Makilien wanted to believe Meniah, but something held her back and would not let go.

She wondered about questioning Meniah more on this, but something about his mood kept her silent. Ever since Captain Rollan's outburst earlier, Makilien had sensed something was wrong. Something terrible and greatly disturbing, but she had no knowledge of what it could be and was too afraid to ask.

These thoughts were interrupted by a low rumbling of thunder. Heavy raindrops began splashing around them, and she and Meniah moved back into the palace. Inside, Meniah turned to her.

"You should get some rest. You will need it for the fight."

Makilien nodded. "Good night."

"Good night, Makilien," Meniah replied with a calming and reassuring smile.

Makilien returned to her bedroom and finally changed into her nightclothes. Although sleep did not come immediately, her mind was calmer.

At first, Makilien thought it was a dream, the faint sound of raised voices that drifted on the edge of her consciousness, but they grew clearer as sleep wore away. Realizing it was not a dream, she sat up straight and listened. Sure enough, she caught the sounds of voices and commotion. Her heart thumped hard in her chest. Had Zirtan's army arrived?

Makilien jumped out of bed and ran to her balcony window. It was gray and foggy outside, but she could see a large number of soldiers gathered in the courtyard below. Something was happening.

Makilien dressed as quickly as she could and didn't bother braiding her hair. Resisting the urge to run, she hurried downstairs and into the throne room. She was just in time to hear Nirgon tell Lord Darand, "They must have used the eastern gate otherwise the sentries would have seen them."

The sharp, angry tone of his voice told Makilien something dreadful had taken place while she slept. Looking around and seeing Vonawyn, Makilien hurried to her side.

"What happened?"

Vonawyn looked at her. No cheeriness lit her hazel eyes this morning. "Captain Rollan and five-hundred men rode out during the night to meet Zirtan's army."

Makilien's mouth dropped open. "Against General Nirgon's orders?"

Vonawyn nodded gravely.

"Do you know what's happened to them?"

"Not yet. The dragons flew out to find them only a short time ago. We won't know until they return."

Uneasiness churned in Makilien's stomach. If Meniah was right, and this was some trick of Zirtan, it would be devastating for Eldor to lose so many men before the battle had even begun.

Everyone was on edge as they waited, particularly Nirgon. Makilien couldn't imagine what Rollan had been thinking, going against his general's orders at such a critical time.

They had not been waiting for nearly as long as Makilien had expected before they received word the dragons had returned. Everyone raced outside, but as soon as Makilien saw the dragons, she knew they did not bear good news.

"Zirtan's force is camped about three leagues from here," Carmine announced. "It appears Captain Rollan and his men did engage them and lost about fifty men. The rest are being held captive."

Shoulders slumped at this horrible news.

"Has Zirtan's entire force re-gathered?" Darand asked.

"Yes. Those who fell back must have advanced during the night."

"So the thousand who went ahead were sent as bait to lure out our men?"

"It would seem so. My lord, we also spotted three riders on their way to the city. They may intend to negotiate for the soldiers. It would seem they'd have no other reason to have kept them alive."

"How soon will they arrive?"

"Soon, my lord. They were only a couple of miles from here."

Darand glanced at those gathered and ordered one of his men, "Saddle my horse. I will meet them at the gate."

Darand and the rest of the men walked toward the stable. Makilien turned to Vonawyn.

"Do you want to go? We can both ride Antiro."

Vonawyn nodded eagerly, and they hurried after the men. At the stable, Makilien bridled Antiro, but did not bother to saddle him. After she led him outside, she brought him to a bench where she and Vonawyn mounted.

In just a few minutes, everyone rode to the main city gate. When they arrived, one of the sentries called down, "My lord, three riders are approaching the city."

"Open the gate," Darand instructed.

Slowly, the massive iron gate creaked open, and they could see the riders coming. Their pure black clothing and armor matched their black horses. One of the men held a blood-red banner. Drawing closer, Makilien was able to make out the design in the middle of the banner—a black, arrow-headed snake entwined around a jagged-edged sword.

Before they could get too close, Darand, Darian, and Nirgon rode out to meet them. Makilien and Vonawyn slid down from Antiro and inched closer to the gate to hear better. The dark riders came to a halt fifteen feet away from Lord Darand. The rider in the middle was the most fearsome man Makilien had ever seen. His black hair and beard matched the rest of his attire as did his eyes, though the blackness there was not from color. They reflected the deep darkness of his heart.

"What business do you have here, servants of Zirtan," Darand asked coldly.

"I am Zendon," the leader spoke in a deep voice that was altogether evil, "general of His Majesty, Lord Zirtan."

He paused for a dramatic moment, and goose bumps rose on Makilien's arms.

"As I'm sure your lizards have informed you," Zendon continued viciously, "we have close to five-hundred of your men held captive. They are alive right now. I am willing to keep it that way and offer their lives in trade."

"We do not bargain with the forces of evil," Darand challenged.

Zendon shrugged unconcernedly. "Then your men will all die."

Darand's saddle creaked as he shifted. He had no choice. "What do you wish to trade them for?"

Zendon let another dramatic moment pass before making his request.

"Meniah."

Eyes widened and tension filled the air. Was he serious?

"I will give you your men, including their weapons and horses, if you give us Meniah," Zendon reiterated.

"But that's absurd!"

"Those are my terms. I need not remind you of what will happen if you do not accept them. You have only until noon to make your decision."

Before Darand could breathe another word, Zendon and his men spun their horses around and galloped off, but Makilien's eyes were glued to the king. Her heart filled with heavy dread. She tried to tell herself Darand would never agree to Zendon's terms—he couldn't—but when Makilien glanced at Meniah, his resigned expression gave her little hope.

The men outside turned their horses. Agony was written on their faces as they came through the gate. It was an impossible situation.

No one spoke until they had returned to the palace. Even then, they were at a loss.

"Is there anything we can do to get Rollan and the men released without giving in to Zendon's demands?" Darand asked Nirgon desperately.

"I don't . . . think there is," Nirgon responded, his voice halting and uncertain. "But without those soldiers . . ."

A long, dreadful silence overcame them. It ended when Meniah announced, "I will go." He shook his head before anyone could protest. "You must have those men to defeat him, and you can't sacrifice five-hundred men for one."

When no one immediately opposed the decision, Makilien spoke in desperation, "There has to be some other way we can rescue them."

Nirgon shook his head, completely extinguishing her failing hopes. "I'm afraid rescue is not an option. Zendon would kill the men before we could ever get close enough. The only way we could attempt it would be at night under the cover of darkness, but we do not have that long."

"We can't give in." Makilien's voice started out strong, but failed at the end as she began to tremble.

Meniah stepped over to her and laid his hands on her shoulders. "It's a sacrifice that has to be made, Makilien."

"But . . . they will kill you!" Tears overflowed Makilien's eyes and spilled down her cheeks. "You told Captain Rollan it could be a trap. He wouldn't listen to you, and he didn't respect you. He insulted you! The men who followed him must have felt the same way. Must you give your life for them?"

Calmly, Meniah answered, "Yes."

But Makilien could not accept that. "Isn't there anything else you can do?" she murmured, pleading.

"No, this must be done."

Overcome with grief, Makilien's tears came in torrents. She did not understand. "We need you," she cried. Tears choked her, and she could not speak further. *I need you.*

Makilien's grief was shared by all, and for hours they made a determined effort to find some other way, but it could not be done. Meniah was right. It was the only way. Finally, he brought an end to their efforts.

"It is getting close to noon. I must go."

"Do you think we can truly trust him to release our men?" Nirgon asked, sounding doubtful.

But Meniah was not concerned. "He is confident in his numbers. Releasing them will not concern him."

Solemnly, the whole group left the palace. Trying to be brave like her friends, Makilien forced back her tears, but she didn't know how long she could keep it up. Outside, Meniah's horse was saddled and brought to him.

No one knew what to say in the moments before his departure. Goodbye was too painful. Not knowing what else to do, Makilien stepped forward and hugged him tightly. Meniah wrapped his arms around her in a loving embrace. Makilien had never felt so deeply loved by anyone—not her family, not even Halandor—and the thought of losing Meniah right before the battle felt as if they'd already been defeated. Mournful tears leaked through Makilien's closed eyelids.

When they finally parted, Makilien looked up at Meniah through teary eyes wanting to plead with him not to go. Gently touching her shoulder, Meniah said, "Don't forget what I told you."

Makilien wanted to speak, to promise him she wouldn't forget, but she could only manage a weak nod as she bit her lip.

Tears glistened in the eyes of every person present as Meniah mounted his horse and rode in silence out of the courtyard. Once he was out of sight, Makilien's shoulders drooped at the immense sorrow filling her heart. How could they do this without him?

With blank stares and aimless pacing, they waited, still gathered in the courtyard. More than an hour had passed since Meniah left. Captain Rollan and the four-hundred fifty men Meniah had given himself up for had returned only a short time ago. In addressing them, Nirgon had been painfully clear in that if they had not been needed to fight, each one of them would have been discharged from Eldor's army and sent away from the city. To their credit, they appeared remorseful and utterly miserable. After Nirgon's intense lecture, he'd sent them to the barracks with orders to be prepared to fight at a moment's notice.

Now they waited only for the dragons to return and give them a report on the activity of Zirtan's men.

Makilien shivered from her place at the palace steps as a damp breeze blew across the back of her neck. She pulled her cloak up higher and glanced at the dark clouds roiling overhead. They blocked out so much sunlight it was as if dusk were upon them already. At midday, Makilien didn't know if she had ever seen clouds so dark and menacing, but she hoped they would pass over without dropping rain to add to their misery.

Suddenly, jagged fingers of lightening stabbed through the clouds, lighting everything for a moment with an eerie glow. It was followed by a shattering clap of thunder that vibrated in the stones Makilien was sitting on. Everyone retreated to the safety of the palace doorway and looked out at the fearful weather. As she watched, Makilien was overwhelmed by an intense feeling of loss and a hopelessness, which could not be explained. She swallowed hard against the lump in her throat and hugged her arms around herself.

What is happening?

In a few minutes, the darkest of the clouds, which had produced the lightning and thunder, passed over leaving only normal gray rain clouds. Cautiously, everyone walked back outside, wondering at the strange phenomenon.

Soon after, the rush of air caused by dragon wings sounded overhead. They gathered in the middle of the courtyard as the three dragons appeared over the wall. Landing amidst the group, the dragons' wings drooped low. With his deep, usually strong voice breaking, Carmine gave them the awful news.

"Meniah . . . is gone . . . they've killed him."

Makilien was overcome with such sorrow it nearly sent her to her knees. Burying her face in her hands, she sobbed uncontrollably. Everyone, including the dragons, shed tears. Indiya gave a low, mournful cry and Emaril nuzzled her cheek as their large teardrops splashed on the cobblestone.

The man they'd all trusted and looked to for guidance and reassurance was gone. Now, when they needed him most. But more than that, the peace and love Makilien had found in his presence was gone too, leaving her heart cold and empty as never before. Meniah had given her hope and courage, but now that hope had utterly deserted her, and fear was devouring every ounce of courage she possessed.

Carmine allowed them to grieve for only a few moments before he said, "My lord, Zirtan's troops were breaking camp and preparing to move. They could be here in as little as an hour."

Darand nodded. He and everyone else knew they must put aside their grief, but Makilien didn't know if she had the strength. She forced her tears to stop, but that was all she could manage. The sorrow only intensified.

"We must be ready to meet them," the king said, his voice determined, but rough. To Nirgon, he ordered, "Get the men into position."

The general gave him a nod. "Yes, my lord." He rushed away to the barracks.

Darand turned to those remaining—Makilien and her friends. "We must arm ourselves." Seeing the sorrow in the eyes of each one of them, he said, "Meniah died to give us a chance at victory. We will not waste it."

This energized everyone but Makilien. Her heart and mind were so distressed, she could hardly think straight. When everyone turned and entered the palace, she followed aimlessly with no clear thought as to what she should do to prepare. The men rushed off toward the palace armory, but Vonawyn made it her duty to aid Makilien.

"I will help you prepare," she said. Her face was drawn, yet resolved. Makilien longed for her strength.

:Chapter Twenty-one:

The War Begins

Makilien swallowed hard, her throat constricting in an attempt to hold back tears. The chain-mail, which had felt so light the last time she had tried it on, now felt like a hundred pound weight draped over her shoulders. Vonawyn tightened the laces of her vambraces, but she only stared straight ahead, still in shock over what had happened. When Vonawyn was finished, she led Makilien to a chair and told her to sit down. Makilien followed numbly.

"I will braid your hair so it won't get in your way," Vonawyn said, her voice sounding hollow and faraway.

The Elf expertly braided Makilien's long hair into a secure Elven braid and helped her up again. Pausing, she looked Makilien in the eyes and saw the turmoil raging. With tears in her own eyes, she asked, "Are you going to be all right?"

"I . . ." Makilien's voice broke, but she continued hoarsely, "Can I be alone for a few minutes?"

Vonawyn nodded. "Of course."

She left the room, quietly closing the door. She too would find a place to be alone. A place to pray, not only for the struggle they were about to face, but for the struggle she knew went on inside her friend.

A moment after Vonawyn left, Makilien stepped in front of the full length mirror. Would her family have recognized her? Her appearance was so different in full battle gear, her chain-mail glinting in the light of a nearby candle, and her sword resting on her hip.

Seeing herself this way made Makilien ask one question—was she crazy? The army marching toward them had just killed Meniah and fifty other men—soldiers. How could she, a weak farm girl who had fought only a handful of goblins, survive an all-out war?

Suddenly, the casualties they'd already suffered made it all seem real—too real. For weeks they had prepared, but now it was here and that terrified her. Overpowering fear gripped Makilien's heart like a pair of icy hands. Her legs started to shake, and she sank down at the foot of the bed, dissolving into tears.

"I can't do this," she sobbed.

The fear and panic that encased her was stifling. Visions of goblins, Shaikes, and the guards from Reylaun closing in around her overran her mind, and she was left to face them alone. Completely and utterly *alone*.

"I can't," she cried again, violent sobs racking her body.

She couldn't face them. She was too afraid. All she wanted was to hide somewhere until it was all over. The urge to run to Halandor and tell him she was wrong, that she couldn't do this, was overwhelming and with each passing moment it grew until it was almost unbearable. She *had* to give up.

But what good would it really do? They were all doomed, all of them. They couldn't face Zirtan. It was impossible. Foolish hope. They would all be killed or imprisoned. So why not fight? Maybe dying in battle would be best. But the thought of death brought a whole new level of intense fear. The darkness and loneliness that had plagued her for weeks descended on her heart with such force it was almost physically painful.

With a new wave of sobs, she wept, "I don't want to be alone!"

In her turmoil there came a gentle whisper, not a true sound, but a whispering in her heart.

You don't have to be alone.

"But how?" Makilien cried in agony. "Even surrounded by friends, I feel alone!"

Just one word came in answer to her question.

Truth.

Makilien clenched her fists and gritted her teeth. *What is the truth? I've searched and searched for it!* Her tears came hot and fast. *I don't know what it is! I don't know how to find it!* She remembered Torick's words in Reylaun.

"The truth is available to anyone willing to believe it."

"But how can I believe it if I don't even know what it is?" Makilien shouted. "I left my home, I left my family, and I have searched! Why can't I find it?"

She had no answer and the darkness, the loneliness, and the fear increased to the point Makilien felt like she was being crushed. It was almost as if the life was being drained from her body, and she had no energy to fight it. Maybe . . . maybe she should just give up and give in. What was the point in fighting it?

But a memory flashed in her mind, hazy at first, but gaining clarity. It was in the throne room the morning they had learned of Zirtan's smaller force. Meniah had spoken to Captain Rollan, but in that moment it had seemed to Makilien the words had been spoken to her.

"Zirtan is a deceiver. He will use all form of trickery and deception to accomplish his purpose . . ."

Trickery and deception . . . the words echoed in Makilien's mind. *Deception is the opposite of truth . . . Zirtan is a deceiver . . . Zirtan is deceit . . . if he is deceit, then truth is . . .*

Elohim.

Understanding dawned in Makilien and grew like a candle's light brightening to light up the corners of a dark room. All this time she had been searching for truth, she'd really been searching for Elohim, and yet at the same time, turning away from Him.

"But I don't have faith," Makilien cried weakly. "How can I believe if I can't see?"

But she realized she did see. Proof of Elohim was in her friends. In their strength, courage, and love for one another.

Yet, the more it became clear to her, the more a dark force poured fear and doubt into her heart. Trembling at the intensity of the struggle and afraid she was about to lose the fight, Makilien cried out, "Elohim, please help me! Give me faith!"

Makilien pushed herself to her knees, fighting against the weight pressing her down, trying to force her to give up.

"Elohim, I've been running from You." Makilien's voice shook and barely passed a whisper, but with each word, it grew stronger. "I do believe You are there, and I need You. Save me from this evil!"

Makilien gasped as the weight lifted. All the fear, doubt, and darkness fled her heart, yet instead of emptiness, it was filled with peace and love. No longer was she alone. Now she understood what Halandor had tried to explain when they'd camped on their way to Minarald. She no longer feared the possibility of imprisonment or even death. Her soul was free.

Weary, Makilien slumped back against the footboard of the bed. Quiet sobs shook her shoulders, and she covered her face with her hands. But this time the tears were not out of despair, but out of joy.

"Thank You, Elohim," she cried softly. "Thank You."

Breathing deeply, Makilien smiled, marveling over how freely Elohim had given her His love even after she had been so steadfast in resisting Him. She wiped her tears and rose to her feet. She was weary, but the growing strength in her heart spread through her body. She looked at her reflection in the mirror and wondered again if her family would recognize her, but this time it wasn't simply her war clothes that made her wonder. Her heart no longer held any uncertainties, and it showed in her eyes.

She was changed.

Makilien straightened and smoothed out her clothes. Taking a deep breath, she squared her shoulders, and a smile broke out again. She *could* do this. She no longer had to face the enemy alone. Elohim was at her side. She was ready.

Makilien blew out the candles, dimming the room, and walked to her door. She was so focused as she walked down the hall she almost didn't notice Vonawyn come from the same balcony where she had talked to Meniah. The memory made her sad, but her heart was comforted.

When Vonawyn reached Makilien, she stopped, deep concern in her eyes. "Are you all right? You look like you've already been through a battle."

Makilien half sighed, half laughed. "I have . . . but Elohim brought me through victoriously."

Tears filled Vonawyn's eyes, and she hugged her friend tightly. "Oh, Makilien, I'm so glad! I knew there was a struggle going on in you so I've been praying ever since I left your room."

Fresh tears came to Makilien's eyes. "Thank you, Vonawyn. I know your prayers helped."

"Come," Vonawyn said with a smile when they parted. "Let's get you downstairs so you can tell the others."

Everyone had gathered in the throne room. Their voices, more subdued than usual, mixed with the jingling chain-mail and clanking of plate-mail. When Makilien and Vonawyn walked in, the men all looked their way. Most eyes settled on Makilien. She walked ahead and met Halandor.

With deep concern for her, he put his hands on her shoulders. "Makilien, are you *sure* you want to do this?"

"I wasn't sure," Makilien confessed. "I was very afraid and wanted to give up, but . . ." she paused, a little smile growing on her face, "I finally found the truth."

Understanding lit Halandor's eyes and grew into a broad smile.

"I am ready to fight," Makilien said confidently. She added a little more quietly, "To fight to honor Meniah's memory."

"As are we all," replied Torick.

Emboldened, Makilien looked at each of her friends and said, "Meniah did not die only for Rollan and the men who followed him. He died for every one of us. If he had not sacrificed himself, we would have no hope of victory. He gave us hope . . . he gave us a way."

All around were nods of hearty agreement.

With Makilien now among their number, everyone prepared to leave the palace. Vonawyn said goodbye to her brothers as Lorelyn embraced her husband. Vonawyn then smiled bravely at her father as her mother touched the faces of each of her sons. It was a sobering moment, each praying they would only be temporary farewells.

After her farewell to her father and brothers, Vonawyn went to Makilien.

"You will do well," Vonawyn said with confidence. "I know you will. You are skilled, and Elohim will be with you every moment of the battle. You will also have my prayers."

"Thank you so much, Vonawyn." They hugged, lingering for a moment before parting.

On the way outside, Makilien glanced at her friends, noting how they had all prepared for battle. Halandor and Torick were equipped similar to Makilien in chain-mail hauberks and leather vambraces. Darand and Darian wore chain-mail underneath silver breastplates and pauldrons over their shoulders. Elnauhir and his sons were wearing Elven plate-mail, which was constructed in a way that would not encumber their swift reflexes. Sirion wore a combination of chain-mail and Elven-style leather armor, which reflected his mixed race.

Outside in the courtyard, the horses had already been gathered, including Antiro. His appearance was almost as different as his rider's. Silver armor, decorated with stars, protected his face, neck, chest, and hindquarters. Though it was still cloudy, each polished piece shined.

Makilien rubbed the soft part of Antiro's nose, right above his lip, the only part not covered by armor. "We've been through quite a lot of adventures together already, haven't we?"

Antiro blew his warm breath into her palm and dipped his head.

"This is going to be our most desperate struggle yet," Makilien went on. "I don't think either of us ever thought we'd end up in something like this. Are you ready to go into battle together?"

Antiro tossed his head and arched his neck proudly as he nickered.

Makilien smiled. "All right then."

She walked around to his left side and mounted.

From the palace, everyone rode together toward the main gate. Soldiers, Elves, and horses crowded the streets, all moving en masse. Their faces were grim, yet determined. It was easy to tell the difference between the various types of soldiers. The soldiers of Eldor's army wore chain and plate-mail with their familiar black embroidered jerkins over the top. The Elves matched Elnauhir and his sons in their armor, and the recruited soldiers from Eldor's villages were dressed in assorted pieces of armor, no one person matching another.

At the wall, the horses were left in an area blocked off near the gate while their riders filed up the various stairs of the wall. Now Makilien wished she'd paid more attention to their strategy.

Moving Antiro close to Halandor's horse, she asked, "What is the plan?"

"We'll defend from the wall for as long as we can. Our goal is to keep them out of the city because once inside, they will destroy as much as possible. We hope to hold out here until Lord Glorlad and Lord Andron arrive. Then we will ride out to join them. But, if the wall is overrun or they break through the gate, we will have to ride out and hold them back. Nirgon will give the signal when it's time."

Makilien nodded in silence, knowing she would have to stay alert.

After leaving their horses with the others, they walked to the base of the wall where Nirgon was overseeing and giving orders.

"I've placed the Elves along the wall above the gate," Nirgon informed Elnauhir. "They can take out the first onslaught of enemies at a distance, and then our archers will join in as soon as they draw closer. The dragons are out scouting. They will let us know when Zirtan's force is close."

Darand and Elnauhir nodded their approval and led the way to one of the stairs. Over sixty steps led up to the top of the wall. It was the first time Makilien had been at the top. The width of the wall was about twelve feet across. She stepped for a moment to the parapet, which reached just past her waist. Able to see far out across the plains, she saw nothing of Zirtan's troops, but it was only a matter of time before the plains were stained by their presence.

Waiting was difficult, not truly knowing what was coming. Makilien tried to visualize an army of seventy-thousand men, goblins, and Shaikes, but it was beyond her imagination. Everything was quiet during the wait as they watched the horizon intently for the first sign of the dragons and the enemy.

In their anxiousness, time seemed to slow down, but less than an hour passed before three shapes appeared in the sky. A few moments later, Indiya, Emaril, and Carmine flew overhead. Armor on their heads, necks, and bellies to protect from arrows flashed as they landed on the wall near Darand and Nirgon.

"They are only two miles away, my lord," Carmine announced. "They will be within sight very soon."

"Thank you," Darand told the dragons. "You can take your positions."

Carmine nodded and moved down the wall while Indiya and Emaril took to the air again.

Nirgon swept his gaze over the army and shouted, "Everyone to your positions. I want all available archers to the front."

The order was echoed by the captains. Makilien cast an uncertain glance up at Halandor. She had her bow, but did she qualify as an archer?

Halandor nodded, and Sirion touched her on the shoulder.

"Come with me."

She followed him a few yards down the wall where the Eldorian archers were lining up. The two of them took their places at the parapet. It gave Makilien a boost of confidence to have Sirion at her side. The feeling increased when a quick glance over her shoulder found Halandor and Torick right behind her in the line of swordsmen.

When she looked down the wall to her left where the main gate was situated, Lord Elnauhir's Elves, including Loron, stood directly over it, ready to send down a deadly hail of arrows. Carmine flanked them on one side while Indiya and Emaril were on the other. All three dragons stood with their front claws gripping the edge of the parapet, poised to launch themselves off the wall and meet the enemy.

Behind the wall, the rooftops of the highest buildings were scattered with griffons. Makilien counted at least two dozen ready, like the dragons, to fly down and attack. The sight of all their plans and preparation put in motion was a magnificent.

Once every soldier had found his place, silence settled over the army as they focused their eyes to the east. Only the sound of the breeze fluttering their flags and banners surrounded them. Occasionally, chain-mail would jingle or plate-mail and leather would creak, but hardly anyone moved. Makilien could just about hear the beat of her heart with each suspenseful second that passed.

Then a quiet murmur rose from the Elves down the wall. The men shifted uneasily.

"They're coming," Sirion murmured.

Makilien squinted, straining to see the approaching army, but it was still out of the range of the Human eye. However, only minutes passed before she did see something, a darkness bleeding into the horizon. Indistinguishable at first, it quickly grew into a solid black mass, oozing across the plains. As the army drew closer, details became clearer. Soon it appeared more like a thick swarm of bugs devouring everything in their path. Makilien was confused they didn't seem to be marching directly toward the city, but in a more northwesterly direction.

"Why aren't they marching toward us?" she asked finally.

"They will march north until the entire force is gathered and attack the city head-on," Halandor answered.

He was right. It took over a half an hour for Zirtan's army to amass in one solid group about a mile north of the city. Makilien drew in a deep breath as the steady, seemingly unending stream of Zirtan's troops surged the ranks of those already gathered in the distance. She had thought Eldor possessed a large force, but now seeing all seventy-thousand of Zirtan's troops at once made their army appear pathetic and small in comparison. It was a frightening sight, the true extent of this army, the most frightening of all she had witnessed since leaving home.

Once they had fully gathered, Makilien waited with bated breath for them to begin their march on the city. But they did not move. For long minutes, they waited with silent expectancy. When Zirtan's force still did not show any signs of movement, the men began murmuring to each other.

"What are they waiting for?" Makilien asked, the suspense churning in her stomach.

"Nightfall," Torick said with low confidence.

Makilien turned to face him and Halandor. "They won't attack until nightfall?"

"Probably not," Halandor answered. "Evil loves darkness so Zirtan's host prefers to fight under the cover of night."

Looking out again at the army, Makilien grimaced. To fight them in the dark when they were most comfortable would be difficult and *very* dangerous. Fear mounted within her and she quickly turned to prayer. *Elohim, I am afraid. Afraid of facing this enemy and being defeated . . . and I'm afraid of losing the friends I've made. I know now that You can protect us all. Please do. And please give me courage.*

Though fear still lingered, calmness seeped into Makilien's heart.

Farther down the wall, Carmine launched into the air and flew toward Zirtan's army. Nirgon must have sent him to spy on the enemy and bring back information. Flying high, far above the danger of enemy arrows, Carmine circled the evil force. His ruby red scales were a stark contrast to the gray sky. He was only gone for a few minutes before returning.

"They are resting," Carmine informed Nirgon. "They will likely not move for a couple of hours."

After this report, everyone was still on edge, but this gave them a chance to rest and prepare as well. Makilien looked up at the sky. With the clouds so thick, she could not see the sun and could not tell the exact time, but she guessed they had only three hours until nightfall. Only three hours until the city was attacked.

Though Zirtan's force wasn't expected to attack until darkness, everyone remained in their positions, watching warily as they murmured with their companions. As she watched, Makilien noticed an occasional dark mass moving through the enemy army. These masses appeared to be much larger than anything else around them.

"What are the tall things I keep seeing?" she asked finally.

"Trolls," Halandor answered.

Makilien swallowed nervously, hoping and praying she wouldn't meet any of them while fighting.

As time wore on, Makilien grew weary of standing. To preserve her energy, she sat down against the parapet. Resting her head back, she thought of all she'd been through leading up to this point. She found her thoughts focusing on her family. It was as if they were a world away. She missed them deeply, and felt she loved them more now than ever. She was very regretful for the way things had been when she'd left. Makilien knew she'd been right to seek the truth, but in doing so, she had not given her parents, especially her father, the respect they deserved. All they had wanted was to protect her, but she hadn't honored that.

Elohim, I want so badly to tell them I'm sorry and how much I love them. Please allow me a chance to do that, and to tell them of all I've learned here.

Makilien wondered what would happen to them if she died. Who would tell them the truth? This caused her to wonder what happened after death. She remembered Torick saying those who did not know the truth would be separated from it forever once they died. But what of those who did know?

From her position, Makilien looked up at Halandor. "What happens to us when we die?"

Halandor's eyes dropped to her. A solemn look came to his face at the mention of death, yet Makilien caught a glimmer of hope also. "The spirit and souls of those who have believed the truth will immediately join Elohim in His Kingdom, an eternal paradise where they will live forever."

The peace and comfort of that filled Makilien's heart. At least if she died tonight, she knew exactly where she'd go.

"And we'll all be there together someday?" she questioned.

A smile came to Halandor's face, his mind touching on his wife and daughter and the other loved ones he'd lost in his lifetime. "Yes."

Makilien too thought of her family again. She wanted more than anything for them to be with her in the Kingdom. But what if that didn't happen?

"What about those who don't believe?" Makilien was almost afraid to ask. It troubled her greatly to think of what might happen to her parents, Leiya, and Aedan.

A sobering expression erased all signs of Halandor's smile. "Eternal separation and suffering."

Makilien swallowed hard. She was desperate to keep that from happening to her family, but it was out of her hands. Looking down the line of soldiers, her heart suddenly filled with sorrow. How many here truly believed the truth and had faith in Elohim? How many tonight would die without it?

Inevitable darkness crept in as evening descended. A shout from Carmine broke the quiet waiting.

"They're coming!"

Makilien jumped up, looking out into the deepening gloom. The torches the enemy had lit raced closer. The sight of thousands upon thousands of torches moving in their direction was terrifying. Immediately, Nirgon shouted orders.

"Everyone back into position! Ready your weapons!"

Makilien took her place again at the front and readied her bow, watching the army's fast approach. Their marching sounded like thunder rolling in from the distance.

Makilien worked to control her heart rate and steady her breathing. Then Sirion said to her, "Once Nirgon gives the order, fire as quickly as you can."

Makilien gave a quick nod, her mouth dry.

Very soon, the army was less than half a mile from the city. An internal battle had already been fought for Makilien's soul. Now the physical battle for the life of every person present and those they fought for was about to be waged.

:Chapter Twenty-two:

The Battle is Waged

Makilien flexed her fingers around her bow. Any moment now, Nirgon would give the order to fire. Zirtan's force was only a few hundred yards away. Makilien could see now that goblins led the charge followed closely by Shaikes. The sharp shrieks of the goblins as they raced toward the wall were chilling.

"Prepare to fire!" Nirgon's order was barely heard over the shrieking.

Makilien drew back her bowstring and picked out one of the many thousands of goblins to aim at.

Next came Nirgon's order for the Elves to fire. All the goblins in the middle of the first line toppled over at once. A moment later, the general commanded, "Eldorians, fire!"

Makilien released her arrow with the rest of the army. Their hail of projectiles rained down on the opposing force. The shrieks and squeals of the dying goblins reached an even higher pitch than those of the living.

Following Sirion's advice, Makilien fired one arrow after another as fast as she could pull them from her quiver. A loud whoosh of air came after her fourth shot, and she glanced to her left. All three dragons flew off the wall. Carmine swooped down toward the enemy first. Passing directly over them, a cascade of molten liquid and white hot flames poured from his open mouth, coating more than a hundred goblins and Shaikes. The dragon's barrage of fire lasted for several seconds before it died away, and he angled high into the air.

Emaril came next to attack. By now, enemy archers had lined up near the front and fired at the dragon. Most bounced off the thick armor protecting his underside, but right at the end, two arrows punctured the membrane of Emaril's left wing. He growled in pain and lifted higher into the air. An enraged roar came from Indiya as she dove toward the archers, spraying them with scorching flames.

Dying screams and the smell of burnt cloth and flesh drifted up to the wall. Makilien wanted to hold her breath, but it would be only a temporary relief. She couldn't help gazing up at the three dragons circling above, wondering how long it would be until they could attack with fire again, but then she remembered she should be firing her bow and pulled out another arrow.

Now many goblins and Shaikes had reached the base of the wall. Makilien wondered how they meant to reach the top, but didn't have a chance to find an answer before the enemy archers released a volley of arrows. Dark streaks shot toward them, and everyone ducked. But some weren't fast enough. The arrows' barbed points punched through armor followed by the cries of the wounded. Other arrows ricocheted off the stones.

Suddenly, something much larger than an arrow flew over the wall, landing with a loud metallic clank a couple of feet away. It was a large, three pronged hook with a thick rope attached to the end. After a strong tug on the rope, the hook clawed up tight against the parapet. All at once, clanking sounded all around as over a hundred of the same hooks sailed up and over the wall.

"Cut the ropes!" The shout came from Nirgon.

Makilien jumped up from her crouched position. She dropped her bow and yanked out her sword. The line of archers now broken, Halandor and Torick rushed to the front and hacked at the rope of the nearest hook. But as many as were cut, more replaced them. In only a few moments, goblins swarmed over the parapet. They lunged for anyone nearby, using their jagged blades and even their teeth to inflict as much damage as possible.

As the wicked creatures surged onto the wall, Makilien gripped her sword with both hands to face them. The moment one was within reach, she swung hard and it dropped instantly. But those behind it were not as unprepared. Her next swing connected with a goblin's sword and she found herself facing three goblins all trained on her.

They lunged simultaneously, and Makilien had to move fast. She jumped to the side to avoid one and swung her sword widely to deter the others. With a downward slash, she severed an arm, leaving only two goblins able to fight. One was not nearly as quick as its companions and was easily defeated, and soon the last was also dead.

Makilien's eyes darted all around. She wasn't in immediate danger, but goblins filled the wall faster than Eldor's soldiers were able to cut the ropes of the grappling hooks. Spotting one hook unguarded in front of her, Makilien rushed to it and cut at the strands of rope.

She had barely managed to hack through half of it when the huge, snarling head of a Shaike popped up over the wall. Startled, Makilien jumped back, nearly tripping over a dead goblin. Lugging its bulky body over the parapet, the Shaike straightened to its full height, facing her. The menacing creature stood almost two feet taller than she did, silhouetted by the torchlight. She gripped her sword so fiercely her hands shook a little as she looked up into the creature's evil, glinting eyes.

"Please, Elohim, help me," Makilien pleaded breathlessly.

The Shaike growled deep in its throat and raised the massive four-foot-long blade of its sword. Makilien swung hers to meet it. Her hands went numb at the impact, and she wasn't sure if she still held her sword as the force of the blow sent it toward the ground. When a little sensation returned to her tingling fingers, she was relieved to find them still curled around the hilt.

Makilien stumbled back, trying to get away from the horrible monster, but it followed, raising its sword above its head. She had no choice but to block. Again, her strength was no match for the Shaike's. One hand slipped from the hilt, and the attack forced her sword off to the side, the Shaike's blade narrowly missing her arm.

Grasping her sword with two hands again, Makilien knew she must do something soon to stop the Shaike. She didn't have the strength or the energy to keep blocking its attacks. Then she remembered Torick saying Shaikes were not very intelligent creatures and stood still as the Shaike swung widely. At the last second, Makilien ducked and the blade cut through the air above her head. Before the creature could even complete its swing, Makilien swung her own sword toward its meaty legs. The Shaike roared in pain as Makilien's sword sliced through several inches of flesh and muscle just above its knee. As it doubled over, Makilien yanked out Aedan's dagger and thrust it up through a gap in the Shaike's armor. It toppled over at her feet, and she returned the dagger to the sheath.

The wall lit up, and Makilien spun around. Carmine skimmed the very edge of the wall, flaming the goblins and Shaikes climbing up their ropes. Makilien put her arm up as he passed to shield her face from the intense heat of his fire.

Distracted, Makilien didn't know at first what caused the horrible pain shooting through her left arm. She cried out at the intensity of it and looked down into the bulging eyes of a goblin. Its mouth was clamped down on her elbow, the only part exposed between her chain-mail and vambrace. Like thick needles, its teeth punctured her skin and scraped against bone.

Makilien slammed the pommel of her sword into the side of the goblin's head, but instead of letting go, it bit down harder. Makilien groaned and raised her sword to strike. Now the goblin did release her arm but lunged for a sword dropped by a fallen goblin. Before it could reach the weapon, a rush of air swept across Makilien's face. The goblin was lifted, shrieking into the night sky and flung over the parapet. Makilien looked up to see a griffon bank sharply to the right and fly farther down the wall. She wondered if it had been Arphen, but it had grown too dark to tell.

Makilien touched her arm gingerly. It ached with a deep, throbbing pain and little rivulets of blood oozed from the puncture wounds, yet she knew she couldn't let it distract her.

Carmine's attack on the ropes had not stopped the goblins and Shaikes for long. Many more swarmed up. Makilien barely had time to breathe before she was assailed by a new slew of goblins. Though the army tried to cut the ropes of the grappling hooks, the number of enemies that had reached the top made it difficult to stop fighting long enough to do so.

Without warning, a new grappling hook flew over the wall, almost hitting Makilien in the shoulder. She scooted sideways, but one of the prongs caught on the skirt of her dress and her chain-mail, pinning them against the wall. Makilien tried to pull away, but it held fast and the hook would not budge because of the goblins already on their way up the rope. She turned to cut it, but two goblins rushed to attack her. Makilien fought them off as best she could without being able to change positions. Realizing she was stuck, the goblins made every effort to keep her from cutting the rope.

Panic flared inside Makilien. The first of the climbing goblins would reach the top at any moment. If she did not get free before then, she'd have no chance. She pulled with all her might against her chain-mail, but her feet slipped on the blood-slicked stones.

"Help!" Makilien cried desperately, but she didn't think anyone would hear her over the din of battle.

Makilien swung hard at the goblins in front of her, but they jumped back jeering at her. They taunted her, jabbing their swords, waiting to finish her off as soon as the others reached the top of the wall. Makilien truly believed she was about to die when a blade slashed across the backs of the goblins, taking them both out at once. Behind them stood Sirion, and relief flooded Makilien.

In the same moment, a goblin reached the parapet and hissed down at her. Before she had a chance to react, Sirion knocked it back over the edge and severed the rope. Without the tension, the grappling hook tipped over, freeing Makilien's chain-mail.

"Thank you," Makilien gasped.

"Stay close," he told her. "I don't think we can hold them off here for much longer."

Makilien did stay close to him, fighting side by side and sometimes back to back. They made a good team, she realized, but Sirion was right. The wall was being overrun.

At last, a voice echoed overhead as Arphen flew over. "Everyone to your horses!"

Fighting all the way, Makilien and Sirion made it to the stairs and hurried down with the other soldiers. Below the wall, Makilien called for Antiro. A whinny sounded above the commotion and she spotted him trotting toward her.

"All right, boy, this is it," Makilien said and swung herself up into his saddle.

She looked around for Sirion. When she saw him mounting close by, she directed Antiro toward him. Glancing around again, she found Halandor and Loron, and Darand and Darian. It comforted and strengthened her to see the faces of friends. Makilien also spotted Nirgon at the gate, and everyone rallied around him, ready to follow him out.

As the gates began to open, Indiya flew along the wall, blasting any of the enemies still on top with fire. When the gate had opened enough, Makilien saw Carmine and Emaril were bombarding the nearby enemies, giving the soldiers an opening to ride.

Though Makilien could not hear him, Nirgon said something and a loud battle cry swept through their army, giving Makilien goose bumps. The order was given and everyone charged through the gate to meet Zirtan's force. Makilien clutched her sword tightly in one hand and Antiro's reins in the other. She didn't know what to expect so she just held on and waited.

Grass and bodies on fire from the dragon's attacks lit up the area in front of the wall, but smoke made it difficult to see anything clearly. Makilien's eyes stung and watered, and she coughed, gagging at the stench of blood and burning creatures.

A deafening crash resonated as the two armies met. Their charge slowed. Some horses went down, whinnying in pain and terror. Metal clashed all around. Enemies surged through the ranks. In seconds, goblins and Shaikes swarmed around Makilien. Raising her sword, she hewed at any within reach.

On and on, beast after beast. Sweat poured from her body, her muscles cramped and ached, and with every swing, her sword seemed to grow heavier. The hilt of it was slick with a mixture of sweat and blood making it difficult to wield. As the roar of battle drummed in her ears, the terrifying tumult all around left her feeling dazed. She was exhausted, yet she had to keep swinging. She must not quit.

She raised her head again to search for her friends, but she was unable to recognize anyone in the roiling mass of bodies and horses. And then, before she could see it coming, the blunt end of a long spear jabbed into Makilien's side, knocking her off of Antiro. She landed hard, her ribs aching and her breaths coming in short gasps. Despite the pain and exhaustion, she stumbled up, afraid of being trampled. She tried to get back to Antiro, but several goblins and Shaikes now separated them.

"Antiro!" Makilien screamed.

She hacked at the enemies, but more and more took their places. Antiro was driven farther away until Makilien completely lost sight of him. Her worst nightmare came to be. She was all alone in the midst of thousands of enemies. Panic took hold of her. She backed away from the battle, but tripping on something hidden in the darkness, she fell. Tears filled her eyes and fear gripped her heart. She didn't think she had the strength to rise and fight again. She tried once, but collapsed.

"I can't do this," she cried.

But then, someone took her arms and lifted her up.

"You are not alone, Makilien."

For a moment, the sound of battle faded away. That voice . . . it sounded like . . . Meniah!

Makilien spun around. But no one was there. She looked everywhere, but no one was near enough to have helped her up or spoken to her. Was she to imagining things?

Yet the determination and strength growing inside her were not imagined. She remembered what Vonawyn had told her right before battle. She was *not* alone. A new surge of energy coursed through her body. Raising her sword, she charged back into battle.

Fighting on the battlefield was much different than fighting from the wall. Now she encountered men as well as goblins and Shaikes. Battling and killing another Human being was not the same, but when she saw the evil and the hatred in their eyes, she knew she must fight them the same or she would never survive.

The longer the battle wore on, the less the dragons were able to attack with fire for fear of killing Eldor's soldiers now mixed with the enemy. But their dark forms flew overhead with the griffons, attacking with their claws and teeth from above. Everywhere was darkness except right near the wall where fires still burned, casting an eerie orange glow on the silvery stones.

Right in the midst of the battle, a tremor vibrated the ground. A moment later, Makilien felt it again. It continued until everyone to her right scattered. Her eyes lifted. Looming up in the darkness was a yet darker silhouette of a giant figure. Fifteen feet tall, it lumbered toward her, vibrating the ground with each step.

A troll!

Makilien dove out of the way as a giant foot stomped down exactly where she had been standing. It was more rounded than oblong and had five stubby toes, more like rocks than appendages. The rest of the creature was cloaked in darkness, but Makilien had no time to study it further. Several more trolls were on their way coming straight for her. Dashing behind the first troll, she moved out of their path.

In no time, their long strides brought them near the wall, and Makilien was able to observe them in the firelight. Their legs were thick and rough like old, gnarled trees, and their skin was the same dark gray as tree bark. With hunched backs, their long muscular arms reached to their knees. Situated on short necks between bulging shoulders, their heads were small compared to the rest of their body. Tangled, stringy hair fell down around long faces sporting square jaws, long crooked noses, and brows jutting out over small, dull eyes. In their long fingered fists, each one carried a club, which Makilien realized were small trees ripped out by the roots.

Five of these club-wielding trolls stopped at the city gate and smashed any of Eldor's soldiers who were unfortunate enough to be within their reach. Once they had cleared the area, four more trolls made their way to the gate. Between them they carried a huge tree trunk with a metal cap on the end, which they used as a battering ram on the gate. The reverberating sound of the metal cap smashing against the iron gates made Makilien's ears ring.

Above the ringing and the commotion, someone shouted, "Stop the trolls!"

Archers, mostly Elves, gathered in a wide semi-circle around the giant creatures and fired, but goblins and Shaikes rushed to attack the archers from behind. Coming to their aid, riders and foot soldiers attempted to create a protective barrier.

Hoping to help, Makilien ran to the group. The first of the enemies she had to face was a Shaike. She groaned. She'd killed a couple of Shaikes since the one she'd fought on the wall, but they had been distracted and easy to kill in the midst of the commotion. This one, however, was focused solely on her.

Makilien raised her sword to block as the Shaike swung its blade down with astounding force. The impact of it tingled all the way up her arms and into her back. Makilien tried to swing at the Shaike's waist, but it easily batted her sword away and swung down hard again. This time, the force of it knocked Makilien to the ground. Thinking fast, she watched the creature put its sword high above its head to deliver a final deadly blow. Right as it brought it down, she rolled away. The blade cut deep into the ground barely an inch from her arm. She rolled back toward the Shaike and onto its sword, her chain-mail protecting her arm from its sharp blade. This sudden move surprised the Shaike, and his sword slipped from his hand.

Makilien jumped up and lunged toward the Shaike, her body weight plunging her sword through the creature's leather armor. The collision sent them both to the ground. Makilien stumbled up and pulled her sword free of the Shaike's body.

A sound like the rushing of a river came from behind, and the back of Makilien's neck heated. She turned to see the dragons attacking the trolls with flames from above. The trolls bellowed, sounding like enraged cows. Three of the trolls lit up, stumbling blindly before collapsing in flaming heaps. Their fire now spent, the dragons attacked with their teeth and claws, but the thick-hided trolls were not easy to wound. Numerous arrows already protruded from their bodies. It was as if they'd been attacked by giant porcupines.

At last, the trolls showed agitation to the arrows, and one at the battering ram dropped its end. Flailing its arms around its head, the troll charged toward the archers in a rage. With the ram unbalanced, the remaining trolls dropped their sections and followed the other. Everyone scattered. The four trolls were so enraged even Zirtan's men were in danger of being crushed. Makilien watched from a safe distance as two of the trolls smashed several Shaikes beneath their feet.

The four battering ram trolls soon disappeared into the midst of the fight, but two more remained at the gate using their clubs to hammer away. Weakened, the gate shuttered and the hinges creaked. If the trolls continued, they would make it through, but Indiya, Emaril, and Carmine wouldn't let that happen. They took turns each swooping down and once their internal fires had rebuilt, they flamed the trolls.

With the gate safe for now, Makilien turned back to the thick of battle. After fighting for so long, her hands were raw. Despite all the practicing she'd done, new blisters had formed on her palms, which had now broken open and stung terribly. But she was learning that blocking out pain was necessary in order to survive.

Makilien had no idea how long they had been fighting when a startling crack like thunder rose above the sound of battle, followed by the roaring crumble of rock. Her eyes rose to the top of the wall to see a huge chunk was missing. Spinning around, she searched through the commotion for what had caused such damage.

A catapult loomed large in the center of a mass of Shaikes carrying torches.

Knowing a catapult could do worse damage than a troll, Makilien hurried toward it. She wasn't sure what she would do when she reached it, but she could try to do something. The catapult was heavily guarded by Shaikes, but Makilien wasn't the only one with thoughts to destroy the war machine.

During the confusion of the fight, Makilien ducked down and snuck past several Shaikes unnoticed. It brought her right up next to the catapult where she found the rope used to crank the arm down. It was nearly as thick as a man's arm. Hoping it would render the machine useless, Makilien raised her sword and hacked at the rope. It took four tries, but finally all the strands severed with a loud snap.

Makilien's victory was short-lived. Before she could get away, the strong grip of a Shaike latched onto her dress and dragged into their midst. She struggled furiously to get away, but the beast would not relinquish its hold. Because she did not have the room to swing her sword with enough force to be effective, Makilien realized this might be the end of her.

A rough hand clamped around her throat, cutting off her air. She clawed desperately at the Shaike's wrist with one hand and thrust her sword blindly with the other, into the dark mass of bodies crowding in. Her head pounded as she gasped for breath.

Suddenly, the Shaike's hand opened, air rushed back into her lungs, and she fell to the ground. As she struggled to get up, a hand—a Human hand—took her by the arm and pulled her out of the fray. Once she'd regained her strength and balance, she looked up into the face of Halandor. The joy of seeing him alive was beyond words, and she would have hugged him if they had not immediately had to turn their attention back to the surrounding enemy.

Desperately, they fought on. Makilien did everything she could to stay near Halandor. Sometimes enemies separated them, but Makilien fought hard to keep him in sight.

Fighting through the midst of the battlefield, Makilien noticed they'd come to the edge opposite the wall. The battle was not quite so fierce here, and she was thankful for a little less pressure.

Above the din, a horn sounded. Though distant, its long, clear note rang out from the west. Makilien turned to look, seeing nothing at first, but then, silhouetted against the slate-colored sky, riders appeared. Thousands of riders. Lord Glorlad and Lord Andron had arrived! Tears of relief rushed into Makilien's eyes. *Thank You, Elohim!* This was just the hope she and their desperate army needed to fight on.

:Chapter Twenty-three:

Aftermath

With a rallying cry, Althilion and Beldon's soldiers joined their allies in battle, felling all enemies in their path. Their arrival energized Eldor's despairing troops, but it also infuriated and emboldened Zirtan's evil horde. The bloodthirsty goblins and Shaikes charged with new viciousness, hacking and biting their way through the ranks as the ferocity of the battle reached its height.

As the light of early morning came at last, Makilien gazed out over the battlefield from a small rise, but was not comforted by the sight. Even with two additional armies, the black-clothed warriors of Zirtan greatly outnumbered their force. *How can there still be so many?* Doom settled cold inside Makilien. Would it really end in defeat after how hard and long they had fought? *Please, Elohim, You must have a plan to give us victory.*

Althilion and Beldon's forces dwindled. Sensing defeat, Makilien fought relentlessly. If she was going to die, she would die fighting, right to the end.

Cutting through a group of goblins, Makilien came upon one of Zirtan's men. Something about his tall and dark form was familiar. She took a closer look and gasped, her eyes widening. *Zendon!* Standing a mere couple of yards away was the man Zirtan had placed over his entire army . . . the man responsible for Meniah's death. The pain of loss stabbed through Makilien's heart.

The evil man stood sideways to her. He raised a longbow and drew it back. She followed his line of sight. Her heart hit her ribs hard when she found his target.

"Halandor!" The words left her lips in a desperate whisper.

Embroiled in a battle with a Shaike, he had no idea of the danger he was in.

Desperation pulsed through Makilien. Zendon had already taken Meniah's life. Would she just stand by and watch him take Halandor's?

"No!" she cried and sprinted forward, raising her sword high.

The moment she was close enough, she swung down hard, connecting with Zendon's arm. His arrow shot harmlessly into the ground as he released the bow. Roaring in pain, he clutched his arm near the elbow. He spun around, and his dark eyes locked on Makilien. His intense, icy stare froze her blood.

Makilien swallowed hard and backed away, but wasn't fast enough. Zendon raised his good arm. Like an iron mace, his studded metal gauntlet slammed into the side of her face. Bright flashes of light exploded in Makilien's head and somewhere in the midst of intense pain, she hit the ground. Her head pounded and her left cheekbone burned as if a fiery knife had cut into it. For a couple of seconds the battle roared in her ears, but then it began to fade away, becoming hazy and far off. Her eyes fluttered open for the briefest moment, but everything blurred into darkness. *Am I dying?* It was her last thought before her mind numbed.

All perception of time disappeared as she floated on the very edge of consciousness. Occasional sounds drifted in—a yell, a clang of metal—but they sounded miles away. Only darkness swirled in Makilien's mind. She tried to move but couldn't feel anything, sinking into darkness . . .

Makilien!

Once again, throbbing pain flooded her senses. She groaned and tried to push herself up, but her arms shook.

"Makilien!" the voice was clearer and close now. A pair of hands took her by the shoulders and eased her into a sitting position.

"Makilien," the voice said quietly this time.

She blinked in confusion, squinting at the light. Finally, a face came into focus. Even covered with blood and dirt, she recognized him immediately.

"Sirion," she breathed.

A smile flashed across his face, but concern in his brown eyes replaced it.

"You're hurt," he murmured. He reached up, his fingers brushing softly against her cheek. Makilien winced even at his slight touch, and when he pulled his fingertips away they were wet with her blood.

"I'm all right . . ."

Her voice died away as she rested back against his arm, becoming aware once again of her surroundings and the battle they had waged through the night. But her expression changed as she listened, though it wasn't a sound that grabbed her attention, it was . . . silence! Her eyes swept the battlefield. Bodies littered the ground, but fighting had ceased. She turned back to Sirion.

"What happened?"

Sirion smiled again, his white teeth a bright contrast to his stained face. "It's over. We've won."

Tears welled up in Makilien's eyes, and her mouth opened a little in astonishment. They'd won? Even vastly outnumbered by unimaginable evil, they'd been victorious.

Makilien threw her arms around Sirion. Smiling, he returned the embrace and helped her to stand.

"Look," he said, pointing east.

Makilien's eyes followed his hand. A black mass of warriors fled across the plains. Riders pursued them on the ground, and the three dragons and a couple of griffons followed from the air.

While they watched, the whole area brightened with dazzling light. Makilien looked up as the sun broke through a bank of clouds. Rays of sunlight bathed the battlefield, and she closed her eyes for a moment, lifting her face to the warmth of it. She truly had not believed she would see the sun again.

Once Makilien opened her eyes, they settled on the battlefield. The city walls were scorched black and scarred deeply from catapult attacks. No grass remained around the perimeter, only charred stalks and blackened heaps of bodies. Almost no green grass showed throughout the battlefield. Thousands of bodies and blood stained a massive, area of land in front of the city. Riderless horses stumbled around with no direction or stood scared and wounded. Hundreds of foot soldiers wandered throughout the battle zone. So much blood stained their clothing it was hard to tell who was wounded and who was not. They shared a sense of joy in their victory, but also solemnness at the display of death all around them.

Makilien looked uncertainly up into Sirion's face. "What of the others? Do you know who . . . who survived?"

Sirion shook his head. "I'm not sure. I saw Lord Darand, but I don't know about anyone else."

Makilien's stomach twisted. She couldn't bear the thought of having won the battle yet losing even one of the people she had come to love.

"Come, we'll search for them," Sirion said.

Before she followed, Makilien searched around her feet for her sword. She found it laying a couple of feet away, but when she picked up the hilt, she found the blade had broken off halfway down. It saddened her in a way, but she smiled thinking of the day Laena had given it to her and how much it had seen her through. Hoping it could be fixed, she brushed off the pieces and returned them to their scabbard.

They had to move slowly to keep from stepping on bodies. Makilien tried not to look, but she couldn't help seeing the dead and the terrible wounds that had slain them. Some of the soldiers were still alive and lay moaning. She wished she could do something for them, but nothing could be done until the people in the city brought stretchers out. She was sure someone had already gone to them, spreading the news of victory and sending them out to help.

The coppery scent of blood filled the air and made Makilien's stomach churn. She rested her hand over it, trying to ignore the nausea and prevent herself from being sick. Finally, when Makilien looked up again, two familiar faces brought a wide smile to her face. Halandor and Torick. They were bloodied and exhausted, but alive. Makilien hurried ahead of Sirion and immediately embraced Halandor. She was so thankful he was alive after nearly seeing him killed.

Makilien turned next to Torick but stopped short of hugging him. The side of his face was caked with blood from a wound somewhere on his head, and he pressed a hand to his right side where his jerkin was torn and stained with fresh blood.

"Are you all right?"

Torick smiled wearily. "I'm fine. Nothing more than a scratch and a cracked rib or two."

Makilien guessed it was more serious than that, but she was relieved it was not fatal.

"Have you seen anyone else?" Sirion asked.

Halandor nodded. "Loron and Lord Elnauhir are near the gate, and I saw Prince Darian there as well."

Makilien sighed with relief. Most of her friends were accounted for.

"What about my uncle?" Sirion wished to know.

"I have not seen him, but he may be with the riders trailing what's left of Zirtan's army."

Makilien looked to the east. By now, Zirtan's army and their pursuers were nowhere in sight. She looked around the battlefield again.

"I have to find Antiro. I got separated from him early on."

"I'll help you," Sirion offered. "I have to find Falene too."

They turned to search the field for their horses, calling out their names as they went, hoping for a whinny in answer. A short time into the search, they came upon Elandir and Elmorhirian. Neither appeared seriously injured though Elmorhirian had a broken arrow shaft protruding from a bloodied hole in his pant leg. His arm was around Elandir's shoulders for support as he walked. Even so, both grinned when they saw Makilien and Sirion coming toward them and greeted them with much enthusiasm.

"Sirion, I must say I am extremely pleased to see you survived without our assistance," Elmorhirian teased.

Sirion smiled wryly. "Yes, I think I did rather well considering you are the one with an arrow in your leg."

"Ah." Elmorhirian shrugged. "It's nothing."

Elandir smirked and said, "Say that when it comes time for Vonawyn to remove it. She ought to love that."

Giving him a hard look, Elmorhirian punched him in the side.

"Ouch! Hey, watch the ribs! They already suffered an unfortunate meeting with a troll's club. Or do you want me to leave you laying here to wait for someone to come along with a stretcher while your wound starts getting infected?"

Elmorhirian did not look very contrite but said nothing. Makilien just smiled at their antics, too weary to laugh.

"Well, we'll see you later," Elandir said. "I'm going to get him to the palace and then come back here to lend a hand."

As the two Elves made their way to the gate, Makilien and Sirion continued searching for their horses. In a few minutes they found Falene. Makilien smiled as she watched the reunion between Sirion and his beautiful mare. It made her ever more anxious to find Antiro. She worried when their search lengthened, but finally one of her calls was met with a nicker. Turning, she spotted Antiro carefully stepping his way to her. She rushed over to him.

"Antiro!" she cried.

Makilien looked him over. His legs were full of scratches and oozing cuts, but that seemed to be the extent of his injuries. A jagged dent in the armor over his hindquarters told her it had saved him from a serious, perhaps life-threatening, wound.

"Oh, Antiro," Makilien murmured, overwhelmingly relieved. "Let's get you to the stable."

Makilien and Sirion led their horses into the city, meeting many people along the way. Men who had not had the skill to fight hurried to the gate with stretchers. Some soldiers helped their wounded comrades along on foot to save the stretchers for the more seriously injured.

At the stable, a couple of the stablemen had already come in from the battlefield. Though still in their battle gear, they worked quickly to take care of the horses. Makilien and Sirion helped remove the armor and tack from Antiro and Falene and left them in the stablemen's capable hands.

Outside, Makilien glanced toward the palace. She was exhausted and her wounds throbbed. All she wanted was to get out of her armor, clean up, and then sleep.

"Go on," Sirion encouraged her. "Get some rest."

But Makilien looked up at him and shook her head.

"Everyone is tired and in need of rest. I'm not sure what I can do, but I won't rest until they do."

Sirion smiled, a look of respect in his eyes that gave Makilien satisfaction.

The two of them returned to the battlefield, navigating streets crowded with men coming and going with stretchers from the empty warehouses, which were converted into makeshift hospitals. At the gate they paused, and Makilien looked around her. She didn't think she was strong enough to help lift the wounded soldiers or carry the stretchers. *What else can I do?* Then she remembered all the horses wandering around. They needed to be looked after too.

"I can take the horses into the city," she said out loud.

Sirion nodded and pointed off to the right.

"Nirgon is over there. You can ask him where they should be taken. We'll find you when we're all ready to return to the palace."

They parted, and Makilien walked over to Nirgon who directed the men.

"General."

He turned and smiled gladly. "Makilien, it gives me great joy to see you alive and well. What can I do for you?"

"I would like to help out, but am not strong enough to help with the wounded. I noticed, though, there are many riderless horses on the battlefield, and if it would be helpful, I could bring them into the city."

Nirgon nodded. "That would indeed be helpful. We all hate to see them wandering around without direction, especially if they are wounded."

"Where should I take them?" Makilien asked.

"Take them to the barracks stables. There should be men there now who can take care of them."

With a determined nod, Makilien turned to the battlefield. Loose horses roamed everywhere. She walked up to the nearest one and took its reins. After going back and forth between the battlefield and the stable a couple of times, she learned she could manage up to four horses at a time if they were calm and uninjured. The wounded and skittish, however, could only be taken one at a time.

At first, Makilien kept count of how many she brought to the stable, but after she passed one-hundred, she gave up. She was sure at least another hundred still needed to be caught. It took hours to gather so many and was very taxing to her already drained body. Pain stabbed through the muscles in her arms and legs, and her wounds stung.

But mental exhaustion overtook physical exhaustion. Makilien could block out the pain, but not the images of the battle and of the destruction everywhere she looked. It was difficult to believe she had lived through it.

Sometime after midday, Makilien felt a little like the lost and skittish horses she tended to. At one end of the battlefield, she stumbled and could not regain her balance. When her arm hit the ground, her wound shot pain down into her fingertips and up through her shoulder. She bit her lip and sat up, holding her arm close to her body. Tears rushed to her eyes and leaked out through her eyelids when she squeezed them shut. But it took too much effort not to cry. She rested her head on her knees and let the tears fall freely.

It felt good to cry. Some tears were in pain, some were joyful over their victory, some were in sadness over the loss of life, and some were out of great thankfulness that Elohim had protected her and her friends during the dark hours of the night.

With each tear drained the last of Makilien's energy. She didn't know if she would be able to get back up, let alone continue to gather horses. After weeping for a time, she felt the welcome comfort of someone gently rub her back. Even through her chain-mail, it soothed her. Slowly, she looked up and met Halandor's compassionate gaze. He understood the reason and the need for her tears. Without a word, he picked her up.

Cradled in his arms, Makilien let go of her attempt to be strong and block out the pain and weariness. Giving in to her exhaustion, she rested her head on his shoulder. Catching a glimpse of Sirion and Loron comforted her, but everything after passed in a blur. When they reached the palace, Halandor took her up to her room and sat her down on the bed.

Gently, he asked, "Are you all right?"

Makilien nodded and gave a weak smile, but then grimaced at the pain it caused her wounded face.

"Sirion has gone to find Vonawyn and let her know you are here," Halandor said.

While they waited, Halandor helped Makilien take off her vambraces. He carefully rolled up her sleeve to inspect her wounds.

"You are bitten."

Makilien nodded again. "By a goblin while we were still on the wall."

When the door opened and Vonawyn rushed in, she was immensely thankful to see Makilien. Halandor left them, closing the door quietly, and Vonawyn helped Makilien out of her battle gear. Being rid of the chain-mail was a great relief.

A tub was brought up to Makilien's room, and while they waited for it to be filled, Vonawyn cleaned the wound to Makilien's face.

"This cut is deep," Vonawyn said, "but I think it will be all right without stitches."

When the tub was almost full, Makilien got in. It was a little cool because it had been filled in haste; nonetheless, it was wonderful to wash away all the grime of battle. Vonawyn remained with her and they talked a little of the fight, but Makilien was too weary to relay much of it. She did not linger in the bath. All she wanted was to get into bed and sleep.

Vonawyn helped her into her nightclothes and applied an ointment to her wounds. Afterward, she bandaged Makilien's arm and her raw and blistered hands.

"Would you like something to eat?" Vonawyn asked.

Makilien shook her head, her stomach still unsettled.

Understanding, Vonawyn guided her over to the bed and pulled back the covers. Makilien crawled in, sinking into the soft mattress.

"Rest well," Vonawyn whispered.

:Chapter Twenty-four:

Unlikely Hero

The gentlest of breezes brushed the side of Makilien's face. It was cool and refreshing, but carried with it a hint of smoke. She rolled onto her back and opened her eyes. Sunshine lit up the opposite wall—morning sunlight. She wondered how long she'd been asleep but was in no hurry to rise.

Makilien let her eyes slide closed again and breathed deeply. A bird chirped from the balcony railing and then flew away leaving the room quiet again. No threats, no urgency existed any longer to mar the days. She sighed contentedly. Ever since leaving home, war had loomed in the future, but now it had passed.

After a few more quiet minutes, she sat up. Every muscle in her body ached, but it was a good ache. An ache that proved she'd fought hard, giving more than she thought she ever possessed, and won. But she knew it was not her own strength that had kept her alive against such a brutal force.

Makilien got out of bed and walked to the balcony's open doorway where she was bathed in sunlight. The warmth of it was almost like a gentle embrace. She closed her eyes, her heart lifted in joy. *Thank You, Elohim, for protecting me from the horrors I saw in battle. You gave me faith, courage, and strength even though I resisted You for so long.* She let out a deep sigh. *Thank You for loving me.*

Makilien opened her eyes and gazed out toward the wall. She had a clear view of the battlefield from here. Men were busy at work. Much would have to be done to clear the battlefield of bodies and repair the wall and gate.

Looking from the battlefield to the streets, she saw they too were busy. Many people were returning to their homes in the outer city.

Makilien turned from the balcony and went to the wardrobe, finding a few new dresses. She picked out a sky-blue one with short sleeves. Summer was now well upon them, and the days were warm. After she was dressed, she walked over to the mirror and fixed her hair. She leaned a little closer to inspect the wound on her face. A four inch cut scarred her cheekbone, and the left side of her face was bruised. Glancing down at the white linen bandages around her elbow and both her hands made her thankful not to have suffered worse.

Her stomach growled fiercely and felt like it was squeezing in on itself, protesting her decision not to eat before sleeping. She left her room and walked downstairs.

The palace was quiet—a relaxing, restful kind of quiet—but voices came from the large sitting room. Stepping inside, she found the men sitting in the various couches and stuffed chairs, and Elmorhirian stood at a long table laid out with a banquet of food. Makilien's mouth watered.

"There she is," Torick announced. "Our brave young warrior."

Makilien looked at him and smiled widely at his compliment even though it made her cut sting. "Now who's a flatterer?"

"Yeah, Torick," Elmorhirian chimed in, sending Makilien a grin as he limped over to an empty chair with a full plate of food.

Torick chuckled, holding his side a little as he did so.

Makilien walked farther into the room and traded smiles with each of her friends.

"Help yourself, Makilien." Elandir motioned to the table. "Lord Darand had breakfast served here since everyone is coming and going."

Makilien went straight to the table. She filled a plate and took the empty seat beside Halandor.

"How do you feel, Makilien?" Torick asked.

"Very well, considering," she answered. "How long was I asleep?"

"Since yesterday afternoon," Halandor told her.

While she ate, Makilien listened to her friends recount their harrowing tales of the battle. Elandir and Elmorhirian were especially entertaining to listen to. Elandir had been among the archers firing at the trolls at the gate. When the creatures had gone on their rampage, Elandir hadn't been able to get out of the way in time. He had been hit in the side by the end of one of the trolls' clubs, but amazingly, he escaped without a single broken rib.

Elmorhirian had been shot by a "pesky little goblin," as he referred to it, which had been hiding behind the body of a dead horse. Torick's side wound had come as a result of a Shaike as Makilien suspected. He had been fighting one of Zirtan's men when the force of a Shaike's blade cut right through his chain-mail. Hearing of all the close calls increased Makilien's thankfulness that all her friends were alive.

Others came and went as they talked. Makilien smiled when Eredan and Bornil joined them. Gilhir arrived a short time later. It was good to see they had survived the battle. With each person came more stories.

Just as Makilien finished eating as much as her stomach would hold, all the lords walked in, followed by Darian and Nirgon. The six of them served themselves breakfast and sat with the others.

"We found Zendon's body this morning," Nirgon announced.

"So he was killed then," Torick said.

Nirgon nodded.

"How?" Elmorhirian asked curiously.

"It appears he bled to death, but from only a small wound to his right arm."

"I wonder who did it," Darand pondered.

"I don't know," Nirgon replied, "but whoever it was saved us all. I'm convinced Zendon's death is the only reason they retreated. Had he survived, he would never have allowed it. He would have forced them to fight to the death, and we all would have been killed. They had the numbers at the end of the battle, but no firm leadership."

Makilien's heart pounded in disbelief as she listened to the discussion. Had Zendon's fatal wound been the one she dealt him when she'd attacked to save Halandor? It must have been. Nirgon's remark replayed in her mind, *Whoever it was saved us all.* In an instant Makilien remembered what Meniah had told her about Elohim's plans. Had He planned all along to use her to bring victory? She did not doubt His power, but felt she was the most unlikely person to accomplish such a thing. She looked at her lap, overwhelmed.

Everyone agreed with Nirgon's statement. Makilien bit her lip in uncertainty. She didn't feel she had done anything incredible so was tempted not to mention her part, but keeping the truth from her friends didn't feel right either.

Finally, Makilien admitted quietly, "I think I may have done it."

Everyone's eyes immediately fixed on her, and she went on, "I think I am the one who wounded Zendon."

Their eyes widened.

"How?" Nirgon stammered. "When?"

"Just before dawn yesterday. I came upon him suddenly on the battlefield and saw he was about to shoot someone. He'd drawn his bow on Halandor." Makilien paused to look at him. "I had no time to think. I just reacted, hitting his arm with my sword to keep him from firing. After that, he hit me and knocked me unconscious." She touched her cut lightly with her fingertips. "Then Sirion found me."

For a moment, everyone was speechless. Finally, Lord Darand exclaimed, "Makilien, your actions saved everyone. They saved Dolennar!"

"But I didn't mean to kill him. I only acted to save Halandor."

"Regardless of whether or not it was your intention to kill him, you acted heroically to save Halandor's life, and in doing so brought our victory. You are a hero."

Makilien shook her head. "Everyone who fought, everyone who died, they are all heroes. Elohim brought the victory through me by His power. Not mine."

Before her friends could say anything, she went on, "I would like to keep this between us. The victory belongs to everyone."

Darand nodded understandingly. "All right, we will respect that decision. It is a noble one."

All agreed.

"Not only is it a noble choice, but I believe a wise one," Halandor added. "Though defeated, Zirtan still has men roaming Dolennar. If they were to find out who defeated their commander, they may seek revenge."

"You are right," Darand said. "We will certainly keep this information to ourselves, for your safety, Makilien."

Immense joy and relief surrounded the city, but a solemn mood tainted the celebration as many mourned the loss of loved ones. Adequate time was needed to grieve before their victory could be fully celebrated.

Many long hours men toiled on the battlefield, carrying away the dead and piling the slain enemy into two large heaps. Four days after the battle, the process was finally finished and the ugly black mounds of enemy bodies were lit on fire. Though the thick, dark smoke that rose from them was blown to the east, fumes still drifted into the city. Most people stayed inside with their doors and windows closed tight. The stench wasn't so bad at the palace, but even so, Makilien chose to take a walk outside the city, well away from where the fires burned.

Leaving the palace, she came to the main gate and turned west. Just a short way from the city, she stopped on a rise and looked back. From here she could look out over the whole battlefield. Giant plumes of dark smoke rose high into the sky and hid the horizon. Though all the bodies and weapons had been removed, the battlefield was still dark—all the grass trampled and the ground stained. It would take rain and time to fully erase the signs of battle.

Makilien continued on her way. She left the rise and walked down into the lush green meadow at the foot of the Irrin Mountains. It was the same meadow where she'd first been introduced to Meniah. The meadow seemed sad and lonely now. Summer flowers swayed back and forth, but there was no sound. Not even the bleating of sheep, which were still gathered inside the city.

For a long time, she sat in silence, reflecting on the battle and the days she'd spent away from home. Curiously, before she rose to leave, warmth, like strong rays of sunshine, soothed her whole body. As she savored the feeling, there came a sudden flash. Makilien jumped up and spun around, putting her arms up to shield her eyes from the dazzling brilliance of the light. When it faded a little, she slowly lowered her arms and gasped.

Standing in the midst of the light was Meniah, dressed no longer as a shepherd, but in pure white. Makilien's heart hammered, and she was overcome by the same awe and fear she had felt at their first meeting, but much stronger this time. Heart racing, she dropped to her knees.

The light intensified, surrounding her.

"Don't be afraid, Makilien." The sound of Meniah's voice was just as Makilien remembered—gentle and full of love and kindness. Peace filled Makilien and all fear faded. She looked up into Meniah's shining face, and the feeling of joy at his presence was so intense, tears trickled from her eyes.

"I thought . . . you died," she stammered.

"I did die. But death has no power over me."

Makilien hardly dared to breathe. "Are you . . . Elohim?"

Meniah smiled. "I am His son."

Makilien trembled a little, overcome.

"Rise, Makilien," Meniah told her.

But Makilien hesitated. Her tears now came out of shame. "I rejected Elohim for so long. I'm not worthy to stand in your presence. I don't deserve your love."

"Makilien," Meniah said gently. "A parent does not easily reject a child when they stray. Elohim's love is far greater than any parent's. You believed the truth. Elohim has taken your heart and made it new. You need not feel guilt any longer. Stand up."

Makilien's shame melted away, and she got to her feet.

"So you *were* there during the battle," she realized. "I did not just imagine it."

Meniah shook his head. "No, you didn't. I was with you from the moment you believed and will always be with you wherever you go."

Makilien felt incredible comfort in knowing that. Remembering the conversation they'd shared the night before Meniah had been killed, she asked, "Was it always Elohim's plan to use me in battle even though I was so resistant to believing?"

"Yes, it was. And there is much more for you to do, Makilien. The people of Reylaun have never heard the truth."

Makilien nodded firmly, filled with determination. "I will tell them."

"In doing this, you will face rejection and hardship, but don't ever forget you will never be alone. Take courage in that always."

"I will."

Sensing Meniah would soon go, Makilien ached to hug him, but she hesitated. However, with a knowing smile, Meniah opened his arms to her. Makilien stepped into his loving embrace. After a moment, she stepped back. Meniah reached up and gently touched her healing cheek. The light surrounding him brightened, and Makilien had to close her eyes. When she opened them again, he was gone, but she knew he truly was still there with her.

She reached up and touched her cheek. The wound was gone. Grinning, she remembered the meaning of her name. Touched by God.

Filled with joy, Makilien ran back to the palace where she shared with her friends all that had just happened. Some were more surprised than others, but everyone shared her joy. The least surprised of everyone seemed to be Halandor. When they were alone, Makilien asked, "You knew it all along, didn't you?"

Halandor nodded, smiling. "Yes."

"How?"

"In my heart, I just knew it."

"Why didn't you tell me?" Makilien questioned.

"Would you have believed me?"

Makilien paused. She wanted to say yes, but realized she could not. "I probably would not have."

"You had to find faith to believe without seeing on your own," Halandor said.

Makilien nodded.

When she and Halandor parted, Makilien went up to her room and walked to the mirror. Turning her head a little, she looked at her once wounded cheek. The wound was indeed gone, but in place of it was a thin scar across her cheekbone.

She touched it lightly with her fingertips and smiled. She was glad it remained. It would be a reminder forever of what she'd been through, and most importantly, what she'd learned.

:Chapter Twenty-five:

Celebration

At the gentle tap on the door, Makilien sat up in bed. "Come in."

The door opened just a little at first, and Vonawyn smiled in at her. "I hope I did not wake you."

Makilien shook her head, and Vonawyn came fully into the room carrying a bundle of clothing. Makilien eyed the clothes and gave Vonawyn a questioning look.

"What are those for?"

"We have a surprise for you," Vonawyn said mysteriously, still smiling, "but you must put these on first."

Filling with curiosity, Makilien crawled out of bed. "What kind of surprise?"

"You'll see," Vonawyn said with a slightly mischievous grin, which reminded Makilien of the Elf's brothers.

Vonawyn handed Makilien a royal blue dress that matched the color of the shirts Eldor's soldiers wore. Over it went a femininely-shaped jerkin and a four-paneled skirt. Both were sewn of soft black suede. Stars were embroidered in silver thread around the collar and bottom hem of the jerkin, and silver clasps adorned the front.

After she was fully dressed in the new garments and wearing a pair of black pants, Vonawyn gave her another item she had brought with the clothing. A black leather belt fitted with a brand new black scabbard. Stars were tooled into the belt, and its tip along with the tip and throat of the scabbard were plated in sliver.

Makilien was puzzled but said nothing as she buckled the belt around her waist. When she was finished, Vonawyn fixed her hair, pulling back a little from each side of her head and securing it with a clip.

"There," the Elf said, pleased with the outcome. "Follow me."

Makilien trailed Vonawyn out of the bedroom and down the stairs. Along the way, Vonawyn peered down the halls as if making sure they were not seen. Finally, they came to the closed door of the throne room. Vonawyn looked around once more before opening the door and ushering Makilien inside. All of Makilien's friends were gathered near Darand's throne. They smiled at Makilien as she and Vonawyn walked the length of the room. They all seemed, like her, to be dressed for a special occasion.

"What is going on?" she asked as she joined them.

"Makilien," Darand said. She turned to face him as Vonawyn backed away. "You have faced many dangers since leaving your home. You came into the midst of a war you were not required to become involved in, yet never once did you choose to remain in safety here or in Elimar. You bravely offered your services many times. In doing so, you helped save both my life and my son's, you saved Sirion, you saved Halandor . . ." Makilien glanced at each one in turn and they smiled warmly. ". . . and you saved Dolennar from the rule of evil. You came to Elohim, acting faithfully, and He used you to accomplish much. We all want to show you our gratitude for your actions, which have saved our countries. Take a knee, Makilien."

With tears in her eyes, Makilien dropped down to one knee in front of the king. Darand pulled out his royal sword and continued speaking.

"By the power granted to me by Elohim, I dub thee Lady Makilien, Swordmaiden of Eldor and valiant warrior of Elohim."

Lord Darand touched both of Makilien's shoulders with his sword. Everyone broke into applause, and Makilien stood, speechless. But Darand was not quite finished.

"As a sign of the service you have shown our country, I give you this." In the king's hand lay a ring. The thick silver band gleamed and in the center was embedded a polished royal blue stone. Makilien gasped. She'd only seen three other rings like it on the hands of Halandor, Torick, and Nirgon. Rings gifted only to those who had done the greatest service for Eldor.

"I am honored, my lord," Makilien murmured as Lord Darand placed the ring on her finger.

Just when Makilien thought she'd received all she could possibly imagine, Lord Darand turned to his son who handed him a sword. The king turned back to Makilien and offered her the sword's hilt.

"And as a token of our gratitude for your service, we give you this sword. May it serve you well should you ever again find yourself in need."

Makilien took the sword, her eyes running over it in admiration. It weighed about the same as her old sword but was much more beautiful. Smooth leather, dyed a dark blue, was wrapped around the grip. The silver cross guard was slightly curved with a star plated in the middle. On top of the rounded pommel there also was inlaid a royal blue stone. Her eyes traveling up, Makilien saw her name was engraved into the fuller of the blade near the cross guard.

"I don't know what to say," Makilien told them, an emotional tremor in her voice. "I don't feel like I deserve any of this. Thank you all so much. I am proud to have fought for Eldor."

She smoothly slid the new sword into the empty scabbard at her side and embraced each of her friends who had become so dear to her.

"Today is a day of celebration for the victory Elohim has given us and to celebrate, between us, what He has done through you," Darand said. "Tonight we will have a feast of celebration and of thanksgiving."

Though much was yet to be done to repair the damage left behind by the battle, the whole city took the day to celebrate victory over their enemies. Soldiers spent the day in the company of their families and friends. Those without family and those from Elimar, Althilion, and Beldon gathered together at the barracks and palace.

Just before everyone gathered for the feast that evening, Vonawyn brought Makilien back upstairs to her bedroom. Spread out on the bed was an array of dresses. Gesturing to them, Vonawyn said, "You may choose one to wear for the celebration tonight."

Makilien's eyes widened. "Any one?"

Vonawyn grinned. "Any one."

Slowly, Makilien walked around the bed, eyeing each of the dresses, each more beautiful than the last, but she could not make up her mind.

"I don't know which one to pick," she said. "They are all so beautiful."

"May I make a suggestion?" Vonawyn asked.

"Please do."

Vonawyn walked around to the end of the bed and picked up a dress made of light blue satin, the color of a pale summer sky with white beaded trim. It was short sleeved with open drapes from the elbows down. The front of the skirt was open with a contrasting white skirt underneath. The sleeve drapes too were lined with the white fabric. Makilien's breath caught a little at the sight of it, and her wide grin told Vonawyn she had made up her mind.

Makilien changed into the dress and looked in the mirror. "I love it."

"You look beautiful in it," Vonawyn told her.

"*Yothaun*," Makilien replied, practicing a bit of the Elvish she was beginning to pick up.

Next was Vonawyn's turn, and she chose a pale pink gown accented with beaded pearls and brocaded elbow-length sleeves. Makilien thought she looked stunning.

Finally, Vonawyn had Makilien sit down in a chair where she worked on her hair. She gave her a beautiful, Elven hairstyle that left Makilien's hair long with a little pulled back and a few decorative braids woven into it.

"There," Vonawyn said in satisfaction. "You're ready."

Makilien stood and stepped in front of the mirror. Her appearance was almost as different as when she'd dressed for battle. She turned to her friend.

"Thank you so much, Vonawyn."

The Elf maiden smiled. "It is my pleasure."

Now that both were ready, they hurried downstairs. The sound of mingling voices drew them to the dining room. Many people had gathered, nearly filling the room. Makilien had never before seen such a beautiful array of colors as she did now seeing the gowns worn by the women and girls present. For a few moments she just stood and stared until Vonawyn gained her attention.

"We have places at Lord Darand's table," she said. "Come, the meal will soon be served."

Makilien followed Vonawyn as she navigated her way through the crowd and in and around a great many long tables set with hundreds of pieces of fine tableware and beautiful white tablecloths. At the head of the room stood one table perpendicular to the others. Here Makilien found most of her friends gathered. They all smiled as she approached.

"Makilien, you look lovely," Torick complimented when she joined them.

Makilien blushed a little when the others chimed in to agree. "Thank you," she murmured with a shy smile.

Halandor then guided her to one of the chairs at the table as everyone took their seats. He sat next to her on one side and Torick on the other.

Shortly, Darand and the rest of the kings and lords joined them, and the cooks came from the kitchen bearing tray after tray of food. More food than Makilien could have imagined. Just before the meal was about to begin, Darand rose and a hush fell over the room.

"Citizens and friends of Eldor. Today we have celebrated our great victory."

A round of applause and cheers filled the room before the king continued.

"If not for the grace of Elohim and the courage of those of this great country and her loyal friends, we would not be here to celebrate. I want to thank everyone from Elimar, Althilion, and Beldon, everyone who left their homes and joined us in our fight. We could not have stood alone."

Darand raised his cup. "To the brave men, and women," he nodded to Makilien, "who have risked and given their lives to defend our countries from evil. And to Elohim, without whom we would not exist nor have countries to defend and would not have achieved victory apart from His will."

A deafening cheer followed. Everyone raised their glasses and drank with the king. *To Elohim*, Makilien repeated in her heart as she sipped the sweet jent wine.

Everyone sat again, and the feasting began amidst much joyful talk and laughter. Tales of the battle and heroics were traded throughout the meal. Makilien enjoyed every minute of it, constantly reminded of how thankful she was for their victory and to be here.

As soon as the feast concluded, and everyone was filled and content, the dining room emptied and the guests gathered in the ballroom. To see it filled and lit with many sparkling chandeliers delighted Makilien.

From one end of the room drifted the sweet sound of music as a group of Elves played a variety of stringed instruments and flutes. Couples paired up and the room soon came alive with dancing. Makilien watched, captivated by the sight—the lovely way the couples glided across the floor, perfectly in sync with each other.

Quite content to just watch for whatever hours remained of the evening, Makilien didn't notice anyone approach until Elandir and Elmorhirian appeared in front of her. She smiled at them, but before she could say anything, Elmorhirian said, "You look very beautiful tonight, Makilien."

Makilien shrugged, blushing again.

"It's true," Elandir quickly added.

"I owe it to your sister," Makilien told them. "I wouldn't even know how to prepare for an evening like this."

An awkward silence fell between them. Makilien waited for the two Elves to say something, but when they only glanced at each other, she grew suspicious. They were definitely up to something.

Then, in the same moment, they asked, "Would you like to dance?"

Frowning, they looked at each other irritably.

Makilien raised an eyebrow. "So that's what this is all about."

"Is that a yes?" Elmorhirian asked, grinning impishly.

"Whoever said you got to go first?" Elandir demanded.

"I asked first," Elmorhirian claimed, which his brother and Makilien both knew was absurd.

Elandir scoffed and crossed his arms. "You did nothing of the sort, and I'm the eldest. I should be first."

"I know how to solve this," Elmorhirian said. "Makilien should decide."

Both Elves turned to her expectantly. Makilien shook her head and raised her hands. "Oh, no you don't. You're not making me choose. You will have to sort this out for yourselves."

And with that, the brothers were arguing again, neither one making much sense. Makilien watched them in amusement but wondered if she would be caught in the middle of their argument for the rest of the night. She knew them too well to believe either one would give in.

Wondering what to do, Makilien felt a tap on her shoulder. She turned, meeting Sirion's smile. Tipping his head, he motioned for her to follow. Stifling a giggle, Makilien quietly walked after him, leaving the Elf brothers oblivious to her departure.

When they stopped some distance away, Makilien grinned at Sirion.

"Thank you," she said. "I have a feeling I would have been caught in that argument for quite some time."

Sirion chuckled. "I'm sure. Now, as long as those two are occupied, would you like to join me in a dance?"

Makilien hesitated. "Well, I didn't have a chance to tell Elandir and Elmorhirian, but I've never really danced before. Not like this . . ."

But Sirion gave her a reassuring smile. "Just follow me."

Makilien smiled in return. "All right."

He took her hand and led her to the edge of the dance floor. Just before they began to dance, Elandir and Elmorhirian's voices echoed from across the room.

"Sirion!"

Makilien and Sirion both broke into laughter but ignored the Elf brothers.

At first, Makilien felt awkward trying to figure out the dance, however, enjoyment soon overcame her apprehension, and she was able to laugh at her mistakes all the while learning how the dance was performed. She found she loved gliding across the polished marble floor, her gown swishing around her feet. It was like living a little girl's dream.

"Are you enjoying the celebration?" Sirion asked her.

"Very much," Makilien answered. "I never could have imagined anything like this. I am very thankful to be here."

"So am I. This is the largest celebration I have ever witnessed. It has been generations since so many from Eldor, Althilion, and Beldon have all come together like this."

"Then I feel even more blessed."

When their dance ended, Makilien and Sirion walked off the dance floor. Stopping at the edge, Sirion turned to Makilien and gave her a little bow.

"Thank you, my lady, for the pleasure of this dance."

Makilien grinned. "And thank you, sir, for putting up with my dreadful lack of skill."

Sirion chuckled. "You are not lacking in skill. You are a quick learner."

"You are a good teacher." Makilien smiled fondly. "And a good friend."

A smile grew on Sirion's face and a look of gratitude softened his eyes, letting Makilien know her words had touched him deeply. "Thank you. I value your friendship." He paused for a moment as the two moved toward the refreshment table. "I don't find I make new friends easily."

Makilien found this strange. She could hardly imagine him having trouble befriending people. "Why is that?"

"I'm afraid of losing them," Sirion said quietly, with an emotion that spoke of deep pain.

It saddened Makilien to hear him speak this way, but she could not bring herself to question him. She longed to give him comfort, but without knowing what had caused such distress she didn't know what to say. However, after a moment, Sirion went on to tell her.

"When I was a young boy, I lost my family. They were murdered by Shaikes." He paused again, and Makilien's heart ached for him. "Gilhir had taken me out hunting that day else I too would have been killed. Ever since then, I've struggled with the fear of losing those close to me. At times I have allowed it to keep me from making the friendships I might have had." Finally, a smile returned to Sirion's face. "I'm thankful I did not this time."

Makilien smiled too. "So am I."

With the spirit of celebration having returned between them, they enjoyed a refreshing cup of tart fruit punch. Afterward, seeing no sign of Elandir or Elmorhirian, they happily returned to the dance floor.

It was a night unlike any other. Makilien wished it could go on forever. She took countless turns around the dance floor with many of her friends. Eventually she did dance with both Elf brothers, but only after Elmorhirian somehow snuck away from his brother and reached Makilien first. The festivities did not end until well after midnight. When it came time for everyone to retire to their rooms, Makilien was weary and a little footsore, but her heart was overflowing with joy and thankfulness. Always this night would be one of her fondest memories to cherish no matter what the rest of her future may hold.

:Chapter Twenty-six:

Farewell

One week after the celebration found Makilien saying goodbye to many of her new friends. The time had come for Lord Glorlad and Lord Andron to journey back to their home countries, and for Lord Elnauhir to return to Elimar. Halandor, Torick, and Loron were joining him so Makilien would too. She was delighted when Sirion decided to come along, but she would have to say farewell to the rest.

Early on the morning of their departure, everyone gathered in the dining room for breakfast once more. Near the end, Darand stood and everyone's attention turned to him.

"Before we leave this room, I want to say how blessed I am to have each of you here at my table. You have all played important roles in the struggle we have faced in the last months, and I am so thankful you are here now at the end of it. As you begin your journeys home, back to your families and your friends, I ask Elohim to grant you safe and easy passage."

Those around the table nodded in agreement, and a comfortable sense of wellbeing settled on all. Makilien looked at each person, noting the diversity she had come to know. What would the people of Reylaun think if they could see?

When the meal had finished, Makilien went upstairs to her bedroom to retrieve her things. She had two bags now—

her old pack containing everything she'd had since the start of her journey, and another, larger pack holding the dresses Lord Darand had given her.

After making sure she had left nothing behind, Makilien walked to the door and turned to take one last look at the room. Would she ever return to it, or even just to the palace? But that was something she chose not to think on right now. Backing out, she closed the door.

The palace was quieter than normal as most everyone gathered outside, but voices still came from the throne room. Makilien entered and found Darand and Darian and a couple of her closest friends. A kind smile from Darand brought Makilien into the group.

"You will be greatly missed here, Makilien," the king said.

"I will miss being here, my lord. Even though I was born in Reylaun, I now look on Eldor as my home. This is where I found truth and, in a sense, was reborn into a new life."

Darand smiled again. "Will you be returning to Reylaun?"

"Yes. I promised Aedan I'd return with the truth. He needs to hear it, and so does my family and everyone in Reylaun. That is what Elohim wants of me, and I am anxious to serve Him."

Knowing the danger Makilien would face returning and spreading the truth in Reylaun, therefore defying Zirtan, Darand said, "You have been blessed with great strength and courage. I admire your faith in Elohim. I know you will serve Him well."

Makilien was touched by his words considering what little faith she'd possessed just days ago. "Thank you, my lord."

"And thank you, Makilien, for what you've done. We are very grateful for the part you played in our lives and our victory."

"I am also very thankful to have been a part of all we've been through."

"You will be welcome here at all times," Darand assured her. "Your family as well."

"Thank you. I hope someday I can bring them here. It is beyond anything they have seen or could imagine."

Realizing time was short, Darand said in farewell, "Goodbye, Makilien. I will pray for your safety and success in Reylaun as well as your return here."

"Goodbye, my lord. I am grateful for your prayers."

Before Makilien moved to say goodbye to Darian, Lord Darand drew her into a hug. Makilien smiled into the king's kind face and turned to his son. Their goodbye was brief, but no less sincere. Makilien would miss them both deeply.

Finally, Makilien and her friends left the palace. A great number of people and horses had gathered in the courtyard, waiting to leave. Makilien was glad she had thought to say goodbye to the dragons and Arphen earlier. It was going to take her long enough just to say goodbye to the rest of her friends, and she didn't want to hold anyone up.

Working her way through the crowd, Makilien found Glorlad and Gilhir first. She had enjoyed their company in the last days, and was sad they were not coming to Elimar. Eredan and Bornil, who she had become good friends with, were next, then Lord Andron, and finally General Nirgon.

At last they had all said their goodbyes and mounted up. After a final call of farewell to Lord Darand, Darian, and Nirgon who stood on the palace steps, the various groups moved out and rode through the city. Outside the city gate, Elimar, Althilion, and Beldon's soldiers had gathered and awaited their lords to begin the march home. Lord Elnauhir and Lord

Glorlad rode to the head of their Elven armies and Lord Andron took the lead in front of his men, and everyone moved out.

In a group with her friends, near Lord Elnauhir and his family, Makilien rode quietly. The sun climbed up behind them as they maintained a steady pace. When they came to the rise where Makilien had first ever looked upon Minarald, she brought Antiro to a halt and turned him so she could look back once more at the city. It was different now with the walls still stained black and scarred, but that did not take away from its splendor.

A horse nickered, and Makilien looked up to see Halandor had stopped with her. They said nothing, but Makilien knew he understood the questions she had inside concerning whether or not she'd ever see the city again. But that was in the hands of Elohim, and Makilien trusted Him.

After four days of travel, the large group made it to the river ford just as night had fallen. Across the river, welcoming light flickered in the houses. Crossing the shallow water, they entered into the beautiful Elven city. As soon as they reached the outskirts, doors opened and Elf children ran out followed by their mothers. Many happy reunions followed as soldiers returned to their homes and families, but Makilien knew many families would be mourning rather than celebrating. Heart heavy with these thoughts, Makilien prayed silently, *Please, Elohim, help the families who have lost loved ones. Give them comfort and strength to endure the grief.*

The somber mood seemed to affect everyone, but entering Lord Elnauhir's house lifted their spirits again.

"Well, I don't know about anyone else, but I am famished," Elandir stated matter-of-factly.

"Me too," Elmorhirian chimed in.

Their father chuckled. "I'll go inform the cooks we have returned and have them prepare us something to eat." He turned to Vonawyn. "Will you show Sirion a room?"

Vonawyn nodded and led Sirion away.

"You are welcome to the same room as before," Elnauhir told Makilien.

Smiling her appreciation, Makilien hoisted her pack up again and walked down the hall. Once in her room, she set her belongings down at the foot of the bed before cleaning up a little in preparation to go to the dining room.

The sun was barely up on Makilien's third day back in Elimar. It had been a delightful, restful two days, but she knew in her heart it had to end. Slowly, she rose from the edge of her bed where she had spent a long time talking to Elohim.

Dressing in a pretty green gown, she left her room. She saw no one as she made her way through the house and out the front door. Outside it was cool, but peaceful. The birds were singing and everything sparkled with dew. Descending the stairs, she walked down one of the winding, leaf covered paths through the city. New summer flowers had grown up for her to enjoy along the way, and still as many butterflies as when she'd first come.

Eventually, the path brought her back around to Lord Elnauhir's house and into one of the gardens. A beautiful fountain sparkled in the center. She circled the wide pool slowly where the water collected, admiring the bright colored fish that swam there. Makilien was so mesmerized she startled slightly when she looked up to find Sirion standing there, watching her. The look in his eyes puzzled her, but in the next instant it was gone, replaced by his smile.

"Good morning," he said.

"Good morning," Makilien echoed happily.

"You're up early."

Sirion joined her at the edge of the pool.

"It's become a habit. Usually I stay in my room to pray and think, but today I decided to come out here." Makilien allowed herself a little sigh and sat down on the edge of the pool. "A part of me wishes to never leave here, but I know I must."

Sirion sat next to her and looked at her thoughtfully. "When will you leave?"

"I think I should leave as soon as Halandor can take me," Makilien said with some reluctance. "I wish I could know if I'll come back or not."

"I believe you will."

Makilien looked into Sirion's warm eyes. The earnestness and confidence in them comforted her.

"Do you?"

"Yes."

Makilien continued to stare at him. She'd known him for the shortest time out of all her friends, yet they shared something special in their friendship. Saying goodbye was something she knew would be very difficult.

Finally, glancing down at the ground, Makilien steered her thoughts and the conversation away from her departure. For a long time they sat and spoke quietly, just enjoying each other's company and the beautiful morning.

As the sun climbed above the trees, the sound of Elmorhirian shouting breakfast was ready came from the house.

"We'd better hurry," Makilien said teasingly as they rose, "or he and Elandir will be upset that we delayed the meal."

Sirion chuckled as they walked together to the house.

Immediately after breakfast, Makilien asked to have some time to talk to Halandor. They left the dining room and entered a small sitting room in one corner of the house.

"I wanted to talk to you about returning to Reylaun," Makilien told him as they each sat down. "I feel it's time for me to go whenever you can take me."

"I can take you as early as tomorrow if that is what you would like," Halandor offered.

Makilien sighed. "I think that sounds best. I've been here three days. The longer I stay, the harder it will be to leave."

Halandor nodded slowly.

"I know what you meant now when you said that when you trust Elohim, you are free no matter what. I may be physically imprisoned again, but my soul will never be. So I am not afraid of going back. My only reluctance comes from having to say goodbye."

"Goodbye is always painful," Halandor agreed, "but for those of us who know Elohim, it is never permanent. The day will come when we are all together in His presence forever."

Makilien smiled, finding great peace in that thought. "I will be ready in the morning then," she said as they stood. "Thank you, Halandor, for taking me back. I know it's no short journey."

"I'm very happy to see you arrive home safely."

:Chapter Twenty-seven:

Homeward

Makilien tugged the cinch of her saddle a little tighter and let the stirrup down. After checking that her packs were tied securely behind the saddle, she led Antiro outside where Halandor waited with his horse.

"Ready?" he asked.

Makilien nodded. They walked back up to Lord Elnauhir's house where everyone was waiting to say goodbye. When they arrived, both were surprised. Three more horses stood saddled and waiting—Torick's, Loron's, and Sirion's. Makilien and Halandor turned to the three questioningly.

Torick stepped forward and spoke first. "I've been with you all this way, Makilien. You didn't think I'd stay behind now, did you?"

Makilien smiled, but asked, "Are you sure, Torick? Riding all the way to Reylaun won't be very comfortable until your ribs have fully healed."

Torick just shook his head in disregard. "I've ridden much farther before in worse condition."

"Maybe in your younger days," Elandir murmured, still loud enough for everyone to hear, and he and Elmorhirian burst into laughter.

Makilien couldn't help laughing a little too as Torick gave the Elf brothers a hard look.

With an amused smirk, Loron spoke next. "The last time you three traveled through Eldinorieth, you almost ended up eaten by mountain wolves. I thought I'd tag along and prevent that from happening this time."

"Thanks, Loron. I surely don't want to end up in some wolf's belly after all I've survived so far," Makilien said with a grin.

Sirion's reason for joining them was much the same. "I'm going along to make sure nothing of the sort will happen."

They shared a smile, and Makilien was delighted with this turn of events.

"Thank you all for doing this for me." Makilien was touched by their loyalty and friendship, and glad she would have a few more days with them.

But goodbyes still needed to be said to Lord Elnauhir and his family. Makilien began with the Elf-lord.

"Thank you, my lord, for welcoming me with such kindness and generosity. I will never forget the time I have spent here."

"We were blessed by your company. As in Minarald, you are welcome here always. Goodbye, Makilien."

"Goodbye."

Makilien said farewell to Lorelyn and then Elandir and Elmorhirian. The two brothers joked and tried to keep everything lighthearted, but Makilien could tell they were sad to see her go.

Finally, Makilien came to Vonawyn, the hardest goodbye so far. Tears formed in her eyes as she tried to smile.

Speaking first, Vonawyn said, "I'm going to miss you very much, Makilien."

"I'm going to miss you too," Makilien replied, trying hard not to cry. "You've been a wonderful friend to me."

She thought of all the times Vonawyn had been with her when she'd felt the most lost and uncertain.

"As you have been to me."

Without further words, they hugged tightly, both shedding a few tears.

"Goodbye, Vonawyn," Makilien murmured as they parted.

"Goodbye, Makilien."

With a teary smile, Makilien backed away and made herself mount Antiro. Each taking hold of their horses, the men mounted too.

"Don't forget," Vonawyn said to Makilien, "wherever you are or whatever happens, I will be praying for you every day. I promise."

"I can't thank you enough, Vonawyn," Makilien said, looking down at her. "I will take great comfort in knowing that."

Encompassing everyone with her gaze, Makilien said one final, quiet goodbye and lightly squeezed Antiro's sides. The men said their goodbyes, though theirs were only temporary, and rode out with Makilien. They hadn't gone far when Makilien looked back toward the Elf family. *Elohim.* Just saying His name in her heart helped ease the pain of her goodbyes. *It is difficult to leave such good friends, but I thank You with all my heart that You brought me here and put them in my life. Even though goodbye is painful, just having known them is worth it.*

When they came to the ford, Makilien looked back once more at the city nestled peacefully in the warmth of the morning sun. She then fixed her eyes ahead as they crossed the river.

Riding horses made the journey much different this time around. Traveling at a good pace all day brought them to the edge of Eldinorieth by nightfall. They set up camp under the boughs of the first trees, and Halandor and Torick fell back into their role of preparing supper.

Though she missed all of her other friends, Makilien enjoyed this time with Halandor, Torick, and Loron, the first three friends she'd made outside of Reylaun, and having Sirion along was even better. She couldn't imagine a better group to travel with.

That night the men set up a system of a two-person watch during each night. Makilien felt capable and confident she could stand watch now, but the men insisted they could manage and Makilien was happy to let them.

Rolling out her bedroll, Makilien laid back against her saddle and stared up at the stars while she listened to the others prepare for sleep. She took particular notice of Torick shifting around, trying to find a comfortable position on the hard ground. She was tempted to say something, but she only ended up smiling to herself as she thought of what his reply might be. Her smiled widened as she considered what Elandir and Elmorhirian might say.

The next couple of days passed smoothly without any incident or mishaps. No mountain wolves bothered them at night and no sign of any goblins or Shaikes were found along the way. It was a pleasant journey, but one Makilien felt passed much too fast.

During their third night on the trail, Halandor told her they would reach Andin the next day. They would stay there for the night and then ride to Reylaun. That gave her only two final days and nights to spend in the company of her friends.

Wanting to remember things just as they were now, Makilien took out her sketchbook to draw them as they all sat around the fire. She opened it up and found only one empty page left. *How fitting*, she thought and began the sketch, trying to capture each of her friends as accurately as possible.

The next day, they left Eldinorieth early, coming to the dry, open grassland leading to Andin. They slowed their pace a little, allowing for conversation, in no great hurry to reach the village since they wouldn't leave it until morning anyway.

This slower pace brought them to the village gate right at nightfall. By this time, all of them looked forward to a good meal indoors. After making sure their horses were comfortable and well provided for at a nearby livery stable, the five of them went to the inn.

When they walked inside, all the familiar sights and smells greeted them and brought back many memories for Makilien. She was an entirely different person than the last time she'd entered this building. Apparently, she appeared different because when they approached the counter, the innkeeper showed no recognition of her.

"Halandor," he said, not quite as gruff as Makilien remembered him to be. "What can I do for you?"

"Good evening, Rindal," Halandor replied. "We'd like a couple of rooms if you have some available."

"I do." Rindal turned and grabbed two keys. He handed them to Halandor. "There you are."

They walked through the crowded common room and into the hall where Halandor unlocked two doors and gave one key to Torick. It was decided Makilien would share a room with Halandor while Torick, Loron, and Sirion shared the other. Even though Makilien knew she could have stayed in a room alone, they all agreed Andin was quite a dangerous place. Makilien had already seen for herself what kind of men frequented the inn, and who knew how many were in league with Zirtan being this far north. For that reason she was glad to have Halandor close in case of trouble.

After depositing their belongings in their rooms, they returned to the common room for supper. While they ate, Makilien and Halandor recounted the tale of how they had met and the trouble Makilien had gotten herself into. She had been so naïve. She couldn't believe she had actually left her money pouch out for all to see. But then, if she hadn't, Makilien realized she may never have met Halandor. She never would have survived without him and thanked Elohim for how He had orchestrated everything.

When they were finished with their meal, they all gathered in one of their rooms so they could talk openly without being overheard. They built a fire in the fireplace and sat near it until late into the night. There was so much to talk about and reflect on. Makilien wished the night would not have to end, but sleep was needed for the last leg of their journey.

Saying reluctant goodnights, Makilien went to her room with Halandor. The small room had only one bed, but Halandor was content to sleep on the floor. As he rolled out his blankets, Makilien got into the bed in the corner, cringing a little at the crunching of the straw mattress and dreaming briefly of the feather bed in Elimar. That turned her thoughts toward home. The next night she knew she would sleep in her own bed in Reylaun. Torick had wondered if the guards would even allow her in again, but Makilien was not worried. She knew Elohim wanted her there so He would get her inside.

Thoughts of home made Makilien think of her family. How would they react to her after being away for so long? She'd left angry and without warning, except for telling Leiya.

"Halandor." Makilien's voice was hesitant, uncertain.

He looked up at her. "Yes?"

"Do you think my parents will welcome me back after I left without telling them and appearing so angry before I did?"

Halandor nodded confidently. "I'm sure they will. From what you've told me about them, I know they love you and will be very happy to have you home. They will be glad to know you are safe."

Makilien let out a sigh, comforted, and the room became quiet as they both drifted off to sleep.

"Reylaun is only another mile up the road," Halandor said, keeping his voice down in case any guards were nearby.

Makilien couldn't believe they were here. It had taken most of the day, but it had come so quickly.

She dismounted and untied her packs. Kneeling on the ground, she sorted through her things and stuffed all her clothes into her larger pack and filled the smaller one with all the things she'd collected. Gifts she had received from her friends—the map Halandor had given her, Aedan's dagger, her sketchbook, a book of stories from Vonawyn, which were much more truthful than Mornash's, several jents from the tree in Eldinorieth, and a few other odd trinkets.

Standing up again, Makilien looked at Antiro. They would not be going any farther on horseback, and she knew her beloved horse could not go with her into Reylaun.

"I wish you could come with me, Antiro," she said longingly, "but I would never be allowed to keep you. The only horses I've ever seen in Reylaun belong to the guards. Their horses are black and if they saw you, they'd want to take you and use you for their own. Neither of us wants that."

Antiro stomped his foot and tossed his head in displeasure.

"I know you're unhappy, so am I, but this is how it must be. You'll be much happier going back to Elimar."

Antiro's neck drooped dejectedly. Makilien stroked his cheek.

"I will miss you, Antiro, very much. There is no better horse in all of Dolennar." Gently raising his head up, Makilien kissed his nose. "Goodbye, Antiro."

The horse nickered softly and nuzzled her cheek. Makilien rubbed his forehead one last time and picked up her packs. Leading the way, she and her friends quietly made their way through the forest. When they spotted the palisade through the trees, they crept along cautiously until Makilien found a familiar old, rotted tree stump.

"The loose stake should be right over there."

Checking to make sure no one was in sight, they left the cover of the forest. At the palisade, Makilien hid her small pack in the long grass. She unbuckled her sword belt and hid her sword with the pack, hoping it wouldn't be exposed to the elements for long.

After this task was accomplished, they went back the way they had come until they found a small clearing hidden by brush. From there they could see the gate leading into Reylaun. Guards stood there, dark and foreboding, just as Makilien remembered, but no longer so frightening.

This was it. All she had to do was approach the gate and ask to be let inside. Somewhere within those walls were her family and Aedan. Being so close filled Makilien with longing and anticipation. But she had one more obstacle to overcome—her final and most painful farewells. She turned to her traveling companions, not sure what to say or how to begin. Sensing her reluctance, Torick spoke instead.

"Here we are, almost exactly where we first met."

The memory brought a smile to Makilien's face. "It seems like a lifetime ago. I wanted to know the truth so bad, I didn't care what might happen if I talked to you. I don't know what would have happened to me if you had never come to Reylaun."

"I never wanted to come here," Torick admitted. "I was going to avoid these villages, but I can see now Elohim prompted me to come."

"Thanks for listening to Him." Makilien paused, not sure if he'd mind if she hugged him, but then Torick opened his arms welcomingly. Makilien embraced him with a smile. "I'm so very glad to know you, Torick."

"And I you, Makilien."

They exchanged goodbyes, and Torick said, "Say hello to your friend, Aedan, for me."

"I will."

Makilien turned to Loron. "Thank you for saving my life the night we were attacked by the mountain wolves, and thank you for your friendship. You certainly showed me the error in the tales I'd heard all my life about Elves."

"I'm glad Elohim brought our paths together," Loron said.

After hugging and saying farewell, Makilien turned next to Sirion. By now it was becoming much harder to hold back her tears. The ache in her heart was especially acute at this goodbye.

"Your friendship has really meant a lot to me," Makilien said, hoping he would understand the earnestness she felt.

"To me as well," he replied softly.

Makilien found herself at a loss. Goodbye was so difficult. Then, quietly and earnestly, Sirion told her, "I will be watching for you."

Makilien smiled. He truly expected her to be back, and she comforted herself with that. The two of them hugged tightly, and he whispered goodbye in her ear.

Makilien then turned to Halandor. Already emotional, she didn't think she could make it through without crying.

"I don't know where I'd be without you," Makilien said, her voice breaking. Halandor had been her father away from home. Her protector, teacher, and best friend. At all times he had been prepared to die before allowing any harm to come to her. She hadn't known such kindness, loyalty, and love existed before meeting him. She had needed him so badly and couldn't imagine being without him now, but it was because of him and all he had taught her that she could return to Reylaun confidently.

As a tear finally slipped down Makilien's cheek, Halandor pulled her into his arms, holding her with as much care and love as he once had his own daughter.

"Thank you so much for everything," Makilien murmured between her tears. "I love you so much."

"I love you too, Makilien."

She did not want to let go, but it was time. With a final goodbye, Makilien stepped back and drew in a deep breath while wiping away her tears. She didn't want to approach the guards looking like a lost little girl, which she wasn't now, thanks to her friends and Elohim. Composing herself, she let a smile return to her face.

"I anxiously look forward to seeing each of you again . . . one way or another."

Shouldering her pack, Makilien focused her mind on her mission ahead and turned. *I will go wherever You lead me, Elohim.* Her heart filling with peace, Makilien left the clearing and strode toward the gate. She was a couple of yards away when the guards noticed her. They stood up very straight and watched her with narrowed eyes.

When she reached them, she stopped.

"Who are you and what is your business here?" one of them demanded in a cold voice, which once would have sent chills through Makilien's body.

Speaking confidently but with caution so as not to arouse their anger, Makilien answered, "I was born here in Reylaun. I don't want trouble, I just want to go home to my family."

The guards looked at each other and glared at her for a long moment, almost as if trying to get her to confess to something. Calling on Elohim for strength, Makilien held their gaze.

"Let me see your pack," the first guard said at last.

Makilien handed it to him and watched him rummage through it. Though he appeared disappointed not to find anything forbidden, he returned the pack to her. She stuffed the dresses back in, which he had left hanging out, and slung it over her shoulder. After another tense silence, the guard finally stepped out of her way.

"Do not cause trouble with the villagers," he warned in a threatening tone.

Makilien did not reply. She looked into the village she'd known all her life. This was her final chance to change her mind—to walk in or turn and run back to her friends. But there was no question. The people here were lost and needed the knowledge she now possessed. Meniah had told her she had much to do, and she would never abandon that charge.

Squaring her shoulders, Makilien walked into the village, following the road she had traveled so many times in the past. Everything was familiar, yet she looked upon it in a new way. Nearing home, she spotted a familiar form on the road ahead. A wide grin broke out.

"Aedan!"

He spun around, his eyes wide in surprise. He blinked once as if he didn't believe what he saw. "Makilien!"

She ran to meet him and dropped her pack so she could hug him.

"You're back!" Aedan exclaimed as they stood facing each other.

"I told you I would be." Makilien laughed happily.

"Where have you been?" Aedan was eager to know. He shook his head in disbelief. "You look so different."

Makilien was pleased to hear so. "Oh, Aedan, I have so much to tell you," she said, her eyes bright and sparkling with enthusiasm. "You won't believe what I've seen and learned."

"I want to hear everything," Aedan replied.

"And I will tell you all of it. I just have to see my family first. How are they, Aedan?"

"They are all right, but they've taken your absence pretty hard. They will be overjoyed to see you."

His words gave Makilien much relief.

"Come on," Aedan said. "I think your father just got home."

They walked quickly the remaining distance, Makilien's anticipation growing with each step. When the little house she'd been born in finally came into view, she wasn't sure whether to laugh or cry. Her mother stood sweeping the porch, and Leiya carried a water bucket to the house. Makilien's eyes filled with tears.

Leiya was the first to spot them coming.

"Makilien!" she cried in pure delight. She dropped her bucket and raced toward them, flying into Makilien's arms.

"Leiya," was all Makilien could manage as she choked back tears, wrapping her arms around her sister. She hugged her tight, finally giving in to the longing she'd had for her family.

"I'm so glad you're home," Leiya murmured.

Makilien brushed the young girl's hair out of her face. "So am I, Leiya."

She looked up then to see her mother standing only a couple of feet away. The tears filling the older woman's eyes were nearly about to overflow.

"Mother," Makilien said emotionally and was swept into her arms.

"Oh, Mother, I am so sorry," Makilien cried as she held her mother tightly. "I should never have left the way I did without telling you and making things right."

Overwhelmed by the reunion, Makilien cried hard into her mother's shoulder. At last, Hanna pulled away gently, her own cheeks wet with tears, and cupped Makilien's face in her hands. "It's all right, Makilien. You're home now. Everything is all right."

Makilien smiled joyfully. "I missed you so much."

But, seeing her father standing just behind her mother, she said no more. Makilien didn't think she'd ever seen him look so emotional.

"Father."

Hanna let her go and more tears fell from Makilien's eyes as her father wrapped her securely in his arms without a word. Laying her head against his shoulder, Makilien was filled with indescribable joy. She belonged here. Whether it be for only a short time or for the rest of her life, right now this was where she belonged. And now that she had found the truth, she knew it would give her courage to face whatever lay ahead and she would never have to feel imprisoned again.

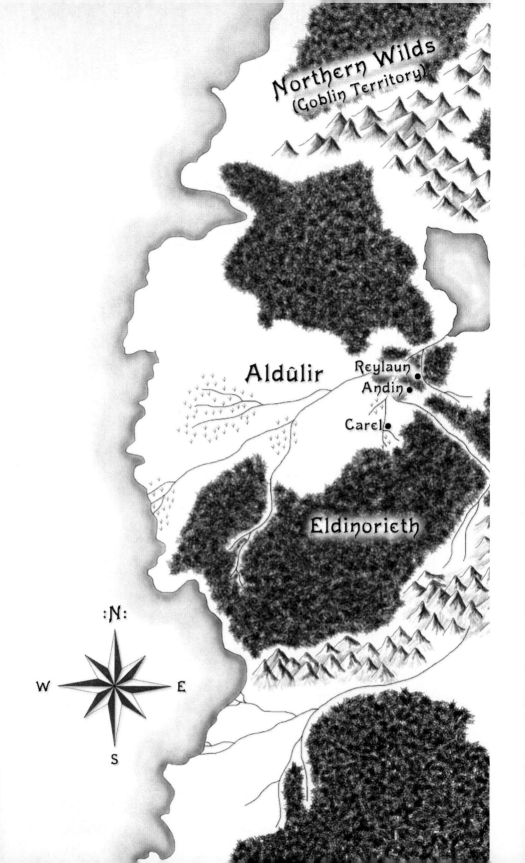

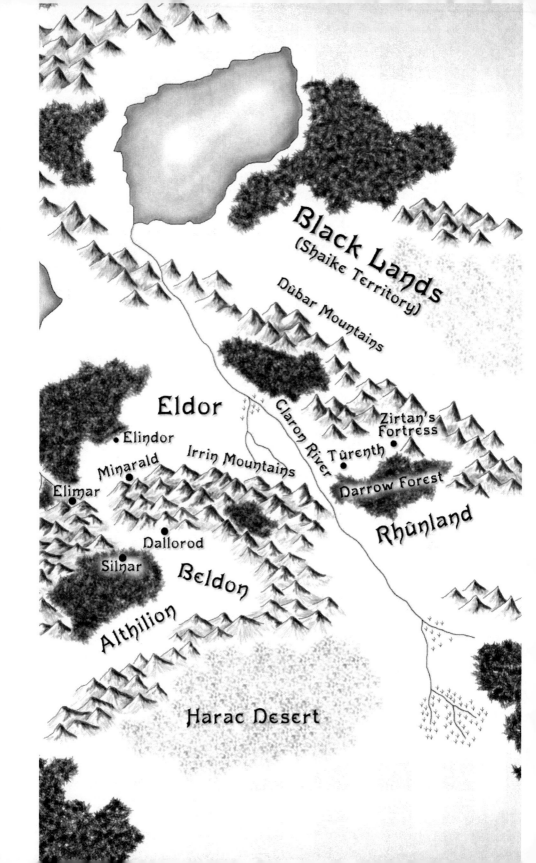

Pronunciation

NAME	PRONUNCIATION
Aedan	Ay - dan
Aldûlir	Al - doo - leer
Althilion	Al - thil - ee - on
Antiro	An - teer - oh
Arphen	Ahr - fen
Baltar	Bal - tahr
Carmine	Cahr - mine
Dallorod	Dal - lohr - od
Darand	Dahr - and
Darian	Dahr - ee - an
Derrin	Dayr - in
Dolennar	Doh - len - nahr
Dûbar	Doo - bahr
Elandir	E - lan - deer
Eldinorieth	El - di - nohr - ee - eth
Elimar	E - li - mahr
Elmorhirian	El - mohr - heer - ee - an
Elnauhir	El - nah - heer
Elohim	Ee - loh - heem
Emaril	E - mah - ril
Eredan	Ayr - e - dan
Falene	Fa - leen
Gilhir	Gil - heer
Gornath	Gohr - nath
Halandor	Ha - lan - dohr
Indiya	In - dee - yuh
Irrin	Ī - rin

Keni	Ke - nee
Laena	Lay - nuh
Leiya	Lee - yuh
Lintar	Lin - tahr
Lorelyn	Lohr - e - lin
Loron	Lohr - on
Makilien	Ma - kil - ee - en
Meniah	Me - nī - uh
Minarald	Mi - nahr - ald
Mornash	Mohr - nash
Néthyn	Nay - thin
Nirgon	Neer - gon
Reylaun	Ray - lahn
Rhûnland	Roon - land
Rollan	Rol - lan
Rommia	Ro - mee - ah
Shaike	Shayk
Silnar	Sil - nahr
Sirion	Seer - ee - on
Thardon	Thahr - don
Torick	Tohr - ick
Vonawyn	Vah - nah - win
Zirtan	Zeer - tan

ELVISH

Cellomwé	Se - lom - way
Yothaun	Yoh - thahn

Want more adventure?
Check out book 2 of the Makilien Trilogy:

Courage

As the evil lord Zirtan amasses an army unlike any that has ever been seen, Makilien, along with her family and Aedan, find themselves thrust into the middle of the struggle. Risking everything to gather their allies, can Eldor achieve victory again, or will evil finally prevail?

BOOKS BY MOLLY EVANGELINE

Makilien Trilogy
Truth
Courage
Trust

Pirates & Faith
The Pirate Daughter's Promise
Every Tear
A Captain's Heart
Finding Faith

Coming 2014

RESISTANCE

ILYON CHRONICLES – BOOK 1

www.ilyonchronicles.com